"*The Moon Pearl* relates another tale of desire, of reaching for something that, in the time and place of the story, seems as impossible to grasp as the icy moon: female independence . . . . The bravery of the (heroines), their willingness to help other women in the village as well as their families (who have disowned them) and their persistence in maintaining their physical, economic and spiritual independence are utterly inspiring and captivating."

    —*The Washington Post Book World*

"Charming. . . . An important book that depicts a largely unknown chapter in the history of Chinese women."

    —JULIA WILSON, Associated Press

"McCunn's beautifully crafted novel brings a new chapter to Chinese womanhood and the inspirational fight for economic and personal freedom."

    —*Honey*

"If you want an easily digestible slice of another world that'll nourish you as you walk through these tough times, *The Moon Pearl* is a very good choice."

    —*Bust Magazine*

"Based on interviews with real women, the novel uncovers an inspiring history of independent women . . . who lived and worked together, ungoverned by men."

    —*Ms.*

"Ruthanne Lum McCunn's new novel *The Moon Pearl* is filled with the heart and songs of old China. Wonderfully researched, it is the vivid and courageous tale of three Chinese girls, who struggle against all odds to forge the beginnings of a powerful silk sisterhood in nineteenth-century China. It is a lovely addition to the growing stories of women who have found the strength to discover new lives."

—GAIL TSUKIYAMA, author of *The Language of Threads*

The
Moon
Pearl

The Moon Pearl

Ruthanne Lum McCunn

BEACON PRESS

BOSTON

BEACON PRESS
25 Beacon Street
Boston, Massachusetts 02108-2892
www.beacon.org

BEACON PRESS BOOKS
are published under the auspices of
the Unitarian Universalist Association of Congregations.

11 10 09 08   8 7 6 5 4 3

This book is printed on acid-free paper that meets the uncoated paper
ANSI/NISO specifications for permanence as revised in 1992.

Text design by Anne Chalmers
Composition by Wilsted & Taylor Publishing Services

Library of Congress Cataloging-in-Publication Data
McCunn, Ruthanne Lum.
The moon pearl / Ruthanne Lum McCunn.
     p.   cm.
ISBN 0-8070-8348-8 (cloth)
ISBN 0-8070-8349-6 (pbk.)
     1. Title.
PS3563.C353   M66   2000
813'.54—dc21
00-008738

This book is dedicated with profound gratitude to the many strangers, friends, relatives, and professionals who carried me through a difficult period after a near fatal car accident, especially Vince Villeggiante, who risked his personal safety to hold my hand; Stan Chamness, who led the first of several teams of professionals that gave me another chance at life; Don McCunn, whose presence in my life spurred me to seize that chance and who repeatedly made the impossible possible; Herbert Randall and Lily Song, who kept constant vigil; Dr. Philip O'Keefe, who was always present; Dr. Gabriel Kind, who led the surgical teams that saved my right leg; Sonny Vukic, who brought the leg to life and taught me how to walk again; Patrick Tribble, who provided crucial fine tuning; Carole Arett, Katie Gilmartin, Robin Grossman, Yvette Huginnie, Mim Locke, Carol Olwell, Lynda Preston, and Judy Yung, who gave and gave—and continue to give.

The limits of tyrants are prescribed by the
endurance of those whom they oppress.
—Frederick Douglass

To change society, you have to start with yourself.
—Han Dongfang

CONTENTS

Author's Note

Even today, single women in America are usually considered somehow less than those who are married, and the word "spinster" continues to have negative connotations. In the Sun Duk district of southern China's Pearl River Delta, however, independent spinsters won acceptance, admiration, and respect during the 1830s.

This novel was inspired by these Delta spinsters, who came to be known as sze saw, self-combers. While the characters sprang from my imagination, the ceremonies, cultural beliefs, and practices depicted are those of nineteenth-century Sun Duk.

Readers interested in my sources will find them in the Acknowledgments.

Prologue

Dragons can shrink small as silkworms or grow large as the sky; their breath can become cooling waters or fiery licks of flame; their roar is louder than that of a big wind; and they can make themselves visible or invisible. But no woman, man, or child has ever seen a dragon grasp the moon pearl. Nevertheless, people hope to succeed where powerful dragons fail.

Look at Sun Duk. A district in the Pearl River Delta, it is laced with silver ribbons of water that rise and fall because of changing ocean tides. Jade-green rice paddies and shimmering fish ponds lie between windbreaks of bamboo, stands of fruit trees, fields with vegetables, mulberry shrubs, freshly ploughed furrows. Here and there, small hills rise. Some are rounded. Others slope steeply, with large outcroppings of rock. Most are wooded or terraced with plantings of tea. All are speckled with tombstones that look like fallen half-moons. Islands and small boats dot the rivers; and along the banks, rows of slate-gray houses with reddish tile roofs snake under weeping willows, banyans, and golden acacias like scaled dragons seeking shade.

In the east, the silver ribbons of water are finer because gentry built embankments across these rivers, then threw large stones and iron pieces into the water around the embankments to block the current so that silt gradually piled up, making new land for growing more mulberry. In the west, most of the rivers still flow freely, and there is less land, fewer fields of mulberry, fewer silkworms that can be raised. But make no mistake, the inhabitants of Twin Hills Village in the west pursue the moon pearl as fervently as those of Strongworm Village in the east.

O N E

1826–1833

Girls'
Houses

YUN YUN's good friend, Lucky, had started passing her nights at one of the many girls' houses in Twin Hills. And, listening to Lucky's excited chatter about the games they played before going to sleep, Yun Yun was eager to join in the fun. But Yun Yun's father had taught her, "Overcrowding is not good for silkworms or people." He'd also shown her what happened to worms heaped in a space too small: the strong fed at the expense of the weak; then the strong *and* the weak became heated and perspired, fell sick, and often died. So Yun Yun was afraid. As she told her parents, "The girls' house that Lucky belongs to already has thirteen members. Yet it isn't any bigger than our house. There are just two sleeping rooms." She counted off the people in their family on her fingers: her father and mother and the new baby brother she was nursing; the two little brothers playing in the courtyard under their grandparents' watchful eyes; herself. "We're only eight. Maybe I should stay at home."

"You silly melon," her mother said over the baby's loud

sucking. "Men don't go into girls' houses, so the members can set up beds everywhere—in the common room as well as the sleeping rooms."

Yun Yun's father set down the basket he was weaving, rested his hands lightly on her shoulders, ducked his head so they were eye-to-eye. "Don't worry. I'm sure there's plenty of space for you."

"Anyway, you're nine," her mother continued. "It's time you went to a girls' house."

Yun Yun's father squeezed her shoulders reassuringly. "Otherwise you might see or hear things you shouldn't."

Frowning, her mother plucked her father's sleeve, and he dropped his arms, fell silent.

Yun Yun leaned against her father. "What things?"

He raised his eyebrows, quizzing her mother.

"Things that are of no concern to girls," her mother answered firmly.

Once her mother's voice turned hard, she was like iron. Even Yun Yun's brothers couldn't move her. So Yun Yun ran next door to ask Lucky. Of course Lucky, although a year older, might not know either, but she had two easygoing sisters-in-law that they could consult if necessary.

Lucky cocked her head at the odorous honey bucket kept indoors for the family's convenience and to prevent theft. "You might see your father or grandfather taking a piss."

Yun Yun laughed. "I see my brothers piss all the time. I even have to help them!"

"Your brothers are babies. I'm talking about men. And not just about their pissing either." Lucky dropped her voice to a whisper. "Men take pleasure in their wives at night, and if you continue to sleep at home, you might see or hear your father or grandfather taking pleasure in your mother and grandmother."

"What do you mean?"

"You'll understand after you've had a few lessons from Old Granny. She comes five, six times a month to the girls' house to teach us."

Except for the three large four-poster beds crowded into the common room, the inside of the girls' house initially seemed the same to Yun Yun as any other house in Twin Hills Village. The slate-gray brick walls were unpainted, and at the far end of the common room, there was a small altar. Then Yun Yun realized there were no spirit tablets for dead ancestors on the altar, and the statue on it wasn't Gwan Gung, the red-faced God of War, but Gwoon Yum, the smiling Goddess of Mercy, seated on a pink lotus. Furthermore, when she and Lucky joined in a game of hide-and-seek, Yun Yun suddenly noticed there was no stone mortar embedded into the earth floor, no farm tools propped against the walls.

"Where can we hide?" she asked Lucky.

"Under the bed."

They'd not crawled in very far when someone called out, "Old Granny's here," setting off a chorus of greetings.

"Game's over," Lucky said, backing out.

Yun Yun, coughing from the dust their hands and knees were scuffing up, scurried after Lucky. Emerging, they hurriedly scrambled to their feet, brushed off their palms and pants, straightened their side-fastened tunics' wide sleeves and high collars, picked bits of dirt from each other's pigtails and bangs.

Across the room, the rest of the members—their pigtails, loose-fitting pants, and knee-length tunics similarly tidied —waited. The older girls were spread out on the two beds pushed against the wall, most of them sitting cross-legged on the straw bedmats, a few perched on the edge. The younger girls were settled on low stools in front of them. Dashing over, Yun Yun and Lucky dropped onto the last empty stools.

Old Granny, as befitted a respected elder, was in the seat of honor, a carved blackwood chair that faced everyone. And since Old Granny was a friendly neighbor Yun Yun had known all her life, she smiled up at the face ploughed with wrinkles, half-expecting the gnarled hands to reach out, as they usually did, with a gift of rock sugar or roasted peanuts. Instead, they gripped the arms of the chair, and beneath her black headband, Old Granny's shaggy eyebrows crossed in a frown so stern that Yun Yun, although seated beside Lucky, shrank within herself, bewildered and afraid.

Hawking loudly into the spittoon by her feet, Old Granny began, "No bride goes to her husband willingly. That is why she weeps and why she must be shut up in the attic for three days and nights before her wedding—to keep her from running away."

One by one she spelled out the losses that a bride suffered.

"She has to leave her family, her friends, all those who cherish her, every familiar person and place and thing, to go and live among strangers."

At each new loss, Yun Yun shuddered. Her skin prickled as eerily as if she were listening to a ghost story, and she sought comfort in the statue of Gwoon Yum. But fragrant smoke from the incense and candles on the altar wreathed the Goddess so that she, too, seemed distant and strange, a ghost. Sucking in her breath, Yun Yun turned back to Old Granny.

"Do you understand?" Old Granny demanded, impaling Yun Yun, every one of the six younger girls, with a fierce stare. Even after Old Granny fixed her gaze on the eight older girls, Yun Yun felt its sting.

"A bride is like a dead person about to cross the Yellow River into Hell," Old Granny continued. "Her coffin is the sedan chair that carries her to her husband and her father-in-law, the King of Hell. If she couldn't unleash her feelings in weeping songs, how could she bear it?"

As if in answer, the older girls leaped to their feet. Beating their chests with their fists like mourners at a funeral, they cried:

> "My matchmaker,
> My death maker,
> I am dying."

Yun Yun swallowed hard. She had, of course, heard many a bride lament. Since they'd been in their houses or wedding sedans, however, Yun Yun had never seen their faces, never paid any mind to the words they chanted. Now, clutching Lucky's arm, she gaped at the singers, listened closely.

"My foot steps into the Yellow River,
My heart beats sore at each further step . . ."

"Louder," Old Granny ordered. "Don't hold back."

Immediately the girls shrilled higher. They not only beat their chests but raked their fingers through their hair, pulling loose their tightly bound pigtails. Yun Yun, caught up in their terrible keening, felt her nose and throat close as if she were being sucked into the dreaded Yellow River. Desperately she gulped air. She reminded herself that Lucky had earned her nickname because she had fallen into the river that wound through Twin Hills Village but had been saved from drowning by her father. Still Yun Yun could not breathe.

Shutting out the girls by squeezing her eyes closed and clamping her hands over her ears, Yun Yun told herself that *her* father would also come to her rescue. But thinking of her father only made Yun Yun wish she were home with him, her mother and grandparents and little brothers, and she let loose a wail, a rush of tears.

Beside her, Lucky began to sob. Long before the song's end, all the girls were openly weeping.

Midway through Mei Ju's eighth summer, an angry red rash prickled across her palms. Strongworm Village was enjoying a bumper crop of lychee, and Mei Ju's grandmother, claiming a connection between the itchy red spots and Mei Ju's favorite fruit, immediately ordered her to hold back from eating more. Mei Ju, however, couldn't resist peeling back the nubby brownish red skin and biting into the sweet, tender flesh whenever she thought no one was looking.

Ma, noting the persistence of Mei Ju's rash, fretted, "Maybe lychee aren't the cause."

"Don't even think of asking me to let the herbalist look at your nuisance child," Grandmother snapped. "I'm not going to throw away hard-earned cash on clearing up a mere rash."

Pulling Mei Ju aside, Bak Ju whispered, "Sister, don't peel the lychee yourself. Let me do it for you."

Astonished, Mei Ju blurted, "How did you know?"

As if she were anointing her sister, Bak Ju rested her thumb lightly on Mei Ju's wide-set eyes, shell-like ears, button nose, and itchy palms, the thick bangs covering her forehead, murmuring, "I looked, I listened, I smelled, I touched, I used my head. Just like Grandmother does. Just like she tells us we should."

"Grandmother didn't find me out. You did."

"Grandmother would have," Bak Ju defended. "It's just that she has so much more than you to worry about."

She did, Mei Ju acceded. For although Grandfather was head of the family, Grandmother made the decisions, not only for inside matters but for outside as well. Moreover, she accomplished this without leaving the house but one day a year: Ching Ming, the Clear Bright Festival for honoring ancestors. In truth, it seemed to Mei Ju that Grandmother, short and square, was like the high gentry who lived in towns and cities, never setting foot in the village, yet whose influence, Grandfather said, dominated the two councils on which he sat.

The Wong clan's Council of Elders governed seventeen families, almost a third of the village, and it met twice monthly to hear reports from those in charge of the clan's genealogical records, accounts, and school; to consider necessary repairs to dikes on ancestral land, possible strategies for defense from bandits, requests from clan members in need of assistance for weddings and funerals; to settle disputes and mete out punishments. Strongworm's Council of Elders, which included representatives from the Council of Elders for each of the village's four clans, met less frequently. Grandfather participated in all these meetings. And Ba—whom Grandmother instructed to listen in as was the right of any adult male—reported that Grandfather always followed Grandmother's directives unless the head of the council indicated they might be contrary to the desires of the gentry.

In their family, no one overrode her. Grandmother established exactly who would stay home to mind the youngest children, go work in the fields and wormhouse, accompany Grandfather to market, or check on their dikes and fish ponds and fruit trees. Grandmother—after carefully questioning her three sons and daughters-in-law, studying the moon and the sky from their courtyard, sniffing the air, and feeling the winds—also decided which vegetables should be brought in from the fields to be cooked or pickled or sliced for drying; when to begin hatching the silkworm eggs for the start of a new season; how to apportion the silkworm waste for fish feed and fertilizer; whether their existing dikes required reinforcing, where new ones should be built.

Mei Ju, then, knew Ma wouldn't take her to the herbalist after Grandmother forbade it. Nor was there any need for the man since the rash cleared once Bak Ju started peeling lychee for her. And even better than saving her from the horrible itching, her older sister was making it possible for her to pass her evenings and nights away from home sooner than Mei Ju had dared hope, for Grandmother ruled, "Although there's eighteen months between the two of you, you'll join a girls' house together."

According to Grandmother, the purpose of the five girls' houses in Strongworm was for training daughters to become daughters-in-law. "The most senior member is the mother-in-law, the rest of the seniors are the older sisters-in-law, and the juniors are the young brides." Whenever Ma and Second and Third Aunt recalled their years as members of girls' houses, however, they spoke gaily of the games they'd played, the friends they'd made, and Mei Ju believed that Grandmother, being old and strict, was exaggerating the importance of a girls' house for training. Indeed, Mei Ju expected to have fun in the girls' house in the same way her grandfather seemed to enjoy his nights in the house he shared with his concubine.

No one in the family ever mentioned this woman. But the

gossips in Strongworm didn't share their restraint. So Mei Ju knew that after Grandmother had given Grandfather three sons, he'd set her aside like a summer fan which was no longer needed. For years he'd dallied with song girls and courtesans in the market town downriver. Then he'd brought back a pretty young concubine.

She was, of course, not the only concubine in Strongworm. But where the other concubines lived in the same households as the wives whose affections they'd supplanted, Grandfather's lived in a small house in which he passed his evenings and nights.

Sometimes Mei Ju when walking past this house, heard singing—wooden fish songs, popular arias from operas. Usually, the concubine would be the one singing. But occasionally, Grandfather's reedy piping would lace the concubine's richer tones. Not infrequently, Mei Ju also heard them laugh.

The first time she'd heard Grandfather laugh, Mei Ju couldn't have been more shocked had she heard one of the statues on the temple altar. At home, the closest she'd ever seen Grandfather come to laughing was a smile so thin it seemed little more than another of the many wrinkles that creased his narrow face. Neither had she ever heard him sing. And Mei Ju guessed that Grandfather had set his concubine up in a separate house as a way for himself to escape from Grandmother.

So too would joining a girls' house be her deliverance, Mei Ju hoped.

. . .

Mei Ju's grandmother selected a girls' house where the most senior member, Empress, was unrelenting in exercising her right to act like a mother-in-law and all the seniors were demanding of meticulous service. If a junior failed to respond quickly enough to an order, prepared a snack poorly, or fanned a senior too weakly or too vigorously, the girl would be fined or scolded or both. Even so, Bak Ju won the seniors' praise for swift and careful service as often as she did from Grandmother, and Mei Ju, to her surprise, was rarely faulted. Then she recognized the reason: the seniors, especially Empress, were too occupied with looking for excuses to punish Rooster, a junior whose family was so poor that they ate gruel and sweet potatoes—famine food—instead of rice, and who had become the butt of village jokes four years ago for calling their son Laureate, the title for the highest degree holder in all China, when he'd barely learned to talk.

Where Mei Ju, like the other girls in the house, wore thick-soled cloth shoes, Rooster wore straw sandals. Her tunics and pants, thin and bleached of color from many washings, had patches on top of patches. And when girls brought crullers, almond or sweet bean porridge, turnip goh, or sugar buns from home for midnight snacks, Rooster—thin as a stick of incense—always devoured her portion like a starved beast, finishing before anyone else.

Mei Ju wanted desperately to give Rooster her share of the snacks. But Mei Ju did not dare. No one did. Not when Empress, pouting out her thick lips, always made a point of re-

fusing a second helping to Rooster and even ordered left-
overs thrown into the nightsoil bucket to prevent her from
retrieving them.

Rooster's eyes, tracking the lost treats, would blaze like
hot coals. Her long, thin fingers would curl into fists. A few
times, she even broke the rules of proper order by fighting back, and on those occasions, Empress exploded in such
fury that Mei Ju was reminded of the terrifying big winds
which struck Strongworm every summer, ripping branches
off trees, blowing tiles off roofs, destroying dikes. Rooster,
thrusting out her pointed chin and narrow chest, appeared
uncowed. But Mei Ju's belly would knot, her chest swell,
thrusting her heart into her throat.

Nevertheless, Mei Ju couldn't stop herself from hoping
that she would find happiness in the girls' house—just as she
couldn't stop herself from eating lychee or from wishing
their neighbor, Shadow, could be her friend.

Shadow

"MAMA, tell me a story," Shadow begged.

"Ai," Mama protested. "Can't you see I'm busy?"

Her chubby arms too short to circle Mama's ample belly, Shadow threw them around a stout leg. "Please?"

"Alright. You win." Laughing, Mama pushed aside her embroidery frame. "Now you know our village is called Strongworm. But the silkworms we raise are actually weak. No, not weak so much as delicate. Demanding, too. They're always hungry."

"Like Mama and me." Baba, who'd been helping Elder Brother make a shuttlecock out of coins and feathers, lurched around on his stool, seized one of Shadow's arms. Pushing back the sleeve of her cotton tunic, he pretended to sink his teeth into her firm, sun-browned flesh, and at the tickle of his warm breath, his short, bristly black beard against her skin, Shadow giggled delightedly.

Mama patted her belly. "Baba and I certainly like to eat. But we can—and do—eat anything. The worms get stomach trouble if the leaves we feed them aren't shredded fine enough, or if we're early or late with a meal, or if we don't keep their trays absolutely clean of dirt. Even the people caring for them must be clean inside *and* out."

Swinging Shadow up from the floor, Baba held her out at arms' length as if she had a bad odor. "So as soon as Mama knew you were in her belly, she had to quit the wormhouse."

Her plump little legs churning helplessly in the air, Shadow squealed for her brother to rescue her. Bent over the shuttlecock he was making, Elder Brother did not respond. So Shadow squealed louder.

Mama raised her voice. "Poor Baba. He had to feed and clean one hundred thousand worms all by himself because Elder Brother was only four and couldn't help him."

Baba, settling Shadow onto his lap, heaved an exaggerated sigh. "Since I had to grow the mulberry for the worms too, I couldn't manage without hiring a laborer. But our profit wasn't enough to fill another rice bowl for long, and we had to let him go after two seasons."

"You were eight months old, and I was almost five, a few months younger than you are now." Elder Brother, having completed his shuttlecock, scooped Shadow into his arms. "But Mama taught me how to feed you spoonfuls of watery rice congee. How to hold you over my shoulder and pat you so you could spit out any wind in your belly."

As Elder Brother acted out what he'd learned to do for her, Shadow burped obligingly. Smiling, Mama took up the story.

"Then I went back to working in the wormhouse, and

your brother quieted you with a rag soaked in sugar water whenever you cried for me. Elder Brother also held your hands for your first steps. He hovered over you when you pulled free and picked you up each time you fell."

Baba reached out and gently pinched Shadow's lips together, forming a duck's beak. "After you learned to walk, you followed Elder Brother just like a baby duck follows a mama duck."

Mama nodded so hard that both her chins wobbled along with her belly. "You stuck closer to Elder Brother than his own shadow."

"My turn," Shadow shrieked, leaping to her feet. "Soon everyone in Strongworm was calling me . . ."

Throwing out her arms, she signaled her parents and brother to join her, and together they belted out, "Shadow!"

During the silk season, Mama had no time for anything except the family's worms and household chores. But after the seventh and final generation of worms completed spinning their cocoons, she would set up her embroidery frame—a rectangle of wood that pivoted on two upright supports—in their common room. And when Baba returned from selling the cocoons in the market downriver, he'd bring back lengths of expensive silk and satin that merchants in the town commissioned Mama to embroider.

In Strongworm, even the rich wore jackets, skirts, and robes of undecorated blue, black, or gray that were scarcely more interesting to Shadow than her own faded cotton tunics and pants. Baby carriers, hats, and shoes were colorful and often elaborately embroidered, but they were also soiled with dirt, food scraps, dust, vomit, and spit.

Shadow, watching the merchants' pristine silks and satins ripple through Mama's fingers, was as dazzled by the hues of sky blue, apple green, deep purple, pomegranate red, and intense pink as if the rainbow had fallen from the sky. And more wondrous than the colors were Mama's scaly, cloud-breathing dragons, her finely feathered birds that looked as if they were about to break into song, her delicately shaded flowers that all but gave off a perfume.

Baba boasted that no other woman in Strongworm could work magic with a needle like Mama, and Shadow had long wanted her mother to teach her that magic. But in response to Shadow's entreaties, Mama would say, "Not until you can thread a needle on your own." Now, at last, Shadow could.

Baba, beaming, presented her with a small, hand-held embroidery hoop. "Your grandmother chose your mother for a daughter-in-law because the matchmaker said Mama was a see fu, master, at embroidery. Learn well, and you'll be sought after for a bride too."

Clutching her little hoop, Shadow paid close attention as Mama instructed, "There aren't many kinds of stitches. Just the long and short, brick, satin, seed, stem, chain, cross, and split. If you're to become a see fu, however, you must not only execute them with absolute precision but you must know which stitch to use when and in what combination. You must also know how to select the appropriate color and thickness of thread."

Under Mama's guidance, Shadow stretched small squares of cotton the size of handkerchiefs within her hoop. Then, her tongue poking through her lips from her efforts to control needle and thread, she cross-stitched lucky symbols and simple designs.

To Shadow's disappointment, her stitches were shockingly uneven, the symbols and designs she created misshapen. Indeed, Shadow was afraid Mama would decide she was too untalented to teach and stop her lessons.

But Mama didn't even criticize.

"If you're to become a master embroiderer," she said, "you must develop your own critical eye."

So Shadow unpicked and tried again—and again. And when the fabric finally wilted from her abuse, she took a fresh square, started over.

Day after day, night after night, Shadow applied herself. Slowly her stitches became more even. The colors she chose and the symmetry of the designs and symbols—although still far from magical—came to please her eye.

Then Mama taught her new stitches, more ambitious designs. And the more skilled Shadow became, the greater her excitement at chasing thread with a needle.

That same winter, Elder Brother started school, and on his first morning, Shadow clung to him sobbing, "Me too," as if she were still a baby and not a big girl of five.

Baba, who had the strength of two buffaloes, peeled her off easily and lifted her up in his arms. "Hush now. Hush."

Comforted by Baba's soft murmur, the beat of his heart against hers, his familiar tobacco breath and scratchy beard, Shadow stopped crying, rested her face against his shoulder.

"When you marry, you'll belong to your husband's family," Baba explained, his voice still soft, his calloused hand smoothing her hair, carressing her cheek. "So paying tuition for you would be the same as throwing money away. Besides, no mother-in-law would take a daughter-in-law with book learning. They want daughters-in-law who're obedient, skilled in wifely arts, and without any interests beyond duty to family."

He set her down. "Be a good girl now. No more fussing."

From behind her embroidery frame, Mama beckoned. "Come. I'll teach you a new stitch."

Wanting to please Baba and torn between Mama's offer and staying with Elder Brother, Shadow didn't move. Elder Brother, a stocky boy of nine, gently patted her back, nudged her towards Mama. But only when Baba sternly repeated, "Mothers-in-law want daughters-in-law who are obedient," did Shadow go. Moreover, while watching Mama demonstrate the chain stitch, Shadow's mind followed Elder Brother and their father out the door and through Strongworm to the small room behind the temple which held the village school. And as she attempted the new stitch herself, Shadow realized with a joyous leap of her heart that if she climbed the flame-of-the-forest tree just outside the temple courtyard, she would be able to stay near her brother without being seen.

Soon as she escaped her mother's watchful eye, Shadow scrambled up the tree, heedless of the rough bark scraping her legs through her worn cotton pants, biting into the tender, exposed flesh of her hands and feet. Then, level with the schoolroom window, she scooted close enough to peer in.

Seated at a desk directly under the window, Elder Brother was clearly bored: his fingers drummed his high forehead, twitched and tugged at his queue; his eyes roved the room. Shadow, staring down at him through the tree's delicate green fronds and bold red blossoms, willed Elder Brother to look in her direction, to see her.

When at last he did, it seemed to Shadow that his pleasure was as great as hers. Grinning, he held his book so the pages faced her and pointed to each character as he called it out.

On every side of Elder Brother, boys—about two dozen ranging in age from seven to seventeen—were also reciting their lessons out loud, and although Shadow strained her ears, she could not distinguish her brother's voice from theirs. The characters, too, were undecipherable squiggles, snarls, and knots.

So Shadow edged closer. Still she could not find her brother's voice among so many. Pointing to her throat, she signaled him to raise his pitch higher, higher yet.

Finally, she managed to hear him. And as Shadow, clinging to her branch, listened to Elder Brother recite the characters over and over, she slowly untangled then memorized the characters the same way she learned stitches and patterns for her embroidery.

. . .

For the four years Elder Brother attended school, Shadow studied with him by climbing the branches of the flame-of-the-forest tree whenever she could escape her chores, and while walking or fishing or flying kites together, she'd recite what she'd learned. Hiding in the twisted roots of the huge banyans surrounding the altar to Seh Gung, the Community Grandfather, Shadow would scratch out characters in the dirt with a broken twig so Elder Brother could make sure she was learning them correctly. He'd also teach her anything she'd missed.

By his last year, though, Shadow was so burdened with work during the busy silk season that she was lucky if she could slip away to join him one day in ten. Even in winter, the only time she could count on being near him was at meals and in the evenings, when he'd practice his calligraphy while Baba repaired a tool or smoked his pipe and she worked at her embroidery with Mama. Realizing that once she joined a girls' house, she'd lose that as well, Shadow begged Mama to let her continue sleeping at home.

Mama clicked her tongue sympathetically. "I know you don't want to go. But you're ten, Elder Brother is almost fifteen. So you've got to stop being your brother's shadow and go to the girls' house. Otherwise people will talk. Anyway, leaving us at night for the girls' house will help prepare you for the larger separation that you'll suffer when you leave Strongworm as a bride."

For the first time, talk of marriage didn't seem like a harmless, far-off dream but terrifyingly close and real, and Shadow balked.

"Why can't I marry someone here?"

"Members of the same clan share the same ancestors, so they can't marry."

"But we have four clans in the village."

"There can be no direct contact between a groom's family and a bride's either during the marriage negotiations or the rituals of betrothal. So your husband can't be from Strongworm or Three Temples across the river or any other village that's close by."

Mama, her voice soft as her folds of flesh, enveloped Shadow in a loving embrace. "That won't be for many years yet, and in the girls' house, you'll learn weeping songs which will help you relieve your sorrow. You'll also get used to being away from us."

Shadow, unconsoled, sought out her brother and pleaded with him to intercede.

"I can't," he told her solemnly.

Her eyes filled with tears.

"Remember how upset you were when I started school?" Elder Brother reminded. "You didn't think you'd get used to that either."

The tears in Shadow's eyes spilled down her cheeks. "I didn't have to. I found a way around it. For a few years anyway."

"Watch." Squatting, Elder Brother ferreted in the soft, moist dirt for a moment or two, drew out a wriggly worm, stretched it flat on the ground between them, and swiftly severed it with a sharp stone.

Shadow, who'd never before seen her brother act cruelly, leaped back as if he'd struck her. The two pieces of worm twitched and writhed, crawled away in opposite directions.

"See," he said. "You thought the worm couldn't be separated, that I had killed it. But it's fine. Both worms are fine. You will be too."

A Bird Snared
in a Trap

MEI JU's grandmother liked to say, "It's not enough to work hard. A person must work smart." And she'd illustrate her meaning by pointing out the shortcomings of their neighbors. "Look at how the Fungs have failed to add to their own holdings despite the earnings of a master embroiderer in their family. Even worse, look at how they let that daughter of theirs follow her brother about. Mark my words, that Shadow will come to no good, and the family will lose what little they have."

Although houses in Strongworm stood alone, they were close enough that when windows and doors remained open —as they usually did except in winter—sounds and smells drifted easily from one household into another, and it seemed to Mei Ju that their neighbors were well content, unburdened by their failure, the doom that Grandmother claimed would be theirs in the future. Mei Ju realized Grandmother would declare this contentment confirmation of the Fungs' foolishness. But Mei Ju envied them.

Yes, Shadow's family ate meat less often than theirs. But they sat down to meals together; Mei Ju and her sister and baby brother and cousins ate with their mother and aunts after their grandparents, father, and uncles were finished. Moreover, Grandmother's tales were lectures more than stories, and conversation generally consisted of her grilling Grandfather, Mei Ju's parents and uncles and aunts. At their neighbors' house, everyone talked, often at the same time, and their stories excited and amused.

Of course, Mei Ju had heard Grandmother say over and over, "Life is no laughing matter." Nevertheless, Mei Ju wanted laughter the way she wanted the sweet taste of lychee in summer, the warmth of her quilt in winter. And she did laugh when she caught glimpses over their courtyard wall of Shadow coiling her father's thick, glossy black queue on top of his head in ever smaller circles so that it resembled a pagoda, which she then decorated with tiny jasmine blossoms for bells; Elder Brother placing the loose end of his thinner, shorter queue under his nose so it became the spindly moustache of a comic opera character whose antics he imitated.

Once, Mei Ju had convinced herself that she could likewise make her own family laugh. But her father had shrugged her off as if she were a pesky fly, and Grandmother had chided, "Nuisance child, can't you see your father is tired? Let him rest."

Her throat aching from the effort to swallow her disappointment, Mei Ju had squeaked, "Shadow . . ."

"Are you deaf or stupid or both?" Grandmother had demanded. "Haven't I told you time and again the Fungs are fools?"

Did that mean she was a fool too, Mei Ju wondered.

When Third Aunt came home with the news that Shadow's mother was asking around about a girls' house for her daughter, Grandmother's jet black eyes glittered as if she were counting silver ingots. "Shadow's mother is bound to be teaching Shadow her embroidery secrets, secrets she could teach Bak Ju and Mei Ju if they were in the same girls' house. Then our family can demand big bride prices for them."

Turning to Mei Ju, Grandmother ordered, "Take your little brother and cousins out to play. Watch them. But keep your eyes open for Shadow's mother. If you see her leave the house, take note of what she's carrying and report to me at once. At once, do you hear? Don't drag your feet."

Soon as Mei Ju returned with the information that Shadow's mother was headed for the river with a basket of clothes, Grandmother grabbed clean pants and jackets from the chest in her room, handed them to Ma. "Shadow's mother is at the river. You know what to do."

Mei Ju, utterly baffled, herded her little brother and cousins as far from their house as she dared go without Grandmother's permission, finally reaching listening distance of the women at the river.

Above the crack of wet clothes hitting rock, Ma was assuring Shadow's mother, "If your daughter goes to the same girls' house as mine, you can be certain my older girl will watch out for her."

Ma's mention of Bak Ju set off a ripple of praise for her from the other women.

"Bak Ju is the best of daughters."

"Truly a ju, pearl."

"Mature beyond her years."

"Not only obedient, but thoughtful and caring."

Shadow's mother, as their neighbor, must have already known everything the women were saying, yet she was ignoring her load of dirty clothes and giving them her full attention, while Ma, her head modestly bowed over their wash, was beating and rinsing and wringing.

The chorus of praise turned to Bak Ju's looks.

"That girl is beautiful, too."

"Yes, she's wonderfully light-skinned."

"And absolutely without blemish."

"I tell you, her face is luminous as a pearl."

People often said she and her sister looked like twins, and Mei Ju, aquiver with excitement, then worry, wondered whether the women's praise would now include her, how her mother would respond if they, like Grandmother, complained, "Mei Ju is a nuisance child." Ma, however, jumped in with a question that turned the conversation altogether.

"Matchmaker Low, didn't you negotiate a good bride price for a girl in my daughters' girls' house?"

"Not one. Several. Wah, I got Old Fung five pigs for his eldest daughter." Matchmaker Low held up her right hand, fingers spread wide. "Five! You see, I can be confident a girl from that girls' house will show proper reserve." She paused meaningfully, then added, "Even with her own brother."

Folding her lips into a tight line, Shadow's mother picked at her wash.

"Isn't Shadow about ten?" Ma asked, abruptly turning the talk again.

Shadow's mother nodded without looking up.

"I thought so," Ma exulted. "She's the same age as Mei Ju. If they're in the same house, sharing the same bed, they'll become girlfriends. Good girlfriends. I'm sure of it."

In Mei Ju, joy vied with stupefaction. Did that mean she wouldn't be faulted anymore for wanting to play like Shadow did? Better still, that Shadow would be her friend, a friend with whom she, Mei Ju, could play and laugh the way Grandfather did with his concubine?

Silently Mei Ju begged Shadow's mother to say, "Yes, my daughter *will* join the same girls' house as yours. They *will* become good friends." When Shadow's mother responded, though, Mei Ju's heart was pounding too loudly for her to make out more than one or two words.

Sometimes the members of her girls' house cried so loudly while chanting weeping songs that Yun Yun was sure everyone in Twin Hills could hear them. The louder they sobbed, however, the more Old Granny praised them.

More than once, Old Granny cautioned, "Remember, it's

as important for you to know how to sing at a death as at a wedding because after you marry, your lives will be controlled by your husbands and in-laws. Both your joys and your sorrows will come from them. But if they make you unhappy, you can relieve your pain by crying out your personal sorrows, your resentments over slights or injustices during the forty-nine days of mourning that precedes a funeral, and these laments can earn you better treatment."

Old Granny also taught them the weeping songs for friends as well as those for a bride, explaining, "A bride's friends are shut up in the attic with her, and they must show their sympathy and support by weeping as loudly as the bride herself."

Sometimes, on nights when Old Granny did not come, the girls played at getting married. The most senior member always acted as the knowledgeable person who would guide the bride. The rest would draw straws for the unhappy role of bride.

Yun Yun, drawing the short straw, wept as Old Granny said a bride should, and she was, in truth, as frightened as her first night in the girls' house.

"We're just playing," Lucky reminded.

Still afraid, Yun Yun took Lucky's hand for comfort. The most senior girl, acting the part of a bridal guide, spit on her fingertips, teased Yun Yun's eyebrows into perfect willow leaves. The other girls laid out the combs, perfumed oils, make-believe wedding jacket and skirt.

Nodding approval at her own handiwork, the guide picked up two long threads, skillfully manipulated them to remove

Yun Yun's facial hair. At the tiny pricks of pain, Yun Yun yelped.

Lucky squeezed her hand. "Distract yourself by singing."

Obediently, Yun Yun quavered:

"Red and green threads used to pluck my face hair,
Tidying my face so I can be a wandering soul."

But when she saw the guide reach for the powder puff, Yun Yun clamped her mouth shut, then her eyes, wished she could somehow seal her nostrils too. Since she couldn't, Yun Yun tried to hold her breath for as long as she felt the feathery touch of the puff skimming her cheeks—but failed, and as clouds of chalky powder streamed through her nose into her throat, she burst into a series of explosive sneezes.

Embarrassed by the unseemly eruption, Yun Yun kept her eyes closed. Nor could she find her voice to resume singing. As the guide removed the ties binding her pair of childish pigtails for the hairdressing ritual, however, Yun Yun heard Lucky, her voice clear and lovely as a temple bell, chant on her behalf:

"Slide the comb from roots to ends,
Clear out all the knots.
Tie up the hair,
But not too tightly."

The other girls joined in. Yun Yun should have too. But the sensations that were rippling through her from the guide's fingers running through her hair, massaging her scalp, and rubbing in scented oil felt so strangely wonderful that Yun Yun gave herself up to them instead.

By the time the guide turned to combing, it seemed to Yun Yun that her hair had become fine and soft as silk, her skull, indeed all her bones, had melted into liquid gold. Opening her eyes, she watched admiringly as the guide divided the gleaming hair into three sections, braided each into a long, neat plait, then wove all into an elaborate wifely bun.

With her free hand, Lucky held out the plain brass pin the girls were pretending was the golden pin Old Granny had told them the groom must send. Suddenly one of the plaits slipped loose, and the guide grabbed the pin, pushed it deep into the bun to secure the plaits, piercing Yun Yun's neck.

Yun Yun howled, tried to pull free. Lucky, tightening her grip, breathed reassurances into Yun Yun's ear. The girls, grasping her shoulders and arms, held her still, chanting:

> "Today misfortune has fallen on you without cause,
> You are like a bird snared in a trap.
> Your tears run like the rivers and streams,
> You cannot escape this trap."

The guide pushed harder on the pin. Blood spurted. Yun Yun screamed. Lucky wept in sympathy:

> "The groom clutches your hair in his hands,
> His golden pin finds its mark."

Only when blood slicked the guide's fingers did she seem to realize the pin was striking flesh and pull it out, causing a fresh surge. Swiftly Lucky lifted her tunic, pressed it against

Yun Yun's wound, stanching the flow. Yun Yun, through her pain and loud sobbing, heard a ripple of sympathetic murmurs.

"The rascal will draw more blood than that," the guide muttered darkly.

In bed, unable to sleep because of the dull throbbing in her neck, Yun Yun tried to puzzle out the guide's meaning.

She knew from the weeping songs that "the rascal" was the groom. But Lucky, asleep beside her, had said that if Yun Yun stayed home instead of going to a girls' house, she might see her father or grandfather "taking pleasure" in her mother and grandmother. From listening to a few of the older girls talk, Yun Yun understood now that this pleasure between husbands and wives took place in bed, that it was somehow different from the pleasure she took in curling up against Lucky.

How, though, could there be enjoyment when all the songs Old Granny taught them, everything she said about marriage was about suffering? And if a husband was in truth a rascal who drew blood from his wife, how could he be anything but hurtful? Deeply troubled, Yun Yun woke Lucky and asked her.

Sleepily Lucky admitted that despite her confident pose, she didn't know any more than Yun Yun what passed between husband and wife beneath their quilt.

"Can't you ask your sisters-in-law?"

"I did. They said I'd find out when I marry."

. . .

Yun Yun, too frightened to wait, blurted out her confusion to her mother the next morning, heedless of her grandmother, who was dozing nearby on a bench by the courtyard wall.

"Will my husband hurt me when I'm a bride?" Yun Yun asked.

Her mother reddened, busied herself with fetching hot water from the kitchen, pouring it into a basin to wash Yun Yun's wound.

Her grandmother opened her eyes, studied her hands, rough and knotted as the fists of mulberry, sighed. "When I was learning to reel silk, I cried every time I had to pull a cocoon out of the basin of boiling water. Ai yah, the blisters and sores on my hand were so painful I was crying even when my hand wasn't in the water! But the next season, I cried less. After a few years I didn't cry at all."

Her grandmother's eyes drooped shut and her head once again bowed in sleep. Had she spoken out of a dream, Yun Yun wondered. Or had her grandmother been answering her question? If she *was* answering the question, what did she mean?

More confused than ever, Yun Yun prompted her mother. "Will my husband hurt me?"

Her mother wrung out a cloth, gently swabbed Yun Yun's wound. "Your father has never hurt me," she said. "And you can be sure we'll tell the matchmaker to find you a good husband. One as good as my parents found for me."

. . .

Yun Yun couldn't picture her father as a rascal, a creature from Hell, someone to fear. When she was small, he'd often lifted her up, nuzzled her neck, and sniffed her hair; he'd whirled her around and around until she chortled with pleasure. And he was still tender, urging her to eat her fill during evening rice lest she feel hungry during the night, reminding her to put on an extra jacket so she wouldn't catch a chill while walking to her girls' house with Lucky. Nevertheless, Yun Yun frequently woke screaming from recurring nightmares of the rascal. And only when she was enfolded in Lucky's arms could Yun Yun return to sleep.

Dreams of Happiness

THE HOUSES in Strongworm were strung out in three long rows, with the river on one side, the village's paved main street on the other. Shadow's family lived near the end of the row by the river, and the girls' house Mama had chosen for her was only one street over, not more than eight or nine houses distant. But on her first night, Shadow asked Elder Brother to accompany her.

Before he could answer, Mama reminded, "I've told you. You're no longer a small girl, so you mustn't walk or talk or sit in public with Elder Brother or any other boy. If you do, people will say you lack modesty and good home teaching. Then no mother-in-law will want you for a daughter-in-law no matter how beautifully you embroider."

Listening to Mama, Shadow's heart twitched and writhed like the worm her brother had cut in two.

Mama pinched Shadow's cheeks affectionately. "Don't look so glum. You only have to stay the night, and you won't have to walk to the girls' house by yourself. I've arranged for Bak Ju and Mei Ju to take you."

Because they were neighbors, both girls were familiar to Shadow, and when they came for her, they treated her warmly, Mei Ju taking one hand, Bak Ju the other. Even so, Shadow hoped against hope that she'd hear Elder Brother chasing after her, his shoes hitting the dirt hard and fast, his deep voice calling, "Come home. I've convinced Mama and Baba you don't have to go to the girls' house. Not tonight. Not ever."

Finally unable to take another step, Shadow stopped, looked back. The street was empty, the door to their house shut tight.

On her way next door to pick up Shadow, Mei Ju had imagined them talking freely, joking and laughing together as they walked to the girls' house. Face to face and hand in hand, Mei Ju barely squeaked out a greeting, Shadow was silent, and Bak Ju launched into a longwinded explanation of the seniors' exacting standards, the system of fines.

Frantically Mei Ju tried to loosen her tongue so she could interrupt her sister's lecture. Shadow's feet dragged slower and slower. Soon she came to a complete stop.

Dismayed, Mei Ju halted too, forcing her sister to a standstill, and as Shadow twisted around to look back home, the corners of Bak Ju's lips turned down like Grandmother's.

"You do know that juniors in the girls' house have to serve seniors the way we all will one day serve our mothers-in-law, don't you?"

Shadow, her eyes shiny with tears, nodded.

Close to tears herself, Mei Ju at last freed her tongue. "We don't have to do that much really. Just prepare the seniors' snacks and pour their tea, fan them when they're hot. Besides, there's seven of us juniors, eight now, counting you, and only four seniors, *and* we take turns serving, so there's still time to play."

Bak Ju resumed walking. "More importantly, we learn from each other. Do you have any special skill to share?"

Wishing her sister would hold back for now from pursuing their grandmother's desire, Mei Ju fell into step with Bak Ju. And as Shadow followed without answering, Mei Ju searched for something she could say that would both distract Bak Ju from her purpose and cheer Shadow.

Nothing, though, came to mind.

"No need to be modest," Bak Ju encouraged.

"I embroider," Shadow said softly. "My work is good enough for Baba to sell. But it's not special like Mama's."

"Work hard and it will be," Bak Ju told her. "Meanwhile we can learn from you, I'm sure."

· · ·

Mei Ju soon understood Grandmother's eagerness for Bak Ju and herself to acquire the embroidery secrets Shadow was learning from her mother. For Shadow could make the most ordinary pattern distinctive through her selection of threads and colors and stitches. She was generous in sharing her skills, too, and Empress took full advantage, asking for one lesson after another.

So when Empress, seated on her chair in front of the altar, called all the members into the common room, Mei Ju assumed it was for yet another embroidery lesson. But when the seniors were settled on their bench left of the chair, the juniors on the hard earth floor between the two beds, Empress did not call on Shadow for a demonstration of her skills. Instead Empress instructed Rooster—who knew more wooden fish songs and had a prettier voice than anyone in the house—to come forward and chant "The Embroidery Song" as a tribute to Shadow. Furthermore, when Rooster inserted Shadow's name into the song in place of the word "wife," Empress applauded loudly.

"Wah," Mei Ju whispered to Shadow, seated between Bak Ju and herself. "Because of you, Rooster finally did something that pleased Empress."

A pink tide rose from Shadow's neck to her plump, dimpled cheeks.

Empress, jumping up from her chair, told Rooster, "Start over so I can sing with you."

Astounded, Mei Ju gazed slack-jawed at Empress and Rooster standing peaceably shoulder to shoulder. The seniors' mouths likewise fell open, their eyes bulged, and all around Mei Ju juniors were gulping, smothering gasps, disguising them as small coughs. There were even a few fawning shouts of, "Ho yeh, wonderful!"

Rooster must have been more shocked than anyone. As usual, however, her sallow face did not reveal her feelings, and her deep-set eyes, which sometimes betrayed her, were blank.

Holding up the wooden fish, she struck it with the mallet to give Empress and herself the beat, and together they chanted:

> "Everybody has gathered
> To congratulate you, Shadow.
> With red and green threads,
> You paint pictures of wondrous beauty.
> Lotus floating in rippling water,
> Ducks flying low over the lake.
> Golden orioles flitting among branches,
> Bats weaving in and out of clouds,
> Lions sitting on a rock face,
> Baring their silver teeth."

Pausing, Rooster glanced meaningfully at Empress's sharp little teeth bared in song, and Mei Ju tensed. Shadow—her face now a deep crimson—stammered that the song accurately described her mother's abilities, not hers.

Shadow's words pulled Empress's attention from Rooster. Even Mei Ju, watching in awe, almost believed Shadow had deliberately interrupted. And Empress, waving genially, signaled for Shadow to be silent, Rooster to continue, the rest of the girls to join in.

Following Rooster's beat, then, they all gaily chanted the final lines as one:

> "Shadow, you are so talented.
> You embroider red peaches and green willows,
> Peacocks fanning out their tails,
> Silver dragons swimming out to sea,
> White cranes soaring up to Heaven.
> Yes, Shadow, our Shadow,
> You are talented indeed."

So talented that she was changing the girls' house into a joyful place, Mei Ju thought gleefully.

To Shadow's surprise, she enjoyed the girls' house. Before, in games requiring more than two people, she'd been restricted to watching her brother play with other boys. Now, when not learning weeping songs, teaching embroidery, or serving the seniors, she played with the other juniors in the courtyard, and Shadow reveled in pitting her strength against them in snapping the dragon, her skills in kicking the shuttlecock, jumping rope.

Between bites of watermelon in their courtyard at home, Shadow regaled her family with a dramatic account of a narrow victory.

Elder Brother snatched Shadow's half-eaten piece of melon. "You'd win more often if you weren't such a fatty."

"If I didn't use your strategies, I'd never win," she laughed, threatening to smear him with her sticky sweet fingers.

Sobering, she let her hands fall. "Rooster never wins."

Mama sopped up the juice dribbling down both her chins with a rag, sliced more melon. "The poor girl's probably too weak from hunger or too exhausted from work or both."

"I'm surprised Rooster has *any* energy for play." Baba spat out a mouthful of seeds. "Old Bloodsucker owns her and her parents and little brother like he owns the house they live in and the fields they work, and you can bet he drives them hard."

Shadow picked up another piece of melon. "Empress drives Rooster hard too."

Elder Brother snorted. "From what you've told us, Rooster is as pig-headed as Empress."

"Rooster's brave," Shadow countered.

"She may be brave," Mama said. "But since Rooster's bravery just drags more grief down on her, she's also foolish."

"Like her parents. Not only did they get themselves deep in debt to Old Bloodsucker, but they insist their son is going to become a laureate and save them, even raise them high." Baba dug a seed out of his melon's pink flesh, threw it into his mouth, and made a show of swallowing it. "That boy has as much chance of becoming a laureate as I have of sprouting a watermelon from this seed. If not for their clan's free school, he wouldn't even know how to read, and soon as he gets big enough to put in a full day's work, Old Bloodsucker is going to force him into the fields."

"Rooster and her family aren't just foolish. They're trouble," Elder Brother, pretending to go after Shadow's melon, breathed in her ear. "So don't you do anything stupid on her account."

The northern winds that brought winter to Strongworm could be bone chilling, and the night was so bitter cold that Mei Ju could see her own breath inside their common room. The girls had piled all their quilts onto the beds on either side of the altar, and they huddled together—the eight juniors in one bed, the four seniors in the other. Each girl had a small pile of roasted chestnuts on her lap. Just raked out of the cinders, they were steaming hot, and Mei Ju, snuggled between Bak Ju and Shadow, was satisfied with savoring the chestnuts' heat through the thick layers of quilt. From the little yelps on both sides of the room, however, Mei Ju realized the chestnuts' delicious fragrance was too tantalizing for some to resist.

"Rooster," Empress purred. "Give us a song while we wait for the chestnuts to cool."

Rooster, leaning over the foot of the bed, jerked the quilts, rattling the chestnuts, setting off a ragged chorus of "Wai," "Watch it," "What are you doing?" while hands, Mei Ju's included, flew protectively to keep them from rolling off the bed.

"Sorry." Rooster grasped the wooden fish from the top of the chest. "It's too cold to get up."

Withdrawing the mallet from the fish's mouth, Rooster swiftly beat out a rhythm and began to chant:

> "Everybody dreams of happiness,
> Yet we all cry at birth.
> Destinies . . ."

"Stop!" Empress ordered. "We've heard that song a thousand times."

With only one saucer of burning oil lighting the room and dark smoke still seeping in from the cinders in the kitchen, Mei Ju couldn't see Empress's face. But there was no mistaking the irritation in her voice, and Mei Ju sucked in her breath—held it as Shadow beside her bravely intervened.

"That song *is* worn. All the songs are. It's been so long since any wandering singers have come to Strongworm. Soon as the weather warms up, though, they'll be on the road again. Then we'll learn some new songs."

Rooster, beating the wooden fish with her mallet, trilled in a high-pitched falsetto, "But if just one of us could read, we wouldn't have to wait for a wandering singer to bring us new wooden fish songs, we could learn from song books."

"Stop that nonsense," Empress snapped.

Mei Ju flinched as though she'd been the one reprimanded, and she silently pleaded for Rooster to obey, for Shadow—who'd begun to tremble—to nevertheless find a way to distract Empress and improve her mood.

Rooster set down the fish and mallet. "If we could read, we wouldn't have to always wait for others to teach us. We could learn for ourselves."

So indisputable was Rooster's logic that Mei Ju nodded.

Her sister jabbed her in the ribs. "You know better than to agree with that troublemaker."

Of course Grandmother—like everyone else in Strongworm—spoke against learning for girls, and until a few moments ago, Mei Ju had accepted their pronouncements without thought. Now, stiffening her neck in obedience to her sister's warning, Mei Ju suddenly realized Grandfather never completed a lease agreement with a landlord until he'd read it out loud to Grandmother. Furthermore, it was she who caught any dubious phrasing that had to be changed. Likewise Ba and Second and Third Uncle relied on Grandmother to interpret the shades of meaning in the almanac whether they were searching for omens or for lucky or unlucky days. Did Grandmother ever secretly wish she could read the almanac and contracts for herself?

The possibility that Grandmother and Rooster might share the same desire made Mei Ju want to giggle. But in the bed opposite, chestnuts were cascading noisily in every direction as the seniors threw off their quilts and scrambled onto the floor; and Mei Ju, terrified they were coming to attack her for nodding agreement with Rooster, pressed silently, soberly against her sister.

The seniors, however, swarmed around the foot of the juniors' bed, scolding Rooster alone. And as her terror receded,

Mei Ju's belly churned with a terrible and all-too-familiar mix of pity for Rooster, relief for herself, shame at her relief.

"So your brother isn't the only one in your family with hopes of becoming a laureate, eh? But remember, you're a girl, and matchmakers look for girls with *no* learning."

"Because 'Learning for girls opens the door to vices.'"

"And 'A virtuous woman has no learning.'"

"Then why has the district magistrate hired a tutor for his daughters?" Rooster shot back.

The seniors, clearly uncertain how to respond, fell silent. But Empress soon recovered.

"It's not for us to question our betters," she roared. "Or to ape them."

Gripping Rooster's bony shoulders, Empress shook her. "Come spring, you'll be starting your apprenticeship in reeling. If you refuse to listen, how will you learn?"

Rooster tossed her head. "If your husband mistreats you, how will you send word to your father for help?"

Again Mei Ju found herself nodding, felt her sister's elbow. Shaking Rooster even harder, Empress yanked her onto her feet, and Mei Ju whispered thanks to Bak Ju for saving her from the seniors' wrath.

"Who will want you for a wife?" Empress sneered.

The rest of the seniors followed Empress's lead. Then some of the juniors chimed in.

"You'd best be wishing for hips, not schooling."

"Yes. You're so skinny, how will a son grow in you?"

"How will he get out?"

As their humiliation of Rooster intensified, Mei Ju thought wistfully of her mistaken belief that Empress was mellowing, the girls' house turning into a joyful place. Shadow, trembling so hard her teeth clattered, burrowed under their quilts. Mei Ju slid in after her, shutting Rooster's attackers from sight, muffling their voices. Mei Ju, however, couldn't escape the sense that Rooster's claims had merit, that her own cowardly silence was as evil as the attackers' abuse.

Wily as
a Fox

SHADOW had understood Empress's warning, "Just as one wrongdoer in a family can shame all its members, one wrongdoer in our girls' house can pull us all down. So if you want to preserve your own chances for a good match, you will tell no one about Rooster's desire for learning." Shadow, however, had seen no reason to hold back from telling her brother.

In the midst of her heated description of Rooster's brave stand against her many attackers, Elder Brother—who'd been stacking dried mulberry branches in the corner of the kitchen—strode over to the door between them and their parents in the common room. As he eased it shut, the tang of burning grasses and mulberry sharpened, the rich aroma from the pot of fish head soup simmering on the stove thickened. Spinning around, he squatted beside Shadow, who was feeding the fire.

"You're not thinking of teaching Rooster, are you?" Elder Brother asked in hushed tones.

Marvelling at how he could see into her heart, Shadow rocked back on her heels, and confided, "I came up with a plan while I was under the quilt with Mei Ju."

"Are you crazy?" he hissed.

Hurt, Shadow protested, "The lessons will be secret, and I'm sure Rooster would never betray us. Nor would Mei Ju."

"Next you'll be telling me you've decided to teach the whole house, even Empress!" Elder Brother spluttered.

"Don't be angry," Shadow pleaded. "At least give me a chance to explain."

"All right," he conceded grimly. "Explain."

"Remember what you told me about how you'd have died of boredom in school if I hadn't given you the excitement of trying to teach me without either of us getting caught?"

"I was a foolish boy."

"It's not boredom that drove me to embroidery," Shadow persisted. "But I did feel as if I'd die if Mama wouldn't teach me. And I know Rooster feels the same about book learning."

"What about Mei Ju? Are you going to tell me she has a burning desire to read and write too?"

Shadow, uncertain whether Mei Ju would dare grasp the opportunity to learn despite her nods of agreement during the attack, admitted, "No. But I felt Rooster's wanting so strongly, I trembled."

"*I'm* trembling over what will happen if people find out I taught you how to read and write. Our parents will be blamed as much as me for my wrong doing, and no family will take you for a daughter-in-law."

"Good," Shadow joked. "I can stay home with you."

"I'm serious." Elder Brother gripped her arm so tight, she winced. "Who's more important to you? Rooster or me?

"You, of course."

"Then forget about teaching her. Or Mei Ju. Or anyone else."

Shocked at Elder Brother's vehemence, Shadow did try to forget. But there was no chance that Rooster could learn from *her* brother. Even if Laureate were willing to teach her, the ancestral hall in which their clan held school had no windows she could look through. Nor could Rooster steal time from slaving for Old Bloodsucker to meet secretly with Laureate. And each time Shadow studied an embroidery pattern or picked up needle and thread, she was reminded of Rooster's inability to satisfy her desire to study a book, to pick up brush and paper.

Rooster's hunger gnawed at Shadow until she could no longer enjoy painting with a needle. Still she didn't dare risk Elder Brother's affection. Then Shadow realized that if she made her plan for secret lessons foolproof, Elder Brother need never know that she'd disobeyed him.

Step by step, over and over, Shadow went through her plan, each time refining it a little more. And when at last she could find no flaw, she sought a sign from Heaven: If she succeeded in emptying the box in which her brother kept his old school supplies without his notice, she could proceed without fear.

In the girls' house, Mei Ju slept between Bak Ju and Shadow. Usually, Bak Ju was the first to rise, and the sudden loss of her warmth coupled with the stirring of their quilt in winter or the rustle of their bedmat in summer would waken Mei Ju. The whispers and the kneading now nudging Mei Ju into wakefulness did not have her sister's deep familiarity, however. And, uncertain whether she was dreaming, Mei Ju opened her eyes to black night, Shadow's plump fingers pressing against her shoulder and hip, rolling her away from Bak Ju towards the edge of their bed.

"Come." Silhouetted against the ghost-white mosquito netting surrounding their bed, Shadow tipped her head towards the door. She raised the netting. "Let's go where we can talk."

Fully awake now, Mei Ju eagerly slid off the bed through the opening. The floor of their sleeping room was cool against her bare feet, but she didn't attempt to find her clogs. She didn't want to take the time. Besides, they'd clatter, and Mei Ju had waited too long for an opportunity to be alone with Shadow to risk waking Bak Ju or the girls asleep in the other bed. Excited, Mei Ju followed Shadow's soft scuffing out the door, through the kitchen, into the damp chill of the courtyard.

To Mei Ju's disappointment, Rooster was perched on a stool, leaning forward expectantly. Of course Rooster always rose before anyone else to replace the burned-out incense sticks on Gwoon Yum's altar with new, to sweep away the fallen ash, then bow her head and pray. But an upward glance proved it was early even for Rooster: stars glowed and the crescent moon was still high in the cloudless spring sky.

"I didn't know how else we could speak in private," Shadow apologized, dragging the bench by the wall over to Rooster, guiding Mei Ju onto it, dropping down beside her. "And I've been wanting to tell you . . ."

Unexpectedly, she broke off in midsentence. Mei Ju, curious yet hesitant to prompt her, shifted on the bench. Across from them, Rooster leaned so far forward that the stool teetered precariously. But she, too, said nothing.

Finally, Shadow started up again. At first she repeated the same words, only she spoke haltingly. Then she ended in a rush, "I can read and write."

Mei Ju, certain she'd misheard, blurted, "Hah?"

Rooster grasped Shadow's knee. "Who taught you?"

"I can't tell you that, but if you want to learn, I'll teach you."

In the darkness, her voice seemed disembodied, what she was saying unreal, and Mei Ju stammered, "Us learn to read?"

"Why not?" Rooster demanded.

Mei Ju, recalling how she'd nodded at Rooster's logic during Empress's attack, also remembered Bak Ju's elbow, her urgent warnings to desist, the lectures against learning for girls in the months since.

"Well?" Rooster prompted.

"No one will know about the lessons," Shadow assured. "We'll set up a bed in the loft for the three of us so I can teach you in secret."

Mei Ju smiled. In the loft she and Shadow would be free of prying eyes and ears, able at last to forge the joyful friendship Mei Ju had imagined for them.

Her smile faded. No, not free. Not entirely. Rooster would be there.

Rooster, leaving one hand on Shadow's knee, seized Mei Ju's with her other. "Let's clean out the loft and set up our bed this morning so we can start our lessons tonight."

Hot with shame, Mei Ju berated herself for her self-interest. Here surely was an opportunity for her to finally show Rooster kindness, as Shadow was.

Rooster's hands slid from Mei Ju and Shadow.

"What's wrong?" Shadow asked.

"We haven't been friends," Rooster answered bluntly. "So there'll be all sorts of questions about why we suddenly want to share a bed in the loft."

Shadow shook her head. "You know Empress has a sister who wants to become a member and one of the other seniors has two cousins. So I'll suggest we make room for them by setting up a bed in the loft. And since there's only room up there for a makeshift one of planks laid over two sawhorses, I'll also offer to sleep in the loft and ask for two more volunteers. Of course everybody except you two will be taken by surprise, so you're bound to beat anyone else to the jump. And it'll appear too natural for anyone to suspect us."

Rooster laughed approvingly. "You're wily as a fox."

"Yes," Mei Ju agreed.

But Bak Ju would doubtless claim their deceit as proof that book learning for girls opened the door to vices. Then again, were they the magistrate's daughters, deception would be unnecessary.

The plan unfolded more perfectly than Shadow had dared hope. Not only were the members of the girls' house blind to the ruse, but they heaped praise on her for the cleverness of her proposal to make more space. And Widow Low, who came to the house to teach weeping songs, commended the three of them for their willingness to give up their own comfort for new members, concluding, "Sacrifice is the most important virtue a woman can possess."

To ensure their secrecy, Shadow told Mei Ju and Rooster they'd limit study to first light, when everyone else was asleep. Nor would Shadow permit Rooster to go down to the altar in the common room to pray lest she wake any girls on her way. Presenting Rooster with a little statue of Gwoon Yum that she'd bought from a peddler, Shadow said, "We can squeeze a small altar to the Goddess behind our bed."

Wisps of sweet smoke, heat from the glowing tips of incense sticks, and the faint swish of a handbroom courted Shadow into wakefulness. Arching her back like a cat, she stretched, rubbed sleep from her eyes.

Beside her, Rooster was on her knees, sweeping up the last bits of ash from the altar. Mei Ju was standing in the middle of their bed, carefully folding back the shutters from the skylight, sending fresh cool air, still slightly moist from rain that had fallen during the night, into the thick, heavy closeness of the loft.

Shadow took a deep breath, dragged herself upright. She

glanced up at the square of sky: pearl gray tinged ever so faintly with pink.

"We'd better get started," she whispered.

While Shadow retrieved Elder Brother's tattered copy of the *Three Word Classic* from under their bedmat, Rooster quickly set down the handbroom, folded her hands in prayer, and reverently bowed—once, twice, three times—to the Goddess. Mei Ju, having finished latching back the shutters, sat cross-legged directly below the skylight.

Shadow joined her, beckoned to Rooster. "Sit on my other side. That way all three of us can see the page."

As Rooster slid over, Shadow held up the book. "This is the *Three Word Classic*."

She expected them to ask her whose book they were using. When neither did, Shadow understood that they didn't have to, that they'd guessed who the book belonged to, who'd taught her. Their silence proved their discretion, and in her head, Shadow told her brother, "See, you're safe."

Out loud, she said, "I'll point to the characters as I read them to you. Then, after I stop at the end of the sentence, you'll repeat it while I move my finger down the page for you, and you'll keep repeating it until you've memorized all the characters. Alright?"

"Yes," Rooster and Mei Ju chorused softly.

Slowly, deliberately, Shadow read, "Man is by nature born good."

When she stopped, Mei Ju recited the sentence haltingly as Shadow's finger shifted from character to character.

Rooster, who'd leaned forward as Shadow had started reading, slumped back, her forehead beneath her sparse bangs creased in a puzzled frown.

Shadow nudged Rooster. "You're both supposed to recite at the same time."

"I know. But didn't you read it wrong?"

Startled, Shadow hurriedly reviewed the first line of the book. "No, I didn't."

"If man were born good, though, parents wouldn't have to scold babies for being bad, and Empress and the rest of the seniors wouldn't be cruel. So how can that sentence be right?"

Shadow struggled for a response. Elder Brother's teacher had never offered explanations. Nor had Elder Brother or his classmates ever asked their teacher questions. It wasn't permitted. In truth, she was sure they'd given no more thought to meaning than she had, and Shadow had assumed Rooster and Mei Ju would be as accepting.

Mei Ju, silently chewing her lips, seemed to be. But then she rarely questioned anything, whereas Rooster pecked and scratched at every little thing. Indeed, both Elder Brother and Bak Ju claimed this was how Rooster brought troubles on herself, and why the seniors' attempts to break her will were for her own good.

With a heartfelt sigh at the difficulties she'd as willfully drawn on her own self, Shadow fidgeted with the *Three Word Classic*, which had fallen shut on her lap.

"This is the book all students learn to read from, and that's what you want, isn't it? To learn to read?"

Mei Ju nodded.

"I'm sorry," Rooster apologized. "I know I sound ungrateful. But that's it, you see. In spite of my prayers to Gwoon Yum, I still can't stop myself from wanting more than I have.

"That's why I want book learning. So I can study the sutras and become like the monks that pass through Strongworm. They're poorer than my family. Hnnnh, they have to beg for every grain of rice they eat. Yet you never hear them raise their voices except in prayer or song. And they look so untroubled.

"But if I can't even understand the first sentence that every schoolboy learns, how can I hope to grasp the meaning of the sutras? How will I ever feel the monks' peace?"

The realization that she hadn't understood the extent of Rooster's longing struck Shadow so forcefully that she sagged beneath its weight. Nor could Shadow see how, with her limitations, she could help Rooster. Unless . . .

"I know this sounds strange," Shadow said. "But hear me out.

"I used to embroider lotus in solid colors on stiff stems. After studying the flower for the longest time and in all different kinds of light, though, I slowly came to see the petals and leaves have graceful curves. Then I experimented with different stitches and thread, looking for the combinations that would best create those curves and show off the shadings of color. I still can't paint them with my needle as well as I want to, but I'm getting there.

"If you give that same kind of attention to the sutras, maybe you'll find the understanding and peace you're looking for."

Smiling, Rooster picked up the *Three Word Classic*, opened it to the first page, and handed it to Shadow. "Not if I don't learn how to read I won't, Teacher."

A Dead,
Stinking Fate

A MONTH before Mei Ju began learning to read, she'd started her apprenticeship for reeling silk. At first all she'd moved were her eyes, which had peered fearfully through a heavy mist of hot steam at Third Aunt plunging cocoons into a large basin of boiling water to soften the gum binding the fibers.

Third Aunt's wide-brimmed straw hat shielded her from the sun beating down into the courtyard. But she couldn't avoid the heat from the fire beneath the basin, and sweat filmed her face and soaked through her tunic.

Stooped over the basin, she squinted in search of the barely visible loosened silk, and her brow furrowed as she manipulated each strand through an agate guide with one hand, wound the threads onto a revolving reel with her other.

So that the silk she was reeling would be unbroken, she had to keep adding fresh cocoons. She also had to remove the spent cocoons' dregs before they could pollute the water. Soon the tips of her fingers were scalded red.

Mei Ju knew from helping Bak Ju spread salve on her badly blistered fingers and palms that an apprentice's suffering was worse. And when Third Aunt said, "You're standing too far away. Come close so I can guide your hand," Mei Ju could not force herself to step forward.

"To be a reeler, you have to accept discomfort," Third Aunt told her kindly.

Bak Ju, who'd recently completed her apprenticeship and was reeling silk at her own basin across from them, assured Mei Ju, "You'll get used to it. I did."

Ma and Second Aunt, bringing in more baskets of cocoons, said they had too.

"Better get going before Grandmother comes out to check on you," Ma added under her breath.

Still Mei Ju did not, could not move. Realizing there was no chance of escape, however, she didn't resist when Ma pushed her forward and Third Aunt took her hand.

To Mei Ju, learning to read and write was similar to learning to reel. When faced with a new character, she tried to figure out the different strokes and commit them to memory the way she tried to separate out and then gather the silk fibers from cocoons. Writing wasn't as complicated as reeling. She had only to hold down her paper with one hand, move the brush with the other. Yet completing a perfect page of calligraphy was just as hard as reeling a perfect skein of silk since a stroke once made could not be touched up any more than a fiber of silk rewound.

Mei Ju, then, found her lessons with Rooster and Shadow in the loft required as much concentration as her lessons with Third Aunt, and both were painful. The characters, unlike the cocoons, didn't have to be plucked out of near boiling water. But the knowledge that she was betraying her sister's, her entire family's, trust was like a stone pressing against Mei Ju's heart.

When reporting their change in sleeping arrangements to Grandmother, Bak Ju had not only repeated Widow Low's praise but added her own: "Mei Ju and Shadow are maturing, and Rooster's conduct is bound to improve from close association with two such thoughtful girls." And to Mei Ju's relief, Grandmother had dismissed the matter with a nod. No one else in the family had questioned the move then or since. They were too preoccupied with Grandfather's failing health.

Before Grandfather had fallen ill, he'd come home from his concubine's house every morning. The woman would accompany him as far as Shadow's house, and he'd walk the final twenty or so steps without her. He'd rarely been on his own for more than a few moments before a family member either saw him or recognized the tap, tap, tap, of his cane and rushed to assist him. Then, when he was ready to go, he'd scarcely be off his chair and headed for the door before Ba or Second or Third Uncle would leap to his feet and seize Grandfather's elbow, murmuring, "Let me help you." As they left, no one in the room ever offered the usual farewell caution, "Walk slowly." It was as if Grandfather were not quitting the house but merely leaving one room for another.

Since the winter, Grandfather had been too ill to leave the house he shared with his concubine. Yet the family continued to maintain the pretense that he was a part of their own household. The coffin he'd bought for himself waited in the loft above their common room. Every day Grandmother brewed strength-giving soups and gave them to a son or daughter-in-law to take to Grandfather as if they had no further to walk than one of the sleeping rooms. They, in turn, offered reports of Grandfather's condition as if Grandmother had just left his side and would return in a moment.

Mei Ju, like the other grandchildren old enough to sustain the charade, asked Grandmother how he was feeling. The younger ones asked to see him. Regardless, Grandmother always responded, "Grandfather's tired today, but he'll be glad to know that he has such filial grandchildren."

Grandfather died in the night. Fortunately, when Third Aunt came to the girls' house just before dawn to fetch Bak Ju and herself, Mei Ju heard her, and she all but slid down the ladder while Shadow and Rooster hid book, paper, brushes, and inkstone.

Mei Ju had long known from other deaths in Strongworm that men for the most part mourned silently while women let loose high-pitched, penetrating wails and chanted laments not unlike the weeping songs for brides. And Widow Low, when teaching weeping songs, often cautioned, "Practicing death laments will bring bad luck. So you have to learn them yourselves by paying close attention whenever you have the opportunity to hear them."

But Mei Ju could never seem to separate herself sufficently from the mourners' sorrow to listen as she should, and she'd memorized no more than a few stock phrases. On their way home, Bak Ju reminded Mei Ju of her ignorance, the need to listen closely to the lamenting for Grandfather.

"I will," Mei Ju vowed.

Stepping over the threshold, seeing Grandfather's coffin before the altar, and hearing sobs from family members already gathered around him, Mei Ju's resolve crumbled. How could she not mourn her own grandfather with her full mind and heart? Mei Ju chewed her lips. How could she mourn him without thinking of his concubine with whom he'd laughed and sung?

At her sister's prompting, Mei Ju took one of the lengths of coarse white cloth Third Aunt was handing them. After Mei Ju poked her head through the hole in her piece, Bak Ju helped her straighten the mourning cloth so it covered both her tunic and pants and handed her a white hood to pull over her hair.

Third Aunt nudged them toward the rest of the family. Also covered in the white of mourning, they were kneeling in proper order of age and importance beside Grandfather, who was lying scarily wraithlike in the open coffin.

Of course his concubine was absent. She'd never once

crossed their threshold. When Mei Ju, as a small girl, had asked her sister the reason, Bak Ju had told her sternly, "The concubine is an outsider. She's nothing to our family."

Now Mei Ju, taking her place between her sister and girl cousins, scolded herself as sternly. "Listen to the laments. Pay close attention."

Thick black plumes of pungent smoke from the incense and candles crowding the altar stung Mei Ju's eyes, and they teared. Blinking hard, she focused on Ma, who was leaning over Grandfather, placing a ball of rice in his hand while wailing:

> "Don't be afraid of the wild dogs.
> Feed them this rice and they won't trouble you,
> They'll let you walk unmolested to the Courts of
>   Hell."

Ma set a few rooster feathers and a swatch of dog hair in the coffin, crying:

> "Don't be afraid because you can no longer see.
> This cock will crow so you'll know when dawn
>   breaks.
> This dog will howl so you'll know when night falls."

She dropped to her knees.

> "Don't be afraid.
> You have lots of descendants.
> Wish your grandchildren peace and good fortune!
> Wish peace to all those who come to pay their
>   respects!"

As she knocked her forehead against the floor in obeisance, another voice rose, strong and bitter:

> "This ill-fated person is your concubine,
> Yet you let me be treated like a stranger.
> Why should I be treated as though I were not kin?
> Why should I be treated like a beggar?
> Ai yah, I am miserable!
> What will become of me?"

Mei Ju wouldn't have been any more shocked had her grandfather sat up in his coffin. Indeed, there were muffled gasps from everyone present. And despite Widow Low's assurances that a woman could go to any house where there'd been a death and say anything in a lament without fear, Mei Ju expected her father and uncles to swoop down on the concubine who must have slipped in unnoticed while everyone's attention was on Ma. But they did not, and the concubine remained where she'd planted herself—kneeling midway between the front door and the foot of the coffin.

At the head of the coffin, Grandmother, her voice thin and cracked with age but no less bitter than the concubine's, cried:

> "This dead-fated person gave you sons,
> This dead-fated person raised them;
> Now you have grandsons as well as sons.
> Yet you valued me less than a blade of grass,
> You didn't treat me well."

Listening, Mei Ju realized Grandmother was not merely criticizing Grandfather but belittling the concubine's pain, pushing it aside with her own. Widow Low had warned the girls that verbal battles sometimes occurred between women lamenting the dead, but Mei Ju had never witnessed such a struggle, and her belly, seized by the singers' distress as well as her own, cramped so painfully that she doubled over.

Bak Ju wrapped her arms around Mei Ju, bracing her. "Don't worry. I'm sure that woman can't outsing Grandmother."

The concubine's response pierced Bak Ju's murmur, Mei Ju's turmoil:

> "This dead-fated person looked after you.
> But you didn't look out for me.
> I cared for you when you were sick,
> Who will care for me?"

Grandmother, sounding more angry now than bitter, shot back:

> "Before my husband had another woman,
> He had no troubles at all.
> He had no headaches or any other problems."

The concubine's tone also changed, becoming that of a humble suppliant seeking to ingratiate:

> "If I were like your wife,
> I would have a good fate.

I would have sons pulling at my jacket,
Sons clinging to my legs.
But my fate stinks,
And I have none."

Pity for the concubine swept over Mei Ju like flood waters
breaking through a dike, and she shuddered. Bak Ju's arms
around her tightened. Burying her face in Bak Ju's shoulder,
Mei Ju struggled to hold back her tears. But she couldn't. Nor
could she bear to listen to any more.

During the forty-nine days of high mourning that preceded
Grandfather's burial, Ba hired laborers to take over the work
in their fields and wormhouse. Ba also engaged a priest to
chant prayers and perform the necessary rituals, to make sure
no mistakes were made.

Widow Low—even more knowledgeable on certain details than the priest because of her long years of participation
in white affairs—came every day to give additional advice
about when each mourner should bow to Grandfather and
how many times; what offerings to make, how to prepare
them, and the order in which they should be presented. Instead of reeling silk, Mei Ju and Bak Ju folded silver paper
into ingots which they then burned in the courtyard—together with paper clothes and houses and servants—for
Grandfather's use in the spirit world.

Before each meal, Ma set a bowl of rice and a platter of taro and dumplings with chicken or pork for Grandfather on top of his coffin, now closed. She also sent Mei Ju or her sister out to the street with a basin of rice mixed with scraps for any hungry ghosts that might be lurking, so they wouldn't slip in unseen and steal from Grandfather.

But no one—not Ba or the priest or Widow Low, not even Grandmother—had the power to stop Grandfather's concubine from exercising her right to lament, to criticize the family for refusing to recognize her in the past, to demand fair treatment for herself in the future. And she returned day after day.

The concubine always dropped to her knees at the front door, scuffing, wearing thin her pants, which had long turned black from crawling across the floor. Her hands, almost as filthy, had smeared her mourning white with ugly smudges since she often beat her chest and tore at the cloth while singing. From beneath her mourning cap, her hair straggled untidily, falling across her face, which was streaked with tears and dirt. Her voice, having grown hoarse, occasionally faltered in the middle of a song. Still she persisted.

According to Widow Low, the male relatives of a singer could kneel beside her and weep to show they sympathized, and Grandmother was surrounded with sons and grandsons shedding tears on her behalf. But outside of Grandmother, who *had* to respond to the concubine's laments, everybody in the family was still acting as if the woman did not exist. Certainly no one knelt by her. Not even once.

Mei Ju knew from the gossips that the concubine had been sold into a house of pleasure as a child. But didn't the woman have a single male relative she could send for? Or was she unable to send for anyone since she could not write, and now, with Grandfather gone, it was unlikely any man in Strongworm would be willing to help her. Was that why she called out so desperately to Grandfather, why her weeping was intensifying, her songs becoming increasingly bitter and unrestrained?

When Mei Ju took food out to the street for hungry ghosts, the laments—penetrating the walls of the house, sailing out of its windows and doors—pursued her, as did the smoke, heavy with ash, that billowed from the offerings burning in their courtyard. The singers' bitterness and the acrid taste of soot choked her throat, stung her eyes and made them water.

Through her tears, Mei Ju sometimes noticed men and women shudder, shake their heads as they hurried past. And above the singing, the crackle of flames, she heard some of them claim the war of words was likely upsetting Grandfather's spirit as it was every living person, every creature within hearing. A few muttered, "The wife has too much pride. She should relent and make peace with the concubine."

How Mei Ju wished these men and women could kneel beside the concubine and add their supplications to hers. But of course they couldn't—or wouldn't—any more than Mei Ju.

The war of words did not end until Grandfather's burial, and because Grandmother had failed to silence the concubine, the village gossips declared the woman victorious. But Grandfather was in the ground less than two days before the concubine—homeless after Ba obeyed Grandmother's blunt, "Evict her!"—walked out of Strongworm alone, carrying all she possessed in a small cloth bundle. Then the gossips gave Grandmother the victory. Mei Ju, though, could not forget that Grandmother, who'd been a wife and was surrounded by dutiful sons and grandsons, had lamented every bit as bitterly as the concubine.

T W O

1836–1837

A Matchmaker's Claims

BEFORE MAMA and Baba had agreed to Elder Brother's betrothal the previous winter, they'd used an elaborate network of relatives, clansmen, friends, and acquaintances to verify the matchmaker's claims that the girl under consideration was healthy, filial, and pliant, a skillful reeler and willing worker. What Elder Brother had wanted to know was whether his betrothed was pretty, and over evening rice, Shadow had asked their parents on his behalf.

As soon as she began posing the question, Elder Brother's neck and ears flushed. Swiftly he lifted his bowl to his lips, but it was too small to hide the spread of color.

"How auspicious," Baba observed with a barely suppressed chortle. "You're turning a lucky red."

Mama's chins and belly shook merrily. "Wah, you're so bright, we don't need any other light."

Burying his face in his bowl, Elder Brother rapidly shoveled rice with his chopsticks. A few grains fell on the table.

Mama raised both hands in mock horror. "Remember, every grain you drop represents a pockmark on your bride's face."

Hurriedly Shadow picked up the grains her brother had scattered, threw them into her own bowl. Under the table, she felt her brother's foot prod hers.

"Come on," she urged their parents. "Don't keep Elder Brother in suspense."

"You know we haven't seen the girl ourselves," Mama said, her chins and belly rippling anew.

Shadow groaned. "How did the matchmaker describe her?"

Behind his beard, Baba's lips twitched. "No one can live up to a matchmaker's exaggerations, so we'd best not repeat them. Otherwise Elder Brother's bound to be disappointed, and that's no way to start a marriage."

Their parents' responses fueled Shadow's curiosity, and waiting for the bridal sedan to arrive, she puffed and hissed like a kettle left on a stove too long.

But when at last the bridal guide led Elder Brother's betrothed into their common room, all Shadow could see of her was that she was half a head shorter than Elder Brother, and her hands, folded demurely, were small, the skin unusually fair. Everything else was hidden beneath her traditional bridal headdress, beaded veil, loose-fitting, elaborately embroidered red jacket and skirt.

Hoping to somehow peer behind the bride's veil as it

swayed back and forth when she bowed to the family's ancestors, Shadow craned her neck, bobbed and twirled her head.

"You're fifteen, not five," Mama hissed. "Act like it."

Breathing deeply, Shadow forced herself to stand still, but she continued to stare. And, while Elder Brother's bride was kneeling and pouring tea for Baba and Mama, Shadow noticed her brother—handsome in his rich black skull cap and long, gleaming black satin robe—likewise studying his bride. Was he able to catch more than slivers of pale forehead, powdered cheeks, and reddened lips between the strands of pearls hanging from the headdress?

As if she were creating a design for an embroidery, Shadow tried to assemble these fragments into a meaningful whole, realized they were too fractured. Neither was she able to satisfy her curiosity during the wedding banquet that followed, for although she sat at the same table as her brother's bride, now her elder sister-in-law, women piling pieces of tender, juicy chicken and duck and suckling pig into the bride's bowl got between them. Furthermore, Elder Sister-in-law didn't once push aside the dangling pearls with her chopsticks to eat. Motionless as a statue, she maintained a steady murmur of thanks while her bridal guide snapped up the tasty, moist morsels of flesh and crispy skin.

Shadow, thoroughly frustrated, decided to spy on the bride-teasing where Elder Brother's friends would try and make Elder Sister-in-law reveal her face.

"You can't," Mei Ju protested.

Rooster agreed. "A girl can't hide in a roomful of men without getting caught."

Shadow hesitated. Although her brother had asked her to question their parents about his betrothed, he would certainly disapprove of her plan to satisfy her own curiosity, as would Mama and Baba. But then, they wouldn't ever know about it any more than they knew she'd given Rooster and Mei Ju lessons in the loft of the girls' house for almost two years.

With a self-satisfied giggle, Shadow drew her friends into her parents' sleeping room, pointed at the wall that divided it from the room her brother and wife would share. "You see how the wall stops short of the ceiling by three, four feet? I'll set a stool on my parent's bed, stand on it, and look down at the bride-teasing on the other side."

"You have to leave with us for the girls' house, or my sister will want to know why," Mei Ju fretted. "She's probably looking for us already."

Shadow slumped onto her parents' bed. How could she have failed to consider Bak Ju? What else had she overlooked?

"Mei Ju and I can put Bak Ju off the scent," Rooster offered.

The furrows of worry creasing Mei Ju's forehead deepened. "We can try. But what if Shadow doesn't get to the girls' house before it's locked for the night?"

Rooster waved her hand airily. "That's easy. We'll climb out onto the roof and watch for her so we can let her in."

Rooster's confidence restored Shadow's, and she threw her arms around both her friends, laughing, "You're more wily than me!"

. . .

From her perch on the stool, Shadow's view of the bridal couple standing near the head of their large, four poster bed was every bit as good as she'd anticipated. But the dark, waxy smoke spiraling up from the half-dozen wedding candles lighting the room tickled her nose, irritated her throat, and stung her eyes, making them water. Blinking furiously, she pinched her nostrils and cut off a sneeze as the bridal guide finished tying back the embroidered blue bedcurtains and directed Elder Sister-in-law and Elder Brother to sit.

Flushing crimson as the wedding sash looped across his broad chest from shoulder to waist, Elder Brother dropped down immediately, and his friends, who'd crowded into the narrow space between bed and door, teased him for being overeager, turning him a darker shade of red. They also showered Elder Sister-in-law with praise for her modesty in hanging back.

The bridal guide repeated the instruction. Elder Sister-in-law remained rooted.

"Wife, sit!" a wag sternly ordered.

The young men closest to the wag took up the cry. Then the ones behind them began to chant, "Wife, sit! Wife, sit!" Soon all the guests, even the ones so far back in the crush that they were outside the room and couldn't possibly see, were demanding she sit.

Head bowed, Elder Sister-in-law edged over to the foot of the bed, obeyed.

"Closer!" the guests in the room demanded.

The rest swiftly followed their lead. "Closer! Closer!"

Elder Sister-in-law didn't shift an inch. Was she less pliant than the matchmaker had led Mama and Baba to believe? Or did young men brag falsely about their exploits during bride-teasings, their success in forcing brides to do their bidding?

Suddenly, Elder Brother slid from the head of the bed towards the middle. His friends bellowed approval, and Shadow, startled by her brother's boldness, wondered whether his eagerness to see his bride might so overcome his bashfulness that he'd draw aside Elder Sister-in-law's veil himself.

"Bride, go to your husband!" one of the guests shouted.

"Yes, the bride must move," another yelled.

Others made the same demand, and their cries soon became a solid chant. Still Elder Sister-in-law remained rooted. Then, as the chant swelled louder, Elder Brother bounced comically from the middle of the bed to the foot, halting mere inches from his bride.

Shadow's eyes bulged. Elder Brother's friends roared with laughter. Now, Shadow thought. Now they'll demand Elder Brother pull back Elder Sister-in-law's veil, and he'll willingly obey. Instead, the crowd pushed Trickster Lee forward.

Gnashing his teeth so loudly that Shadow, up on her perch, could hear him, Trickster Lee hurled out an arm in the large, exaggerated manner of an actor and dangled a purple-red plum on a string between the bride and groom.

"Bite the plum," he commanded with droll ferocity. "Bite."

Instantly the rest of the guests called out, "Bite."

Of course! The bride, biting into the plum, was bound to expose her face. Then why was Elder Brother lunging at the plum and snaring it with his teeth?

Angling the stick from which the plum hung, Trickster Lee jerked Elder Brother's face so close to Elder Sister-in-law's that they would have touched had she not ducked. As she dove, the pearl veil swung wildly. But her head was bowed so low that Shadow doubted even Elder Brother, turned the color of the plum, could see her face. Certainly Shadow, leaning over the partition as far as she dared, couldn't.

"Bride and groom must bite the fruit together," Trickster Lee scolded.

"Together!" the guests chorused. "Bite into it together."

The bridal guide nudged Elder Sister-in-law. But she didn't respond to the guide any more than she did to the guests' loud clamoring.

All at once, Elder Brother took the entire plum into his mouth. Moments later, he spat out the pit.

His friends shouted their disapproval. Some stamped their feet. When a few went so far as to raise their fists, Elder Sister-in-law shrank against the bedpost. Trickster Lee shook his stick at her.

Leaping up, Elder Brother capered, playing the fool. And as his friends' angry shouting turned into guffaws, Shadow understood her brother was trying to protect his bride from them. From her, too, although he did not know it.

Scrambling off the stool, she slipped out and ran to the girls' house.

· · ·

Months later, after they'd become friends, Elder Sister-in law—her face round and white as the moon, her ready smile warm as the sun—told Shadow, "When I saw your brother doing everything he could to take his friends' attention away from me during the bride-teasing, I knew he was as exceptional as our matchmaker claimed."

By then, Strongworm was buzzing with talk about Young Chow's wedding, the girl coming to be his wife.

"The bride's name is Yun Yun."

"Double Gift, eh? Double Sacrifice, more like."

"Where's this Gift, this Sacrifice from?"

"Twin Hills."

"That's almost a half-day's journey by boat from Strongworm!"

"Any closer and the bride's family would've heard talk about the Chows."

"And know the matchmaker's lying."

"You got that right. No lies, no bride. Not for a rotter like Young Chow."

"Maybe a bride will sweeten him."

"Not a chance!"

"If you ask me, getting married made his old man meaner."

"That's because Old Lady Chow is as tough as he is."

"Old Man Chow's got the fists. Old Lady Chow's got the mouth."

"I'll take his fists to her mouth any day. That tongue of hers is sharp as an executioner's blade!"

The same could be said of the gossips' tongues, Shadow

thought. Yet they didn't exaggerate. Her girls' house was next door to the Chows, and she'd heard their loud quarreling more nights than she cared to count. Moreover, as far back as she could remember, Young Chow had been a vicious bully.

Once, she and Elder Brother had been flying a dragon kite that had taken him months to make. Their faces turned up to the sky, Shadow had been admiring the way the dragon's gold scales glittered in the sun, Elder Brother had been shouting out his pleasure at how its body twisted and leaped in the wind, when, suddenly, Young Chow had appeared from nowhere and cut the kite's string.

Young Chow was as mean now as he'd been then, and Shadow understood why his parents said the wedding would take place within a month of the betrothal: the more time between the two events, the greater the risk that the bride's family might discover the truth behind the matchmaker's lies.

A Red
Affair

YUN YUN had noticed no stranger in Twin Hills, no sign of her parents negotiating with a matchmaker on her account. So she was stunned to see the traditional betrothal gifts of tea, cakes, and betel nuts on the table in their common room. And while her head was yet reeling, her mother removed one of the small golden cakes from the box on the table, formally presented it to her with both hands.

The cake was one of Yun Yun's favorites. About to bite into it, however, Yun Yun realized the light, fluffy pastry signified not just betrothal, but the marriage that would follow, and with it, the loss of her good friend Lucky, her family, everyone and everything she'd ever known.

Crying, "No," she set the cake back in the round lacquer box.

"Silly girl," her mother said, retrieving the cake and holding it out to Yun Yun. "Don't you know you must eat it to show you accept the betrothal?"

Not knowing what else she could do, Yun Yun reluctantly took the cake, broke off a little piece, put it in her mouth. The morsel was dry on her tongue, bitter as ash, and she had to force herself to swallow.

"Silly girl," her mother repeated. "You should be happy. Your betrothed's parents, the Chows, own their land instead of leasing like we do. Better yet, where we still mostly grow rice here in Twin Hills, the Chows' village, Strongworm, is almost entirely given over to silk production, which yields a greater profit."

Yun Yun's blood quickened: when peeling off the paddy leeches that clung to each other's ankles and calves during rice planting, she and Lucky had often dreamtalked of marrying into villages where silk was king.

"True, Strongworm is nearly a day's walk from Twin Hills. But the two villages are considerably closer by boat."

And she and Lucky would convince her parents to find her a husband either in Strongworm or close to it.

"Furthermore, Young Chow—like your father—is an only son. There'll be no need for you to vie with sisters-in-law for favor with your mother-in-law, no squabbling over who inherits what."

Yun Yun, thinking of the warm camaraderie Lucky's easy-going sisters-in-law enjoyed, felt a stab of disappointment, dismissed it. With Lucky nearby, the absence of sisters-in-law wouldn't matter.

Eager to talk to Lucky, Yun Yun stuffed the unfinished betrothal cake into her mouth.

"The Chows want the wedding next month, before the new silk season begins."

The sweetness on Yun Yun's tongue soured: she and Lucky would be separated for months, maybe longer.

The rush of preparations did nothing to ease Yun Yun's distress. Worse, when Lucky asked her parents to find her a husband in Strongworm, they refused. "We couldn't bear to have you so far from us."

Too late, Yun Yun realized she and Lucky should have told their parents sooner of their hopes to be married into the same or neighboring villages. And, shut up in her family's loft for a bride's ritual period of mourning with her friends, Yun Yun dropped onto the floor. Lucky did likewise. Knee to knee, they then poured out their regret and sorrow in weeping songs.

On her wedding eve, Yun Yun was still crying:

"What is happening is so unexpected."

And Lucky, her tone as desperate as Yun Yun's, echoed:

"Happy in our companionship,
We failed to see misfortune descending."

Tears streaming down their faces, the two continued to call and respond:

"We've laughed together."
"And played together."

"We've picked flowers."

"And strolled down paths."

"I'd hoped to enjoy more time with you."

"But we're fated to part."

"Tomorrow I go to the rascal."

"And there's no return."

"Let's pledge friendship for a hundred years."

"Let's pledge friendship forever and ever."

Yun Yun, too distraught over their coming separation to go on, buried her face in her hands.

Lucky, embracing her, railed, "Even your parents' cabbage and livestock are fully matured before they sell them. Why couldn't your parents wait a few more years before they sold you?"

In truth, Yun Yun—small boned, with a delicately shaped head above a slender, graceful neck and narrow shoulders— did feel more child than woman, unready to leave home. But her mother had told her, "I was also sixteen when I married." And her father had said, "A matchmaker doesn't come along every day with an offer from a family as ideal as the Chows. I couldn't refuse."

Yun Yun was convinced her parents had accepted the offer for her sake, not their own. As she'd pointed out to Lucky, the bride price from the Chows had not included cash. Nor did the cost of their gifts, added together, come to a huge amount.

Yun Yun, then, defended her parents with an improvised song of gratitude that she sobbed into Lucky's chest:

"A sugar bowl in the honey pot,
Is no sweeter than my life at home;
A shock of rush inside a shoe of straw,
Is not better protected than I by my mother's side."

Yun Yun even blamed herself for their coming separation, crying as she dragged herself from Lucky's arms and descended the ladder for her final meal with her family:

"I am worthless as a weed.
Had Father and Mother been fortunate,
I'd have been born a son;
Father would have hired many people
To fetch a maiden.
But Father and Mother were unfortunate;
A daughter was reared,
And soon that daughter will be dead to them."

Throwing one last lingering look up at Lucky, Yun Yun took her place at the table, accepted the bowl of sweet rice her mother placed in front of her, and joined in the ritual chorus of "Sik faan, eat rice."

All around the table, chopsticks clicked as slowly and deliberately as Yun Yun's. Her mother and father were usually measured in their eating. And her grandparents, with only a few blackened stumps of teeth left, always chewed and chewed and chewed before they swallowed. But Yun Yun was used to her three younger brothers racing through their meals as they did everything else. Now they were laboring over the clumps of tasty rice like she was. Were they also

thinking of how she'd taught each of them to use their chopsticks? How she'd planted stems of bak choy in their rice as
trees for them to fell. How she'd guided their little hands,
circling their bowls of soup like birds, then swooping down
to snap up crunchy bits of lotus root and sweet red dates. Did
the rice they were swallowing seem like lumps of stone to
them too? Were they, their parents and grandparents forcing
themselves to eat, as she was, because the stickiness of the
sweet rice symbolized their close relationship, the hope that
their ties would not be entirely severed?

Every grain scoured from their bowls, Yun Yun's mother
rose and sang:

> "All daughters must leave home,
> But few have your luck.
> Your mother-in-law's house is a rich fish pond.
> You'll doff your cotton tunics,
> And wear only silk.
> Yes, you're entering the Dragon Gate of Fortune.
> You'll ride to the sky on a white crane."

Of course the future her mother painted was one Yun Yun
wanted—but without losing those dear to her. As her mother
had just reminded her, however, remaining home wasn't a
possibility, and Yun Yun returned to the loft to dress with a
heavy step and even heavier heart.

Waiting for her was not only Lucky but the bridal guide
her mother had hired. This guide was a brusque, middle-
aged stranger from another village chosen for her expertise
in red affairs and her good fortune: she'd given birth to nine

children, six of them sons, all of them living. Tall and heavy-set, she loomed over both Yun Yun and Lucky. Yet the woman gave directions with such clarity and conviction that Yun Yun was glad of her presence. Slipping on her shimmering, sequined, dragon-and-phoenix wedding jacket and skirt, Yun Yun even found herself savoring their weight, the plea-sure of silk caressing her skin.

Then the guide opened the jar of pow fa, the sticky paste made from wood shavings that keeps hair in place. And as the loft filled with its pungent, bitter odor, the guide began the ritual haircombing that would replace Yun Yun's childish pigtails with a complicated wifely bun, thereby transforming her from a girl to a woman.

At the first pass of the comb, Lucky chanted, "Slide the comb from roots to ends." And Yun Yun—remembering how they'd played at red affairs in the girls' house, the horror of having her head pierced by the groom's pin—shuddered. Indeed, had she not gripped her stool with both hands, she would have bolted.

She and Lucky had long ago figured out from watching chickens and dogs mate just what the groom's pin repre-sented. Now the memory of the animals' squawks, sharp nips, yelps, and drawn-out howls of anguish stoked Yun Yun's panic.

Quickly she reminded herself of her mother's promise. "Your father has never hurt me. And you can be sure we'll tell the matchmaker to find you a good husband. One as good as my parents found for me."

While discussing with Lucky how escape from hurt might

be possible, Yun Yun had long ago wondered out loud
whether there were husbands and wives who coupled like the
moths in the wormhouse. To her, these creatures looked as if
they were performing mysterious, tender, intimate dances.
Dances that sometimes aroused a delicious trembling in the
pit of her belly.

"Mine too," Lucky had confessed.

Within the curtains of their bed, they'd since awakened
these pleasurable shiverings in each other by pretending they
were moths, fluttering their eyelashes and trailing their fingers along each other's bare skin. . . .

Loud blasts of a horn jolted Yun Yun back to the loft.

"The groom's golden pin finds its mark," Lucky intoned.

In a single smooth sweep, the guide picked up the groom's
pin, slid it expertly across Yun Yun's skull, into her womanly
bun. Yun Yun's eyes filled with tears.

"Lament as much as you want, but don't cry," the guide
warned. "Tears will make tracks in your face powder."

Without breaking the rhythm of her chant, Lucky seized
the handkerchief from the table, dabbed gently at Yun Yun's
eyes, pressed the square of red silk into her hands. The guide
set the elaborate headdress in place and secured it, completing the haircombing ritual as Lucky shrilled the final lines of
the song.

> "Head crowned with five golden phoenix,
> Pearls dangling from their mouths,
> Hiding the beautiful bride."

Yun Yun's head drooped under the weight of the headdress,

and the strands of pearls clattered together noisily. Blinded now as well as thrown off balance, she would have fallen had Lucky not grabbed her elbow and steadied her. Relieved she didn't have to descend the ladder on her own two feet, Yun Yun climbed onto the guide's broad back, and the woman, panting hard, carried her down to the common room where the family waited.

With a loud grunt, the guide set Yun Yun inside a large, flat bamboo sieve. Yun Yun—squinting through tear-swollen eyes between swaying strands of pearls—tried to find her pair of new red shoes for a happy new life, failed.

Crouching, Lucky scooped up the shoes. Yun Yun leaned on Lucky, and together, they worked each foot into a shoe, their fingers touching, intertwining—slowly parting.

The guide, still breathing heavily, steered Yun Yun over to her grandparents, parents, and brothers. Soaking her handkerchief with her tears, Yun Yun called out sad farewells to them one by one.

"Faster," the guide urged in a whisper. "We have a long journey ahead."

Yun Yun, pretending she didn't hear, forged on:

> "Other daughters are just a village or two
> From grandparents, parents, and brothers.
> I will be separated from mine
> By ten thousand layers of clouds."

The guide nudged Yun Yun.

"But with ghosts and goblins approaching from all
    sides,
I can do nothing but sing my sad song."

The guide cleared her throat, then coughed with increasing irritation. Yun Yun, realizing she couldn't spin out her leavetaking any longer, completed it with a vow to keep her family in her heart forever.

Swiftly the guide herded Yun Yun into the bridal sedan, slammed the door shut, ordered the bearers forward. The men stepped lively, and Yun Yun rocked in the suffocating darkness, helpless as if she were bound hand and foot.

"In this chair
I am held captive.
My brows locked in sorrow,
No peace in my heart.
Who will have pity on me?"

Passersby shouted their approval.
"How filial!"
"She knows so many songs."
"What learning!"
"She'll make a good wife."
A few villages later, Yun Yun's voice cracked, then disappeared altogether. Still she continued to lament.

When the bearers stopped and the guide threw open the door, Yun Yun slammed shut her eyes against the glare, gratefully gulped the rush of cool air, the happy realization that Strongworm was not as far from Twin Hills as she'd feared.

Stiff as the breeze gusting in, she tried to rise. The guide pushed her back.

"Just throw out your handkerchief."

Yun Yun gasped. Lost in her laments, she'd forgotton about the ritual that marked the end of her right to express her unhappiness at leaving her family.

"We're just half way to Strongworm?" she stammered hoarsely.

"Yes, so hurry, or it'll be night before we get there."

Fresh tears flooded Yun Yun's eyes.

"No more crying or lamenting," the guide reminded.

Yun Yun daubed at her eyes with her handkerchief, now a sodden wad.

"What did I tell you?" the guide demanded.

She grasped Yun Yun's arm, propelled it out the door.

"Drop the handkerchief. Drop it and sing."

Yun Yun, remembering how Lucky had placed the red square of silk in her hand, tightened her grip. With an exasperated grunt, the guide pried Yun Yun's fist open, and the handkerchief, deeply creased and heavy with tears, fell into the dirt.

Yun Yun stared at the red stain. Then, raising her eyes, she saw behind the guide a scrap of cloudless blue sky. And, reminded of the glowing future awaiting her in Strongworm, Yun Yun mustered what voice she could and chanted:

"This handkerchief of sorrow
I drop onto the ground.
It stays on the ground,
And the sky turns bright.
All the tears I've shed
Sink into the sea.
All the curses I've uttered
Sink into the sea too.
Good fortune carries me on this road,
This road that is free of worry,
This road that is filled with peace,
This road that leads to my husband's home."

Wife

HORNS BLARED, cymbals clashed, startling Yun Yun from damp, hot sleep into the cramped, dark rocking of the wedding sedan, a terrible sense of yearning and loss spilling out in song:

> "You, Lucky, are in the West,
> I am going to the East,
> Departing . . ."

A deafening series of explosions blasted Yun Yun into full wakefulness, and she realized with horror that the horns and cymbals must have been announcing her arrival in Strongworm so the Chows could set off firecrackers in welcome. Had anyone in the village heard her weeping song? Or had the horns and cymbals drowned her out? Shivering despite the heat, she prayed the noise of the firecrackers was not only driving away evil spirits but any bad luck she might have drawn on herself with her song.

The sedan lurched into a hard halt, and Yun Yun felt the impact of fists pounding against the door. A moment later, the door flew open, and she tumbled into dense clouds of smoke, the stink of burned powder, her bridal guide's arms.

Dizzy and weak from the long journey, Yun Yun found she couldn't stand without the woman's help. Nor could Yun Yun see clearly through her tear-swollen eyes, her bridal veil. But desperate to create a favorable impression on her new family, she propped herself up against her guide and listened closely to her promptings for the wedding rites.

One by one, Yun Yun bowed to the Chows' ancestors before the family altar, then Old Man Chow, Old Lady Chow, and Young Chow. Finally, she poured tea for her husband's mother and father, now hers.

To Yun Yun's consternation, the blurry glimpses that she caught of her in-laws were of a healthy man and woman, neither of whom were anywhere near the age of her grandparents. So why had the matchmaker given old age and infirmity as the Chows' reasons for insisting on a short betrothal? Moreover, the altar and the room's furnishings seemed modest for people with means. Were the Chows perhaps avoiding ostentation? Was that why there were only three tables for the wedding banquet?

Seated at the women's table, Yun Yun wished her husband had a younger sister. A girl near her own age. A girl she, Yun Yun, would not be afraid to approach with her questions. A girl who would become her friend.

In truth, Yun Yun wished for her good friend in Twin Hills, for Lucky.

. . .

Out of a confused mixture of modesty and fear, Yun Yun hadn't attempted so much as a glancing peek at her husband while performing the rituals that made her a wife.

During the bride-teasing, however, Young Chow surrendered so readily to the men's boisterous demands that Yun Yun's fear turned into pity. Indeed, she worried he was suffering as much as she over the embarrassments that were being forced on her through him, and she wondered how she could show her husband that she didn't fault him for being weak, that she valued gentleness over strength.

When the men, growing ever more rowdy, shouted for Yun Yun to draw aside her veil and look at her husband, she hesitated for only a moment before bravely reaching up, gathering the strands of beads between her trembling fingers, raising her downcast eyes in search of his.

As she faced her husband squarely, the men roared.

"A bold one!"

"Better watch out."

Yet Yun Yun did not drop her gaze. She couldn't. She was too terrified by what she saw: eyes set deep in a sea of flesh, eyes glittering like a rat's when it sees fat.

No sooner did Young Chow dismiss the bridal guide than he pounced, pushing Yun Yun onto her back so roughly the side of her head struck the bedpost with a loud crack.

Crushed beneath him, she could hardly breathe. The straw bedmat bit into her buttocks, her back. And as he mauled her breasts, tore off her pants, and pried apart her legs, she sealed her eyes shut against his brutishness, her shame. She bit her lips to keep from crying out.

But she couldn't close out the stink of his breath. The terrible sound of grunting as he labored to drive his blade into her most private parts. The searing pain when his blade, finding its mark, drove into her, tearing and ripping as it sliced deeper and deeper. The memory of her good friend's tender pleasuring, her mother's promise to find her a good husband, a man like her father, a man who would never hurt her.

Two nights in her husband's bed felt like two years to Yun Yun. The cold faces and sharp tongues of her parents-in-law made the hours out of his bed difficult to endure as well.

That her bridal guide had changed from brusque to sympathetic helped a little. What sustained Yun Yun, though, was the knowledge that on the third day she could return to Twin Hills with her guide.

Of course, Yun Yun understood that at the day's end, she would have to come back to the Chows. Alone. But for the space of a watch, perhaps an entire afternoon, she would have the warm comfort of her grandparents' and parents' smiles, her little brothers' hugs, Lucky's embrace.

While dressing for the ritual third-day visit, however, Yun Yun reconsidered. Her parents would be looking for confirmation that she was happy in her new home, and even if she were clever enough to answer their questions with lies, which Yun Yun doubted, how could she hide her clumsy gait, her face?

Hard as she tried, the pain between her legs made it impossible for her to walk normally. And from the tenderness that she felt when she washed her face, Yun Yun guessed the crack against the bedpost on her wedding night had bruised her skin. One glance and her parents would know they'd failed her. Badly.

So Yun Yun, citing the distance between Twin Hills and Strongworm as her reason, offered to forgo the ritual visit, and her mother-in-law pounced on it. Tipping her bridal guide generously from her own small store of cash, Yun Yun asked the woman to buy some fried sesame dumplings, steamed sponge cakes, and turnip goh for her parents.

"Don't you mean stinky beancurd and bitter melons?" the guide said.

Yun Yun understood the woman's meaning. But Yun Yun wanted to believe, *had* to believe that her parents had not failed entirely, that when she learned how to please her husband and in-laws, they'd soften, become kind.

So Yun Yun, pressing the string of cash into the guide's hands, begged, "When you take the sweets to my family, don't worry them by repeating what you've seen and heard. Tell them the sweets are a gift from the Chows. Say I'm happy."

In the girls' house next door, Mei Ju heard Yun Yun's in-laws and husband yelling at her night after night. And out on the streets and in the fields, it seemed to Mei Ju that Yun Yun had the look of a frightened dog: when walking, she skulked against the walls of houses; if approached, she cowered, her eyes darting fearfully.

One morning, as Mei Ju and her sister and Shadow were leaving the girls' house for home, Yun Yun limped past them, leaving such a heavy scent of linament in her wake that their noses pricked and their eyes stung.

Mei Ju, turning so as not to embarrass her, saw Shadow wince.

"I'd rather be Eldest Cousin," Bak Ju muttered.

More than ten years had passed since Eldest Cousin had died. Mei Ju, only five at the time, hadn't understood their cousin was dying, hadn't grasped their second uncle's intention when he'd started bundling his daughter's quilt around her. But Eldest Cousin, not quite eight and wasted from the spitting blood disease, must have known, for as soon as her father loomed over her, she flailed her arms and legs, mere skin over bone, and mewled pitifully between rasping breaths, "Don't. I'll get better. I will."

Second Uncle, his face strangely twisted, stolidly continued to cocoon Eldest Cousin in the quilt. Confused, Mei Ju turned to her sister. For once, however, Bak Ju looked as bewildered as herself.

Frightened now, Mei Ju cried for their mother. Bak Ju, staring at uncle and cousin, wrapped her arms around Mei Ju. Ignoring them, Second Uncle scooped Eldest Cousin into his arms, stalked out of the room toward their front door.

Mei Ju broke free of Bak Ju, chased after uncle and cousin, shrieking, "Ma," in a long, drawn out wail.

Ma, hurrying into their common room, peered uneasily into Grandmother's sleeping room, quickly shut the door, grabbed hold of Mei Ju.

"Didn't Grandmother tell you to go help your aunts in the wormhouse?"

Mei Ju sniffed, wiped her nose with the back of her hand. "Eldest Cousin wanted water, and Second Uncle . . ."

"Open the door for your uncle," Ma snapped.

As Bak Ju obeyed, Mei Ju butted her head against their mother's belly. "Why? Where's Second Uncle taking Eldest Cousin?"

"You fool," Second Uncle choked. "I'm trying to protect the family."

Poking her head around Ma, Mei Ju saw him carry her cousin outside. Bak Ju shut the door, hurried back to Mei Ju.

"Where's Second Uncle taking Eldest Cousin?" Mei Ju repeated.

Ma shook her finger sternly at them both. "If you'd gone to the wormhouse with your aunts like good girls, you'd have been spared what you can't yet understand."

Bak Ju hung her head.

"Where's Second Uncle taking Eldest Cousin?" Mei Ju insisted.

"You know your cousin's been very sick for a long, long time. Now she's dying. She won't last out the day whether she's in her bed or not. But if she dies under our roof, her hostless spirit can harm the family."

Bak Ju's head jerked up. "Second Uncle took Eldest Cousin outside to die in the open?"

Mei Ju's eyes welled with fresh tears. "I don't understand."

"Didn't I say you're too young?" Ma came back.

Bak Ju quickly took Mei Ju's hand. "Come on. We'd better go."

"No." Mei Ju pulled free, tugged on their mother's jacket. "What's a hostless spirit?"

Ma glanced uneasily at Grandmother's door, turned back to Mei Ju. "Each person has three souls. One that remains in the body at death and is buried, one that undergoes judgment in the Courts of Hell, and one that enters the spirit tablet."

She pointed to the spirit tablets—each a long piece of wood with the name of a dead ancestor painted on it—resting on the family altar. "Daughters must marry before they can have a tablet, a host for their spirit."

"Can't we get Eldest Cousin a host some other way?" Mei Ju pleaded.

"Don't worry." Pulling out a handkerchief, Ma wiped Mei Ju's face dry. "Grandmother will find a family with a dead son that Eldest Cousin's ghost can marry. Then she'll have a host for her spirit and people who'll send her offerings."

"Will Eldest Cousin be happy then?" Mei Ju asked.

"Yes," Ma assured her. "Very happy."

．　．　．

Despite her mother's reassurance, Mei Ju had been haunted for months by the image of her cousin lying helpless and alone in the open. Now Mei Ju fretted over her sister's meaning when she'd responded to Yun Yun's hurts by muttering, "I'd rather be Eldest Cousin." After all, their cousin had been dead when she'd married a ghost. Bak Ju was alive.

Day after day, Mei Ju waited for Bak Ju to say more, to explain why she would consider marrying a dead man, becoming a ghost wife. When Bak Ju didn't, Mei Ju asked her friends.

She was just climbing into their bed. Shadow, already settled for the night, grimaced.

"To avoid a husband like Young Chow."

Seated cross-legged beside Shadow, Rooster looked up from the book of sutras she was studying. "To avoid the bother of a man in bed."

Mei Ju, uncertain exactly what couples did in bed, didn't know whether a man was, in truth, a bother. But from watching her mother and aunts with her father and uncles, Mei Ju guessed it was the wife who did the pleasuring, the husband who was pleasured. In any case, she couldn't believe the pleasure was greater than the thrill of exchanging ideas openly with her friends. And, kneeling so she faced them both, Mei Ju suggested, "Bak Ju could avoid a husband altogether by becoming a nun."

Snatching Rooster's long pigtails, Shadow wielded her fingers like scissors. "You mean cut off her hair and shave her head?"

Rooster thrust out her pointy chin. "I'd do that gladly except nuns have to beg for their livelihoods, and thanks to Old Bloodsucker, I've had my fill of begging for this lifetime." She pulled her pigtails free and tapped Mei Ju's shoulder with them. "What about you?"

"I don't want to be a nun. But my mother and aunts have to ask Grandmother's permission for every little thing. Isn't that begging too?"

"Yes." Rooster shut her book. "Maybe that's why Bak Ju wants to be a ghost wife."

"As a ghost wife, Bak Ju would have a dead husband, but her parents-in-law would be alive, and she'd have to serve them and beg their permission for things the same as any daughter-in-law," Shadow pointed out.

"My sister wouldn't mind," Mei Ju said. "And since she never fails to please our grandmother, I'm sure she could satisfy the most demanding mother-in-law."

"So it must be the marriage bed that Bak Ju wants to avoid. I do too, because Empress was right when she said no baby will get through these." Rooster placed her hands on her narrow hips. "If my belly were to swell with child, I'd almost certainly die. My child as well."

Insides Turned
Upside Down

TOO TROUBLED by Rooster's and Bak Ju's distress to sleep, Mei Ju waited impatiently for the night to pass so she could calm herself by reeling silk.

She'd long ago become used to the heat from the fire and steaming water, the stench of boiling cocoons and hanks of raw silk. She'd also become so skilled in manipulating the cocoons with chopsticks that she rarely burned her fingers.

The moment she completed unwinding silk from one cocoon, she replaced it with another so as to maintain an even thickness in the thread. She immediately removed the spent cocoon from the hot water, thus preventing the oil in the chrysalid from marring the appearance of the silk. She also made certain the fire was big enough to keep the water boiling, yet not so fierce that smoke would sully the water, robbing the silk of its lustre.

The challenge of performing multiple tasks simultaneously excited Mei Ju. And since she'd completed her three-year apprenticeship, there'd been the added pleasure of escaping Grandmother's rule through reeling. For when there were no cocoons left at home, Mei Ju and her sister and Third Aunt went to work outside of family.

Where Grandmother scolded Mei Ju for being slow, Master Low, the landlord for whom Mei Ju reeled silk, praised her for being careful. He'd even told her, "You have the makings of a master reeler."

What Mei Ju liked best about reeling, however, was that the concentration it demanded left no room in her head or heart or belly for troublesome thoughts and feelings.

Rooster had said she found the same solace in practicing calligraphy. "From the moment I start grinding the inkstick and smelling the blackening ink, I stop fretting, and after I've written for a while, I forget about all the things I don't understand. I feel completely at peace. But the feeling vanishes the moment I stop. That's why I have to keep studying the sutras. Because only when I understand them will I know real peace. Peace that has no end."

Mei Ju, though, didn't see how Rooster would ever understand the Buddhist scriptures. Not because Rooster was stupid. But because she didn't know enough characters. And when Mei Ju and Shadow tried to help Rooster figure out characters by breaking them down, identifying and then piecing together the radicals they recognized, there were so many irregularities that they were usually defeated.

For a few months after Shadow had stopped their lessons with a regretful, "There's nothing left that I can teach you," Rooster had picked up new characters by hovering around her brother Laureate whenever he was reading out loud. But Rooster had been forced to give that up since he'd made a fuss about her disturbing him.

"I know I leaned a little too close and blocked his light," Rooster had seethed. "But I apologized and backed off immediately. Laureate lashed out anyway, and you know he's big for a twelve-year-old and strong, so I started bruising almost as soon as he started hitting me. Yet our parents said nothing to him about it. They were too busy yelling at me, accusing me of deliberately bothering my brother, making it impossible for him—and therefore our family—to succeed.

"I tell you, their attack hurt me more than Laureate's. How could I not defend myself? So I told them about my prayers to Gwoon Yum back when Old Bloodsucker tried to pull Laureate out of school to work for him. All that did, though, was make everyone angrier. Ba slapped me for talking back to my elders. Laureate shouted that it was his brains alone and not my prayers to the Goddess which won him the support of the Low elder who stopped Old Bloodsucker. And Ma added ill temper and stubborness to her long list of my sins."

Suddenly, Rooster's voice had lost its fire. "Well, she's right about that. I do flare up when I shouldn't and I am stiff-necked. I'm envious too. Not of Laureate, but of his chance to study at our clan's school. To have lasting peace within his reach."

．　．　．

"Where there is proper order, there is peace," Mei Ju's grandmother liked to say. "And under proper order, children must obey their parents, wives their husbands, juniors their seniors." Of course Grandmother made certain everyone at home observed proper order. Yet Mei Ju had never found it a place of peace.

For if Bak Ju should strike Grandmother's back lightly with her fists, murmuring, "It's damp today. Your old bones must be stiff. Let me loosen them up," Grandmother would croon, "At least I have one grandchild I can count on." Then Ma and Ba would beam as though they were being praised, while Second and Third Aunt and Uncle would set their children to shelling peanuts for Grandmother or amusing her with a rhyme, a story, a song.

In response, Grandmother might snap, "Peanuts are yeet hay, overheating. Do you want me to get sick?" Then Ma and Second and Third Aunt would fall over themselves running to the kitchen for leung cha, cooling tea. Or Grandmother might complain, "Ai, all that prattle makes my head ache," sending them racing for her pungent medicated oils. And should she single out one child for praise, the rest of the children, urged by their parents, would try to prove themselves helpful and clever too.

Empress—until she'd left to marry—had likewise manipulated the members of their girls' house into jostling for her favor. So had her successors. And their matchmakers had praised every one of these seniors for running a well-ordered house. Mei Ju, however, felt no peace in the girls' house either.

Except in the loft with Rooster and Shadow. But even there, Mei Ju could not be completely at ease since there was always the fear that someone might overhear them and thereby discover—worse, expose—their secrets.

Sometimes Mei Ju dreamtalked with her friends of a place where they wouldn't have to speak in whispers or hide their books and brushes. A place where they could escape the rule of seniors and family—the way her grandfather and his concubine had in their little house.

A house for three girls was, of course, impossible. And self-rule was against all proper order. In truth, Mei Ju's insides turned upside down just thinking about it, and she was reminded of when, as a small girl, she'd somehow slipped outdoors unnoticed during the height of a big wind. Swept off her feet and tossed into the air, she'd screamed, terrified she'd end up alone among strangers, perhaps badly hurt. But she'd also screamed, at least a little, from the delicious thrill of sailing above the earth like a bird on the wing.

Yun Yun could not please her new family. The water she heated for her parents-in-law and husband to wash in was too hot or too tepid or too cool. The tea she served them was too strong, not strong enough.

"Look at the color, you fool!" her mother-in-law would shout. With her long, sharp nails, she'd peel back Yun Yun's eyelids. "What are your eyes for? Just to stare at food?"

Cleaning up after their morning rice, Yun Yun threw away the few grains that had dropped on the tabletop and floor during the meal. Her mother-in-law's long face stretched even longer, and she carped at Yun Yun for being wasteful. "You could have used that to feed the chickens!"

The worm trays were heavy, too large and awkward for Yun Yun to pick up. When she dragged them as she'd always done at home, her father-in-law, built like a bull, scolded her for being weak, her husband accused her of being as inept at work as she was in giving pleasure.

Over and over Yun Yun's parents-in-law and husband abused her for being lazy, a useless rice bucket, a stranger to work. But Yun Yun was, in truth, accustomed to labor from childhood. She'd been barely five when her grandmother had taken her into their wormhouse and taught her how to pick the dead ones from the live. The following year, her grandfather and father had shown her which mulberry leaves to pick, how to shred and feed them to the worms. At ten, she'd learned to reel silk. Only her grandparents and parents had always corrected her gently and with warm affection. They'd encouraged her diligence through praise. Nor had her neighbor's parents and brothers and sisters-in-law been any less kind to Lucky. And although Old Granny, their teacher in the girls' house, had sometimes frightened them, she'd always been fair.

Crushed beneath her husband at night, Yun Yun recalled the stone mortar for hulling rice that was set in the earthen floor of her family's common room, the pestle fastened at the end of the beam which rose when her father stood on the other end, fell when he stepped off to release it. While she was still in split-bottomed pants, her father had let her clamp her arms and legs around the beam so she would have the pleasure of bobbing up and down. And after she tired of the game, she'd curl in her mother's lap, where she'd be lulled to sleep by the beam's rise and fall, her mother's voice chanting wooden fish songs to the beat her father made with the pestle. He'd been so careful whenever Yun Yun rode the beam, ready to catch her if she should fall. How could he have let her become the grain in the mortar, pounded cruelly, relentlessly by the pestle?

Of course matchmakers—sly and skilled at exaggerations, even outright lies—did outsmart fathers. That was why Old Granny had taught the girls the lament:

> "Sick at heart, my brows are knitted,
> My insides are turned upside down.
> My tears fall like rain,
> They flow like rivers and streams.
> All because my kind father
> Listened to the treacherous words of the
>   matchmaker."

And Yun Yun's father *was* kind, so trusting that her grandfather, too infirm with age to go to market himself, would shake his head over his son's poor bargains and sigh, "You're as blind as Day Jong Wong, the Earth King."

Yun Yun, when a child, had thought her father's sight actually did fail him at times. She had once even feared she'd become similarly blind.

·   ·   ·

It had been spring, she recalled. Water buffaloes had been dragging heavy plows, breaking up the soil for receiving seed, and Yun Yun's mother had sent her out to their rice fields with hot tea for her father.

As always, he wouldn't take a single swallow until he'd freed the buffalo from the plow and led it to the river where it, too, could slake its thirst. Yun Yun, waiting for the buffalo to drink its fill, threw herself onto the tall, soft grass that lined the river, and as the cool damp of the soil seeped through her thin cotton tunic and pants, tickling, she squealed gleefully.

Her father, finished with their buffalo, dropped down on his haunches beside her. "Do you see any buffalo in the clouds?"

Eagerly Yun Yun propped herself up on her elbows, squinted up at the sky. Not only could she find no buffalo, but the sun's harsh glare soon sealed her eyes in a frightening golden glow.

"I've become blind like you and Day Jong Wong," she cried.

Her father eased Yun Yun onto her back and gently stroked her eyes closed. "No, you haven't."

Cautiously she opened her eyes. "But I . . ."

He trailed his fingers across her lips, quieting her. "You can't see buffalo in the sky because there are none. Not now. Long ago, however, buffaloes walked freely among the Gods."

The animals, he said, had been beautifully dressed, capable

of speech as well. Then people cried out to the Gods that they were too small, too weak to plow without assistance. Seh Gung, the Community Grandfather, and Day Jong Wong, the Earth King, could see that what the people said was true, and they asked the buffaloes to go down to earth and help.

No buffalo wanted to do it.

"Why should we work?"

"We'll spoil our clothes."

In response, people promised to reward the buffaloes generously. Still none would go.

"Talk is worthless."

"Why should we believe you?"

So people sent up many wonderful offerings of delicious food and fragrant incense. They pleaded sweetly. And Seh Gung and Day Jong Wong—convinced that plowing would truly be easy for such large animals and certain of the people's goodwill—assured the buffaloes that they would live as well on earth as in the sky, perhaps better. All they had to do was take off their clothes while they worked.

"If what I'm saying isn't true, may I never have a roof over my head," Seh Gung vowed.

"May I lose my sight," Day Jong Wong added.

The buffaloes, thus persuaded, took off their clothes and went down to earth to give people the help they needed. But plowing was much more difficult for the buffaloes than people had said. Indeed, the work was so hard that the buffaloes suffered terribly. Nor did people reward the animals as they'd promised. Some even mistreated the creatures.

Watching the animals struggle, Seh Gung and Day Jong Wong realized that not only had the two of them been duped but they had, in turn, fooled the buffaloes, who'd placed their trust in them. Deeply ashamed, the two Gods sought to show their remorse and prove their integrity: Seh Gung gave up the roof over his head, Day Jong Wong his sight.

There was no going back to their old lives for the buffaloes, however, and they continued to eat bitterness. The more bitterness they ate, the more of their speech the buffaloes lost. Soon they could only cry.

While learning weeping songs, Yun Yun had wailed, "I know I cannot escape this trap," many times. So she understood that a woman, once married, could not leave her husband's family any more than the buffaloes could return to the sky. And, like the buffaloes, she wept.

Struggling
Woman

THE CHOWS were either too poor or too miserly to hire
help, and their fields and ponds were widely scattered. But
Yun Yun didn't mind the burden of additional steps. The
greater the distance between the fields and ponds, the more
she was able to avoid working near her husband and in-laws.
The long walks also gave her a chance to see all of Strongworm.

Although Yun Yun's mother had told her the village was
dedicated almost entirely to silk production, the sight of field
after field devoted to mulberry—with only a small scattering
of rice paddies, vegetable patches, and fruit trees—still startled. Surveying the narrowness of the river and the maze of
canals criss-crossing the fields, Yun Yun guessed much of
Strongworm's land must have been reclaimed. But there was
no one she could ask for confirmation: her mother-in-law
had strictly forbidden her to talk to anyone outside of the immediate family, and with them there was no conversation in
which she was included.

Then, on Yun Yun's way home from the fields one day, the sky suddenly blackened with heavy clouds that burst open, letting loose torrents of heavy rain.

"Over here," a woman's voice called.

Mindful of her mother-in-law's orders, Yun Yun hurried on without looking up.

"You'll get soaked," the voice warned.

Cold rain, driven by a strong wind, was already rendering Yun Yun's widebrimmed hat useless, stinging her face, piercing her tunic and pants, dribbling between collar and neck, down her back.

"Come on," the voice urged.

Yun Yun, glancing in the direction of the voice, saw a woman so stout she almost filled the doorway of a mud hut several yards from the flagstone road. As their eyes met, the woman's dumpling-like face broke out in a huge smile and she beckoned warmly. Impulsively Yun Yun ran towards her, dashing through wet grass, shooting through the door into thick smoke, the sound of men's voices.

Frightened, Yun Yun would have retreated. But the large woman had her firmly by the arm and was drawing her further in, telling her, "We're almost neighbors. My daughter Shadow is a member of the girls' house that's next door to you."

Yun Yun, captivated by the woman's friendliness, could not summon the will to resist when she took her hoe, propped it against the wall. Still concerned over the possible presence of men, however, Yun Yun peered through the smoke—saw a cluster of five or six old men squatting in the far corner, sucking on their pipes, spewing billows of bitter smoke.

That the men were grandfathers was a relief. Nevertheless, Yun Yun shifted her eyes, hands, and feet, uncertain whether she should retrieve her hoe and plunge back into the downpour.

"No need to worry," the woman soothed. "Your mother-in-law can't fault you for stopping here. This hut is a shelter for just such occasions."

One of the grandfathers hawked a huge gob of spit, and Yun Yun shrank back against the woman's soft, comforting bulk.

"The hut wasn't always a shelter," he said, grinding his spittle into the dirt floor with his heel. "It wasn't a single room either, but a half dozen or so rooms in a row, one of many such houses that the Low gentry built when they were reclaiming land from the river."

"Gentry, hah!" another grandfather sneered. "Leeches more like. They were trying to rent out the land while it was forming, not yet ripe enough to grow much of anything. All the same, they wanted tenants to turn over half their harvests in rent."

The rest of the grandfathers jumped in.

"Who could live on what was left?"

"Hnnnh, we showed those leeches they couldn't suck our blood."

"Wah, that was a great day, when no Strongworm man would agree to those terms."

"Great how? Didn't those leeches just go ahead and build mud huts on common land then fill them with Tankas willing to farm for them?"

"What are Tankas?" Yun Yun, caught up in their talk, asked.

"Outcasts who live in boats for houses and drift about on rivers and seas."

"Men and women so poor their clothes rot on them and their children run about naked."

"People too desperate to refuse starvation terms."

"People the Low gentry drove out when the land ripened sufficiently for proper cultivation and we wanted to work it."

"Isn't that always the way?"

"Right. Big fish eat little fish."

"Little fish eat shrimp."

"And shrimps eat mud."

When Yun Yun came home dry, her mother-in-law pinched her ear, demanding, "Didn't you hear me tell you to return directly?"

Yun Yun tried to defend herself by explaining she'd taken shelter in the hut. But Old Lady Chow only became more furious because under her grilling, Yun Yun revealed she hadn't been alone, that men had been in the hut too.

Grabbing the hoe, Old Lady Chow knocked Yun Yun to the floor and accused her of shamelessness.

"They were grandfathers," Yun Yun pleaded.

Old Lady Chow threw down the hoe, seized Yun Yun by her collar, yanked her onto her knees.

"I know how brazenly you leered at my son during your bride-teasing," Old Lady Chow hissed.

"I . . ."

Old Lady Chow's hand struck Yun Yun's mouth full force, silencing her. "I should never have believed the matchmaker's claims about your good home teaching. But *I* will teach you. And you *will* learn."

Each hand gripping one of Yun Yun's ears, Old Lady Chow twisted viciously. "Your first lesson is to use these."

Releasing the ears, Old Lady Chow once again smacked Yun Yun across the mouth. "Not this."

The next morning Yun Yun's ears felt swollen and sore, but she shielded them from prying eyes with her hair; the painful welt from the hoe was already invisible to others. Old Lady Chow's last slap, however, had split Yun Yun's lips, puffing them out beyond the farthest reach of her tongue. During the night, Young Chow had also deliberately smashed her nose and blackened her eyes. "Now see if you can get any man to look at you."

Deeply ashamed, Yun Yun begged permission to stay indoors until she healed.

"Release you from work? Reward you for doing wrong?" Old Man Chow roared. "Never! Let people see you for what you are. A worthless daughter-in-law in need of teaching."

Trying desperately to hide her disgrace, Yun Yun tipped

her hat far forward and walked with her head bowed. Even so, she heard passersby catch their breath, click their tongues, and mutter their disapproval.

When she went to wash the family's clothes at the river, Yun Yun avoided the women already there. Nor did any come near her. All the same, they must have noticed she'd been punished, for their talk centered on remedies for breaking up bruises and bringing down swellings.

Burning with humiliation, Yun Yun was nevertheless grateful for the women's sympathy. She was also thankful that the Chows lived next to a girls' house. Watching its members come and go freely, listening to their happy chatter, Yun Yun was warmed by their camaraderie, the memories of Lucky that they conjured.

Shadow looked so much like the woman in the hut that Yun Yun easily picked her out, and sometimes she'd try to pretend that she too was a member, that she had only to finish washing the family's bowls and dishes and chopsticks from their evening rice before she could run next door and join in their fun. Inevitably, however, the Chows' never-ending demands would shatter these imaginings almost as soon as they began.

Yun Yun understood a new bride was supposed to be the first to work, the last to eat and sleep. But if she wasn't cooking, she was chopping up slop for the pigs, gathering eggs from the chickens, fetching water from the well, or carrying nightsoil to the fields. There were also worms to feed, mulberry to pick, and cocoons to reel.

Seeking relief, Yun Yun lamented in her head:

"My shoulders look like rough granite,
My feet are full of holes.
Ai yah, pity this struggling woman.
If I told of all I suffer,
It would be like fire melting iron.
Ai yah, pity this struggling woman."

Shadow, like her friends, pitied Yun Yun. To Shadow's dismay, though, there were people in Strongworm who claimed Yun Yun brought her troubles on herself.

Whenever someone expressed sympathy for Yun Yun, Mei Ju's grandmother would decree, "A mother-in-law is *always* right." And more than a few women agreed. "If Yun Yun were diligent and careful, her mother-in-law and husband would have no cause to hit her."

Others said Yun Yun needed humbling.

"She's too proud to talk to us."

"She overlooks us alright."

"She barely mumbles a greeting."

There were also men who justified Young Chow's treatment of Yun Yun, contending, "Old Lady Chow is living proof of the maxim, 'Spare any woman a beating for three days, and she'll stand on the roof and tear the house apart.' Young Chow just doesn't want to end up with a harridan like his mother for a wife."

Even Elder Brother wondered out loud whether Yun Yun's parents might not have been cheated by matchmakers, whether *they* might have been the ones in a hurry for the wedding, not the Chows.

Appalled, Shadow blazed, "You must be delirious with fever to be spouting such nonsense."

"Not nonsense. Not accusations either. But the fellows at Young Chow's bride teasing did say Yun Yun was bold."

"Like she was with those rheumy-eyed grandfathers in the hut," Mama snapped.

Shamefaced, Elder Brother backed down hastily.

"If only Yun Yun had gone home for the ritual third-day visit, she could have come back with her father," Elder Sister-in-law said.

Baba shook his head. "You think Yun Yun's father could shame the Chows into doing right? Take my word for it, he couldn't. No one can. The Chows are far too thick-skinned."

"Are you saying no one can help her?" Shadow spluttered.

"All I did was try and save Yun Yun from getting wet," Mama reminded. "The next day her eyes were bruised black and her nose was swollen big as a cabbage."

Elder Sister-in-law gazed down at her belly swollen with happiness. "Maybe that's why Yun Yun didn't go home, why no one has ever heard her cry when she's beaten. Because she knows no one can help her."

Alone with Elder Brother, Shadow confided her fear that when the time came for her to marry, she might be as unfortunate as Yun Yun.

Elder Brother rapped Shadow's head with his knuckles. "No, this isn't wood. So you're not a muk tau, wooden head. Yet you seem to have forgotten how carefully our parents went about selecting a wife for me, the happy result. Can you really believe they'll be any less careful when choosing your husband?"

Propriety prevented husbands and wives from open displays of affection, but Shadow frequently caught Elder Brother leaning close to Elder Sister-in-law and whispering in her ear, making her laugh softly behind her hand. During meals, he'd drop his chopsticks and brush his hand against her leg when he stooped to pick them up. Out in the courtyard, he'd chase invisible moths, mosquitoes, and flies, and in his attempts to catch them, he'd graze his fingers against her back, her arm, her cheek. Each time, Elder Sister-in-law's plump cheeks would dimple with pleasure, her movements and speech would become more animated. Moreover, Elder Sister-in-law was always ready with hot water for Elder Brother and Baba the moment they returned from the fields, massaging Mama's neck and shoulders for her after a long day in the wormhouse, helping Shadow with her chores.

Shadow, then, gladly acknowledged the happy choice their parents had made in Elder Sister-in-law, her certainty that Baba and Mama would try to secure her similar happiness. "Since we've succeeded in keeping my knowledge of book learning from them, however, isn't it possible for a matchmaker to fool them too?"

Elder Brother tousled Shadow's bangs the way he used to

when she was little. "I'll make sure our parents aren't fooled, alright?"

Shadow nodded. But the first weeping song Shadow had learned in her girls' house was about matchmakers:

> "To get new shoes, Matchmaker,
> You'd lure birds from the trees
> With sweet words.
> To get more wine, Matchmaker,
> You'd draw monkeys out of the hills
> With your sweet tongue."

And Shadow, without a matchmaker's honeyed tongue, had kept her lessons in the girls' house loft a secret from her brother as well as their parents.

The
Big Wind

WHEN SHADOW'S embroidery had become good enough for Baba to sell at the market town upriver, Mama had given her a little trunk. "You can store your earnings in this."

The elaborately carved trunk, small enough for Shadow to easily carry herself, seemed absurdly large for the nine coppers Baba had stacked on the table, and she laughed.

Mama reached out, cupped Shadow's chin, gently tipped it so they faced each other. "Listen well."

Sobered by her seriousness, Shadow gave Mama her full attention.

"Sons turn their wages over to their fathers because they stay home and inherit all. But daughters keep their earnings since they must go to strangers when they marry and will have only what they take with them to call their own."

Mama picked up the little pile of coins, placed them in Shadow's hands, which were then still childishly pudgy. "This money is yours. But after you marry, you'll have to give every single coin you earn to your mother-in-law. So you should save while you can. If I hadn't brought savings with me when I married Baba, I would've had to ask your grand-mother for every little thing."

Shadow blinked in confusion. Each time they went to make offerings at the family graves, Mama would heave her considerable bulk down onto her knees one by one, bow deeply, and pray, "Ancestors, give my daughter a mother-in-law as kind and generous as mine. Mother-in-law, watch over your granddaughter. Help her learn the skills that will bring her favor as a daughter-in-law." If Grandmother had been as kind and generous as Mama claimed, why had Mama's sav-ings been important?

Shadow looked down at the coins, hard and cold, on her silk-smooth palms, folded her plump little fingers over them one by one. "Wouldn't Grandmother have given you what you asked for?"

"She did. But having my own money meant that if a ped-dler had a piece of fabric I liked, I could buy it on the spot, that I didn't have to wait and ask permission, or wonder if Grandmother might think I was taking advantage of her good nature, or consider me wasteful. Be frugal now, and you can enjoy that freedom as well."

Shadow had opened the trunk, dropped in the coins, and at their merry jingling, she'd felt a sudden surge of satisfaction. Now she realized the coins in her trunk would not save her if she married into a family like the Chows. Neither would her ability to write to her parents. Nothing would. Furthermore, even if she married into a family with a husband and in-laws as kind as her brother and parents were to Elder Sister-in-law, she would not only lose Elder Brother and Mama and Baba, but her good friends Mei Ju and Rooster, their nights in the girls' house loft, every single one of the freedoms and privileges she now enjoyed.

In truth, Shadow felt like a person who'd been applying a wet finger to a papered window so as to create a transparency through which a little could be seen. Slowly the view had become less and less clouded, and now that she could see with absolute clarity, she knew she didn't want to be a wife—not to a husband who was alive and kind, not to a husband who was dead.

Shadow was aware that she wasn't the first girl to recoil from marriage. Only last year four members of a girls' house in a neighboring village had bound their feet and hands together with two long cords, then jumped into the river loudly proclaiming it was better to die than become wives. Over the years she'd also heard occasional whisperings of other girls in the district who'd embraced death alone—by eating opium or hanging—for the same reason. Shadow, however, didn't want to die.

Nor did she want to become a nun. Not because she'd have to shave her head so much as she didn't want to exchange the rule of husband and in-laws for the rule of an abbess. She wanted to rule herself.

She and Mei Ju and Rooster had talked more than once of living together in a house where they ruled themselves. But they'd merely been dreaming out loud. Now, trying to figure out how to turn their dreamtalk into reality, Shadow reminded herself of Strongworm's newly awakened dragon.

The district had been suffering an unusually wet and stormy summer. So Strongworm's Council of Elders had sought to appease the Sky Dragon by replacing the tattered ceremonial dragon with a new.

The dragon's brightly painted plaster-and-wood head was massive, the cloth body so long it could circle the temple courtyard three times over. And before the most senior member of the Council opened the dragon's eyes by painting in jet black pupils, the creature lay motionless in the dirt, without life.

Sighted, its whiskers and ears wriggled, its jaws gaped wide in vain attempts to seize the large, luminous moon pearl that hovered just above its head. Then its long, serpentine body writhed, shimmering silver and green and gold, rising higher and higher off the ground until it was dancing, kicking up clouds of dust that it rode in soaring leaps.

However high the dragon jumped, though, the moon pearl continued to elude it; and rainstorms and big winds continued to menace the area.

As yet another big wind threatened, all the able-bodied men in the village ran to bolster the dikes, every woman and most of the children rushed to gather as much mulberry as they could before the storm struck. Clouds, black with rain, already crowded the sky, and Mei Ju, sent by Grandmother to pick leaves in their family's most distant field, worried whether she and her sister and cousins and aunts could bring in a sufficient supply of dry leaves to feed the family's worms. Not only during the storm, but afterwards, while the sun was drying out the mulberry in the fields. For damp leaves didn't store well. They moldered. And moisture on the leaves would bloat the worms and make them sick.

Each autumn, her father and uncles cut their mulberry close to the ground, and each spring, suckers came up which grew to five, six feet by the end of the season. The shrubs were now just past Mei Ju's waist, and despite her haste, the need to fill her baskets, she was careful to pick whole, undamaged leaves, to avoid those at the end of a branch so there'd be something left to draw the sap and force the plant into new leaf.

Stooped over and intent on her task, she ignored the dimming light, the stiffening breeze that riffled the mulberry beyond the shrubs she was disturbing with her urgent plucking. But then the breeze sharpened into a brisk wind, and a wild gust sliced between the two rows of mulberry Mei Ju was picking, whipping her pants against her legs, tearing loose the ties to her widebrimmed straw hat, lifting it off her head.

Reaching up to catch it, she felt the full force of another blast, doubled over, saw the basket she'd been filling tumble, spill, the leaves fly.

"No," Mei Ju yelped, abandoning her hat and throwing herself protectively over the basket.

Grit, stirred up by the wind, flew into her mouth. She spat, heard Bak Ju yell, "Over here, Mei Ju!"

"In the canal," Ba added.

Realizing her sister and father must have come for her in the family's skiff, relief washed over Mei Ju, and with it, a surge of strength. Righting the basket, she shouted, "I'm coming!"

When she attempted to stand, however, the wind knocked her down. Squatting, she used the mulberry shrubs as a windbreak and pushed the half-empty baskets toward the canal, her father and sister.

Whorls of dirt burned Mei Ju's eyes, burrowed into her nose, suffocating, compelling her to breathe through her mouth. Even with her teeth clenched, she swallowed throat-scratching dust. Yet she prayed it wouldn't rain so the leaves would stay dry and there'd be no chance of their spoiling or causing sickness in the family's worms. She even made a laborious detour to reclaim two of the baskets of leaves she'd picked earlier.

As she neared the canal, lightning and thunder shattered the sky, pelting Mei Ju and the leaves with rain. Without her hat she was soon drenched. The already oversoaked soil puddled, turned into muck. Still she swiveled on her heels, twisting herself back and forth, pushing the half-empty basket, dragging the two that were full: once she reached her father's skiff, the baskets would be sheltered, and the bottom leaves might be saved.

Hands reached down, took one of the full baskets.

"Leave the half-empty one," Ba ordered.

Bak Ju seized a handle of the remaining full basket.

"Hurry," she urged.

Reluctantly, Mei Ju released the half-empty basket, grabbed the handle opposite Bak Ju. Towing the basket between them, they scurried after their father, heedless of the mud splattering from his heels, their own.

The boat pitched wildly in the roiling water. Together Mei Ju and her sister hoisted each basket up to Ba, who—crawling on his hands and knees—secured them under the awning. Then, one by one, he hauled Mei Ju and Bak Ju onto the deck, which was slick with rain, river water, crushed leaves, and—in what Mei Ju guessed was a desperate effort to balance the skiff—positioned them on opposite sides, ordering them to lie flat against the gunnels, to hang on tight.

Clinging to the top of the gunnel, Mei Ju peered through the blinding rain at her father in the stern, struggling to maneuver the skiff despite the fierce winds, the torrents of floodwater cascading through broken dikes. How could he possibly keep them afloat, bring them home safe?

All at once, the River Dragon lashed his tail, hurling the skiff into the air. The boat landed hard, knocking the breath out of Mei Ju. Bak Ju flew across the deck. Instantly Mei Ju tried to reach out and catch her. But before Mei Ju could pry loose a single finger from the gunnel, Bak Ju tumbled over the side, disappeared.

She didn't resurface either, at least not close enough that Mei Ju could see her. Nor did Mei Ju hear Bak Ju cry out. Or perhaps the water pounding against the hull, the rain beating against the awning and deck, and the screech and wail of the wind muffled her cries.

Second Uncle said every family in Strongworm suffered losses. Theirs, though, was hit the hardest. Trees, uprooted by the big wind, fell across many of their dikes, which crumbled, flooding most of the family's fields and fish ponds, destroying the greater part of their mulberry crop, letting many of the fish escape in the ponds' overflow.

Covered by the awning that curved across the middle of the family's skiff, most of the leaves Bak Ju had picked and a third of Mei Ju's remained dry and could be fed to the worms, otherwise they, too, might have been lost. But Mei Ju and Ba, out on the open deck, were chilled to the bone, and for days afterwards racked with intense fits of shivering, periods of scorching fever. Bak Ju's body was never recovered.

The village gossips laid the responsibility for the family's misfortunes at Grandmother's feet. Some said that Grandfather's spirit, angry at his wife for treating his concubine too harshly, couldn't rest although almost four years had passed since his death. Others claimed Heaven itself was avenging the concubine. But Mei Ju couldn't see how any of her family's losses could possibly benefit the concubine, how their distress could ease hers.

Nor could Mei Ju understand why Grandfather's spirit would take Bak Ju. While their mother was lamenting Grandfather, she'd begged over and over:

> "When you come at night, please come silently.
> Don't touch your grandchildren with your hands.
> Just look at them.
> And when you go, please go silently."

Until his burial, Ma had set out food for Grandfather every time they sat down as a family to eat. And in the years since, she'd never once failed to place generous offerings before his spirit tablet on the altar the first and fifteenth day of each month. So even if Grandfather's spirit *was* angry with Grandmother, why would he take Bak Ju?

Then Grandmother proclaimed Bak Ju had come to her in a dream and said, "I offered myself to the River Dragon as a sacrifice."

But Mei Ju, revisiting their final moments together on the deck of the family's storm-tossed boat, saw only her failure to shout for help, to reach out and grab Bak Ju as she tumbled across the deck, fell into the dark, churning water.

THREE

1837–1838

The
Best Thing

SHADOW had hoped to present her friends with the gift of a flawless plan for how they could refuse marriage and rule themselves. She was still trying to perfect it, however, when Mei Ju choked, "I thought we'd have at least two, maybe three, even four years left together, but Grandmother's marrying me off this autumn to help make up our family's losses from the big wind."

"The way Old Bloodsucker's pressuring my family for money, you can be sure I'll be married off by year's end too," Rooster responded gloomily.

Shadow, no less upset than her friends, blurted, "You don't have to marry. Nor do I. We can make vows of spinsterhood just like nuns. Instead of shaving our heads or living in a cloister or on charity, though, we can comb our hair in a bun so everyone knows we're not girls under our parents' rule but women, and we can rent a room here in Strongworm and support ourselves through reeling and embroidery. That way, we won't have to answer to anyone except ourselves."

Mei Ju and Rooster, like herself, were seated cross-legged on their bed, and as Shadow spoke, they leaned toward her just as they had the morning she'd revealed her knowledge of book learning, her plan to teach them. Indeed, their faces were so close to hers that Shadow could feel their sharp puffs of breath, their awe; then their frustration when the night-watch passed, calling out the hour, beating his brass gong, forcing her to stop because she couldn't be heard above his clamor.

As the gong's last reverberations faded, Mei Ju murmured dreamily, "If only we could."

Rooster's deep-set eyes shone with desire, but her shoulders drooped with defeat. "*If* is right. None of our fathers would ever give us permission. Not even yours, Shadow."

Shadow grinned. "We won't ask. We'll force their hands."

"You mean threaten suicide unless they let us do what we want?" Mei Ju sighed. "That might work for you, but it won't for Rooster or me."

Rooster, who'd been studying Shadow through narrowed eyes, rubbed her chin. "I do believe our wily fox might have some other ruse in mind."

"I do." Shadow's grin stretched wider. "We can make our vows of spinsterhood in secret and before Heaven. Then no one can stop us, and our families will be forced to honor our choices."

"Ho yeh, wonderful!" Mei Ju praised, holding out both her fists with their thumbs up. "Even my grandmother wouldn't dare risk the wrath of Heaven by overriding such vows."

Turning so she faced their altar, Rooster raised herself onto her knees and reverently knocked her forehead against their bedmat. "Thank you, Goddess, for answering my prayers."

She swiveled back. "Nuns make their vows to Gwoon Yum. Although we won't be charity spinsters, so can we."

Shadow shook her head. "No, we can't risk being seen at the temple. And it wouldn't be fair to involve the other girls in this house by making our vows up here in secret. But we can go to the altar for Seh Gung, the Community Grandfather. It's shielded from the road by the banyan trees, and we can further lessen our chances of being seen by going in the final hour before dawn, leaving here a little after the nightwatch has passed."

"Seh Gung lost the roof over his head from making a vow too," Mei Ju observed.

"Didn't you hear me say we'll rent . . ." Aghast, Shadow slapped both her hands over her mouth. How could they keep their intentions secret if they went around Strongworm asking about rooms for rent?

"Hmmmm, our fox isn't as wily as I thought." Taking Shadow's hands in hers, Rooster turned the palms up and examined them as if she were a seer. "But there's no need for despair. These lines here show there *will* be a roof over our heads. Not much of one, mind, since it's straw. The walls are bad too. They're mud and have more cracks than an old tortoise shell. There's not much in the way of furnishings either. A narrow bench. An ancient scarred table. A few rough boards on two sawhorses. . . ."

"No," Mei Ju broke in. "Not the rain shelter."

Rooster wagged a finger at Mei Ju. "Don't *you* start with the no's."

Shadow, as repelled by Rooster's proposal as Mei Ju, swiftly swallowed the protest she'd been about to make. "We shouldn't have to stay in the hut long. A few days at most."

"We can also carry Gwoon Yum to Seh Gung's altar and make vows to them both," Rooster said.

A bubble of laughter rose in Shadow's throat. "Why didn't I think of that?" She stretched her arms and arched her back. "We've still got many more details to work out, but now we have three heads instead of one."

"And a couple more months," Mei Ju said. "No one marries during the silk season."

Rooster shook her head. "We could be forced into a betrothal any day, and once betrothed, we'd be good as married. We wouldn't be able to make vows of spinsterhood."

"Ai," Shadow groaned. "I didn't think of that either."

"We could watch for matchmakers going in and out of our houses," Mei Ju suggested.

At Mei Ju's easy solution, Shadow brightened. "Sudden bouts of house cleaning and the appearance of special treats are hints a matchmaker's been sent for too."

"You know how careful parents are to hide those sorts of things from their daughters' notice. Why take that kind of a chance?" Rooster demanded.

"Since my family won't have my bride price to help them, I'd like to finish out the silk season so they'll at least get the benefit of my wages from reeling," Mei Ju admitted.

With Elder Sister-in-law unable to reel because of her big belly, Shadow's father needed her as well. "If I leave home before the end of the season, Baba will have to sell this final generation of worms as cocoons instead of skeins of silk, and he's counting on the extra profit to help make up our losses from the big wind."

"Are we trying to save our families or ourselves?" Rooster exploded.

Mei Ju flinched. Shadow sucked in her breath, pointed warningly at the ladder leading to the girls asleep below.

More softly yet no less intense, Rooster continued, "Shadow, I'll wager your mother's embroidery sales this winter will make up most if not all of your family's shortfall. Mei Ju, the biggest bride price added to your wages for a full season couldn't cover what your family's lost. Likewise, I could let Old Bloodsucker squeeze me dry, and it wouldn't lessen my father's debts. Not the way Old Bloodsucker keeps piling on interest. So the best thing we can do for all three of our families is include lucky words in our vows for Heaven to shower them with blessings. And the best thing we can do for us is make those vows without delay."

"Wah," Shadow gasped admiringly. "If your brother's brain is anything like yours, he really will become a laureate."

Since her sister's death, Mei Ju's first thought on waking was of their years before the girls' house, when they'd shared a bed with their grandmother.

Their mother and aunts rose at dawn so that as soon as Grandmother cleared her throat, signaling she was awake, they'd be ready with her tea, a basin of hot water for washing. And at Grandmother's first cough, Bak Ju would sing out, "Good morning, Grandmother. Did you sleep well?" Grandmother, spitting nightphlegm into the spittoon beside the bed, would respond with a nod, an affectionate pat, and Bak Ju would leap out of bed to open the door for Ma and Second and Third Aunt.

Bak Ju would also help them pour Grandmother's tea, rinse her washcloth, ease her into her outer pants and jacket, comb her hair into a neat bun; slide her black headband around her forehead, over her ears, and under the bun; set her shoes where she could step right into them. But Mei Ju would stay curled in the far corner of the bed, praying she'd escape notice by pretending sleep. The few times she'd attempted to join in, Grandmother had faulted her for not wringing out the washcloth sufficently, carelessly dragging the clothes on the floor, setting the shoes too far or too close to the bed.

Throughout the day, Ma and Second and Third Aunt—although busy with chores, looking out for the children who were still too young to care for themselves—continued to serve Grandmother as well as Grandfather and their own husbands. Watching them, Mei Ju understood her mother and aunts were living out the maxim, "A good daughter-in-law is never thirsty, never hungry, never sleepy, never tired, and never in need of going to the toilet." What she couldn't figure out was how they succeeded in doing all. Or how Bak

Ju always managed to be by their sides, ready with a bowl or spoon or cloth that was needed.

When Mei Ju asked her sister, Bak Ju told her, "The trick is to anticipate." And Mei Ju tried. But absorbed in a piece of sewing or feeding their chickens and pig in the courtyard, she didn't hear her father and uncles coming home from the fields, so how could she bring them water for washing? Running after their little brother and cousins, making sure they didn't fall into the river or some other mischief, it didn't occur to her, as it did to Bak Ju, that they could also look for and harvest the tender bamboo shoots Grandmother favored.

Over and over, Mei Ju punished herself with the thought that if she *had* mastered the trick of anticipating, she might have saved her sister by recognizing Bak Ju's intention to sacrifice herself and convincing her not to, or by reaching out to catch her as she'd hurtled off their father's skiff. Now, her head and heart burning from Rooster's fiery "Are we trying to save our families or ourselves?," Mei Ju resolved not to repeat her sister's mistake, her own.

Together, she and Shadow and Rooster worked out the wording of their vows. By the end of the fifth watch, the hour Rooster usually rose to pray, they'd also made a list of what they would need in their new life and divided responsibility for acquiring the items that were not already in the loft: Their clothes they'd each bring from home; Mei Ju would retrieve their bowls, chopsticks, and dishes from the girls' house kitchen; Rooster would get the necessary offerings; Shadow would borrow her sister-in-law's pins and pow fa, sticky paste, for their hair, one of her family's tiered baskets to carry all.

"After I tell my family we've combed up our hair and made vows of spinsterhood, I'll buy a cooking pot and some rice for us to get started with," Shadow concluded.

Rooster tilted her face up to the skylight, the pale rays of morning sun streaming in. "This time tomorrow, we'll be sworn spinsters."

Was it really possible, Mei Ju wondered.

Despite her resolve, Mei Ju's intestines knotted in panic as soon as she was away from her friends. Even reeling couldn't calm her. Indeed, for the first time since her apprenticeship, Mei Ju burned her fingers and tangled her threads.

During morning and evening rice, she forced herself to eat just enough to prevent questions. Afterwards, she hurried to the outhouse and threw up every mouthful. Then, stirring the stink in the honeybucket to hide her vomit, she retched again, squeezing out bitter dregs from her belly that seared her nose and throat.

Inside the kitchen, she rushed through her nightly wash, pulled on her three pairs of pants, the longest last. She did the same with her three tunics. Fumbling with the buttons, she broke out in a sweat. Yet the breeze from the small barred window high above the stove was strong enough to stir the soot clinging to the walls.

Soon as hot, shivery, and wet with perspiration as she'd

been at the height of her fever, Mei Ju feared she might faint. Desperately she panted for air, the courage and strength to walk through the common room and bid Grandmother, the rest of the family, "Jo tau, rest early," without betraying herself and her friends.

In truth, Mei Ju arrived at the girls' house without any knowledge of how she'd managed to achieve it. The evening, too, passed in a dream. Somehow, though, she succeeded in lingering over the cleanup in the kitchen until everyone else had gone to bed, then wrapping her friends' bowls and dishes and chopsticks without dropping any. Reaching for her own, she noticed her sister's. Impulsively Mei Ju took them as well.

Vows of
Spinsterhood

SHADOW had not slept in two nights. She was burdened by
the tiered basket, blinded by a damp, cloying mist that intensified the predawn gray. Her heart, however, was glad, and
she walked briskly. On either side of her, Rooster and Mei Ju
matched her pace, took turns helping with the basket.

To reach Seh Gung's altar, they had to leave the main
street, which was paved with large slabs of smooth stone, and
cut through a stretch of tall grass wet with dew. Yet their
progress continued swift and sure.

Even when confronted with long twists of banyan roots,
Shadow did not falter. Recalling the many happy times she
and Elder Brother had met in secret under these same trees
for lessons, she plunged through the roots that drooped like
whiskers from low hanging branches; she leaped nimbly over
those that ridged the ground, arriving only slightly breathless at the altar where she set down the basket.

Moments later, Mei Ju and Rooster joined her. Before
them, Seh Gung's stone altar curved in a half-circle that

reached out like a grandfather's kindly embrace. At their back, the banyan trees sheltered them from any chance passer-by, the possibility of discovery. Thus warmly enfolded, Shadow unpacked and lit the candles they'd brought; Rooster unwrapped and set the statue of Gwoon Yum in the center of the altar; Mei Ju laid out their offerings of wine, rice, and fruit.

Reverently, they each lit incense, bowed deeply once, twice, three times to the Commmunity Grandfather and Goddess of Mercy. Lifting their heads from their final bows, they unbraided their maidenly plaits, shook the strands loose so that their hair surrounded them like waist-length, gleaming black veils.

Slowly, deliberately, Shadow drew a comb through her hair in three long strokes that began at her temples and ended at her waist; and with each stroke, she asked Heaven for the blessings they'd decided on together. "First comb, comb to the end. Second comb, may my brother enjoy bountiful wealth and many children. Third comb, may my parents and friends enjoy wealth, happiness, and long life."

One after the other, Rooster and Mei Ju did likewise, and Shadow heard in their voices the same deepening pride and joy she felt bubbling within. Indeed, it seemed to Shadow her friends' faces shone bright as the rising sun.

Smiling, she brought out the box of pins and small jar of pow fa so they could start dressing their hair in the style that would signify to all they were no longer girls but women. This process, long and complicated, was always done for a bride by someone else, but to demonstrate their self-reliance, they were doing it for themselves. None of them had actually combed their hair into any kind of a bun before, however. And although Shadow and her friends had decided they would avoid the elaborate styles designated for brides, she soon understood why families hired hairdressers for their daughters.

Combing up her girlish bangs and applying the sticky pow fa was not hard, but making the hair stay in place was. By the time Shadow got every strand plastered down firmly, shafts of sun pierced the branches of the banyan trees. Hurriedly she gathered the rest of her hair, began braiding it into a single plait.

Her childhood pair of plaits had allowed Shadow to drape her hair over each shoulder for braiding. The single plait meant she had to somehow accomplish the braiding behind her back, and her arms, held at awkward angles, quickly tired. Worse, strands of hair clung to her palms, which were moist with perspiration, and the plait she was making felt increasingly loose, about to unravel altogether.

Wishing she and her friends had thought to practice on each other before trying it alone, Shadow abandoned the plait she'd been weaving, checked how Rooster and Mei Ju were faring. Rooster was doing no better than herself. Mei Ju had not only completed her plait but had wound it into a neat bun that she was pinning into place.

Straightening her tunic, Mei Ju made her vows of spinsterhood in a strong, sure voice. "This woman named Wong Mei

Ju will henceforth remain unmarried. She will remain pure, and she prays that you, Seh Gung, and you, Gwoon Yum, will give her your blessings and protection."

Inspired, Shadow returned to her task with renewed energy. Sunlight warmed the backs of her hands, her neck. And the closer she came to completing the transformation from girl to woman, the more powerful her pride, her joy, so that when at last she lowered her arms and made her vows, the words all but burst out of her.

While planning for their new lives, Shadow had suggested that to signify their independence, they should go alone to their families to announce their vows of spinsterhood. "When we're finished, we can meet at the rain shelter."

Her friends had agreed, and Rooster had added, "You and Mei Ju will have the furthest to go, so I'll drop the basket off at the hut. To be honest, I won't mind the delay since my parents are bound to be furious when I tell them what I've done."

She also warned, "You know my pockets are empty as always, and Old Bloodsucker won't give me wages for the reeling he's used to getting for free. Fact is, he's so spiteful he'll probably throw his weight around to make sure no one else in Strongworm will hire me—or you two either."

Mei Ju paled. "What'll we do for money? I gave my savings to Grandmother after the big wind, and I've been turning over all my earnings to her since."

Shadow shrugged off her friends' concern. "This silk season's almost over anyway, and between my savings and selling our embroidery, we can make it."

"How will we get our embroidery to market?" Mei Ju fretted.

"I'll ask Baba to sell for you like he does for Rooster and me."

Rooster squinted skeptically. "Old Bloodsucker doesn't realize your father's been helping me hold out on him by taking some of my embroidery to market along with yours. For your father to sell our work after we make our vows, though, he'd have to openly go against him. We'd best plan on selling through the sui haak, water peddlers."

That Baba, who went out of his way to avoid trouble, wouldn't want to confront Old Bloodsucker, Shadow readily acknowledged. Baba was also likely to be angry with her for choosing spinsterhood. He'd been worrying over the need to increase the family's income. And how could he accomplish that without more land, land he might have acquired with the cash from her bride price? Having overheard Mama sympathizing with Elder Sister-in-law's homesickness, however, Shadow wasn't afraid to face him.

"I'd be lying if I didn't tell you that after twenty-three years, my heart still aches for my mother," Mama had sighed. "And it won't be long before I'll have to part with Shadow. Fact is, a woman's life is filled with loss." She'd patted Elder Sister-in-law's belly, the baby growing within. "If we're lucky, this will be a child who won't have to leave us, a son."

Surely Mama and Elder Sister-in-law would be pleased she'd found a way to remain in Strongworm. And Shadow was likewise certain of her brother's support.

The only time he'd ever been upset with her was when she'd confided her desire to teach Rooster and Mei Ju, and his anger then had sprung from his concern that if her knowledge of book learning—and his role in it—was discovered, it would be difficult for their parents to arrange good marriages for them. Now that was no longer a consideration.

More importantly, where women with learning were condemned, women who vowed chastity were admired. So there was no reason Elder Brother shouldn't share her happiness, and Shadow couldn't wait to see his face when she took off her hat and revealed her womanly bun.

Setting off for home, Shadow stretched her legs in long, eager strides. Her arms free of the basket, she knocked aside low-hanging branches with a toss of her hand, a swing of her elbows. Then Shadow noticed that where Mei Ju had easily kept pace with her earlier, she now lagged behind. Mei Ju had also turned white as mourning, and she was chewing her lips so brutally that they were bleeding. Clearly she was dreading her family's reception as much as Rooster. More.

Hurrying back to Mei Ju, Shadow linked their arms together and said, "Everything will work out. You'll see. Mama will be happy that I won't have to leave Strongworm, and Baba always bows to her in what he calls 'women's business.' So if he's angry with me for refusing marriage, which I'm guessing he will be, she'll calm him down. And Elder Brother and Elder Sister-in-law will help her. Then, when Baba comes around, which he will, he and Mama can talk to your father and grandmother and Rooster's parents and bring them around as well."

When combing up her hair and making her vows, Mei Ju's hand had been sure, her voice strong. As she and her friends put on their wide-brimmed straw hats to hide their buns until they reached home, however, her heart quailed.

Trying to bolster her courage, Mei Ju told herself that if someone was abroad this early and noticed they had no plaits dangling down their backs or over their shoulders, it wouldn't really matter because they weren't going home to ask their families for permission to refuse marriage but to announce they'd vowed to remain pure forever, and no one would dare dismiss what had been declared before Heaven.

Still Mei Ju's heart and legs trembled, her belly quaked, and she tasted blood. In truth, she couldn't have walked out of the banyan grove and through the village without Shadow's steadying arm and warm assurances.

To avoid prolonging the ordeal, Mei Ju had planned to announce, "I've vowed to remain unmarried forever," to the first person she encountered at home. Just as she stepped over the raised threshold between street and common room, however, her arm brushed her father's, and Mei Ju, startled, stammered, "I don't want to marry."

Ba, who'd been reaching for his hoe by the door, grabbed it. Ma, lighting fresh incense on their family altar, hastily snuffed out the taper with her fingers, headed toward them.

"Don't want to marry?" Ba roared.

He shook his hoe at Mei Ju, and her innards tossed as they had during the big wind.

"If I tell you to marry a chicken, you'll marry a chicken. If I tell you to marry a dog, you'll marry a dog."

"Of course she will," Ma said, stepping between Mei Ju and Ba.

Mei Ju's head spun, and she seized the back of the nearest chair to keep from falling.

Ma, gently plucking at Ba's sleeve, eased him out the door, all the while murmuring soothingly, "As Earth turns to the left, Heaven to the right, so man calls and woman obeys. This is the proper order to the universe. Our daughter knows that."

Ma's tone turned hearty. "Mei Ju is like her name, a beautiful pearl. Yes," she told his retreating back. "Mei Ju will fetch a large bride price, perhaps large enough for us to avoid borrowing."

"No," Mei Ju wanted to cry. But her throat closed as it had on Ba's skiff when she'd been too frightened to shout out an alarm, and although she opened her mouth, no sound came out.

Ma whipped around. "Nuisance child!"

Struggling to respond, Mei Ju tried to take off her hat to show she was a woman. But her fingers clung to the back of the chair as tenaciously as they had to the skiff's gunnel, and she couldn't pry them loose.

"How dare you try and upset the order of the universe?" Ma demanded. "Don't you realize a woman without a man is a vine without a stake to support her?"

"I earn my own money," Mei Ju forced out in a barely audible whisper. "I can support myself."

"Maybe you *can* feed yourself in life. But are you really such a wooden head?" Her words tumbling faster and faster, Ma repeated what Mei Ju already knew. "If you have no husband, no son, there will be no one to feed your spirit when you die. You'll be a hungry ghost, wandering without a home, without any chance of rest."

"My ghost can marry a ghost like Eldest Cousin's did," Mei Ju rasped.

"Your cousin had a family to make those arrangements for her. Your sister, too. You won't."

Stunned, Mei Ju sank onto the chair.

"Do you think you can disobey your father yet remain a member of this family?" Ma pressed. "Even count on us to find a host for your spirit when you die? Exactly which one of us were you expecting to do that for you? Your grandmother and father won't. You can be sure they'll teach your brother not to either. And why should they trouble themselves on your account?

"I'm telling you, the most you'll get as a ghost from anyone in this family will be a few scraps once a year during the Festival of Hungry Ghosts—just enough to hold you at bay."

While Ma threatened, Mei Ju pulled together the tattered remnants of her courage by silently repeating, "I'll have Shadow's family to call mine." She prized her fingers from the chairback one by one, then tore at the knot under her chin, finally loosening it sufficiently for her to duck out of her hat, exposing her slicked back hair, her bun.

"What are you playing at?" Ma snapped. "Comb that bun out at once! You're just lucky your grandmother is in the outhouse and no one else is around."

Determined to get her announcement out at last, Mei Ju said, "I've made vows of spinsterhood."

"You're not only a nuisance, but stupid! Charity spinsters shave their heads."

Stung, Mei Ju came back, "I'm not a nun dependent on charity. But I *am* a spinster. A sworn spinster. I vowed to Seh Gung and Gwoon Yum that I'll remain unmarried forever."

Gwoon Yum's
Song

Shadow, her head pounding from the family turmoil that announcing her spinsterhood had unleashed, stumbled out of her parents' house into the street. Blinking back tears, she secured the ties to her hat and plastered on a smile for any neighbors and acquaintances she might pass on the way to her friends in the rain shelter.

Behind her, the door to the house slammed shut. Shuddering, she willed herself not to look back, to hope Elder Brother would throw it open and come running after her, shouting belated congratulations. Because he wouldn't. He was too worried about Elder Sister-in-law, who—coming into the common room from the kitchen at the same moment Shadow had pushed open the front door and slipped off her hat—had misstepped and almost fallen.

At the time, Shadow had attributed the near accident to Elder Sister-in-law's protruding belly. Now Shadow wondered whether it might have been the sight of her combed-up hair that had thrown Elder Sister-in-law off balance.

When borrowing Elder Sister-in-law's pow fa and pins, Shadow had said they were for playacting in the girls' house. So how could Elder Sister-in-law have instantly understood the full significance of the womanly bun? Yet wasn't instant recognition and support what she, Shadow, had expected from Elder Brother?

Too late, Shadow wished she'd taken both her brother and sister-in-law into her confidence. Then they would've been sitting in the common room waiting for her return, ready to help explain to Mama and Baba why she'd vowed spinster-hood and combed up her hair. Instead, Elder Sister-in-law had tripped and would surely have fallen had Elder Brother not leaped off his stool and caught her.

Although Elder Sister-in-law was safe, the scare had upset everyone. Shadow, unable to order her thoughts, couldn't speak convincingly. She wasn't sure Elder Brother, fussing over Elder Sister-in-law, was even listening. And Mama, furiously fanning Baba and herself, must have completely misheard. Why else was she spluttering like oil in a red-hot wok?

Desperate to persuade her, Shadow brought up the little trunk in which she kept her savings, reminding Mama that it had been her gift, that she'd emphasized the importance of a wife retaining a measure of freedom by taking money of her own into her husband's family. But before Shadow could finish, Mama began scolding her for failing to see the difference between a measure of freedom and turning Heaven and Earth upside down.

Then Baba, his face purple with anger, lashed out at Mama

for talking about freedom at all and for not being stricter. "Haven't I always said raising children is like raising silkworms? For good results, care must be taken from birth."

Mama claimed he was the one teaching deceit by selling pieces of Rooster's embroidery for her on the sly. Elder Brother, raising his voice above theirs, shouted that Elder Sister-in-law was complaining about a pain in her belly and asking for white flower oil.

Instantly Mama abandoned the argument and gave Elder Sister-in-law her full attention. Baba turned from yelling at Mama to accusing Shadow of possibly harming his unborn grandchild. When Shadow tried to defend herself, Elder Brother bellowed for quiet, adding, "Haven't you done enough damage already?"

That Elder Brother would blame her for Elder Sister-in-law's distress cut Shadow to the quick. Since he'd asked for quiet, however, she didn't dare speak, not even to apologize or offer help. She simply flung on her hat and hurtled out the door.

Now, bolting blindly through the village, Shadow feared Elder Brother might have taken her departure as proof of her thoughtlessness. Worse, she might really have harmed Elder Sister-in-law and her baby.

Motes of dust hung in the shaft of sunlight pouring through the rain shelter's one window. Yet the air seemed dank to Mei Ju. Breathing as shallowly as she could, she'd decreased the frequency of her sneezes. But she couldn't stop sneezing altogether, and with each explosion, Mei Ju jounced Shadow, seated beside her on the hut's narrow bench.

Shadow, sunk into gloom, didn't seem to hear either the sneezes or Mei Ju's apologies. Perched on a stool across the table from them, Rooster greeted each fresh assault with a bright, "Dai gut lai see, good fortune!"

Bobbing her head in acknowledgment, Mei Ju thought dolefully that they could certainly use every one of Rooster's wishes and more. In truth, surveying the hut's crumbling walls and festoons of cobwebs, Mei Ju couldn't understand how Rooster could sustain her joy.

"Cheer up, you two," Rooster urged. "I know talking to our parents was like chickens talking to ducks. But can't you see my near escape is proof of Heaven's approval?"

Mei Ju, wanting desperately to believe her, begged Rooster, "Tell us again what happened."

Her eyes aglow and her voice so highly pitched with excitement it reverberated off the mud walls, Rooster obliged.

"Well, you know how Old Bloodsucker prides himself on squeezing cash out of people with none? He apparently forced my parents into negotiations with a matchmaker, and they've been meeting at Old Bloodsucker's and had already picked out a groom and matched horoscopes and done everything except present betrothal gifts.

"So you see, if we'd delayed making our vows by so much as a day, it would've been too late for me. I would've been trapped into marrying.

"Hnnnh, if we hadn't made our vows to Seh Gung and Gwoon Yum, my father would've ripped the pins out of my hair and combed it back into two plaits himself!"

Retrieving her statue of Gwoon Yum from the basket, Rooster held it tenderly against her cheek, and Mei Ju imagined the clay image cooling her own heated skin.

"The Goddess really saved me," Rooster said, wiping off the rickety table with a broad sweep of her sleeve.

A cloud of dust billowed into Mei Ju's nostrils, causing a flurry of sneezes.

"Good fortune, good fortune, good fortune," Rooster crowed.

She set the statue on the table, rotated it so Gwoon Yum faced Shadow. "You bought her for me, remember?"

Mei Ju, wiping her eyes with her handkerchief, sensed rather than saw Shadow nod.

"Gwoon Yum hasn't forgotten either," Rooster assured softly.

Smiling, she began, "Gwoon Yum was born the daughter of a king. Yet she didn't care about earthly riches or power. What she wanted was to remain pure. To shave her head and become a charity spinster, a nun. Her father, however, wanted her to marry, and when she wouldn't, he ordered her beheaded."

As Rooster paused for breath, Mei Ju eagerly took up the familiar tale.

"Of course, the executioner didn't dare disobey the king. But when his sword struck Gwoon Yum, it shattered without hurting her. Then Gwoon Yum's father ordered her suffocated, and when her soul left her body, it descended to Hell."

Rooster cocked her head encouragingly at Shadow, and Mei Ju, recognizing Rooster's intent, fell silent. But the only sounds were their breathing, the buzz of flies foraging in the mounds of rubbish littering the floor, gnats circling their faces and necks, their wrists and hands.

Mei Ju waved away the gnats, laced her fingers through Shadow's, murmuring, "Come on."

When there was no response, Rooster pushed the statue of Gwoon Yum forward, and Shadow—hesitantly at first, then more strongly—at last picked up where Mei Ju had left off.

"Gwoon Yum's presence in Hell turned it into Paradise. So, to save his kingdom, the King of Hell restored Gwoon Yum's life, and she was transported on a lotus flower to an island in the Southern Sea, where she lives as a healer and from which she sails on her Boat of Mercy to help those in trouble."

Steadying the statue with one hand, Rooster curled her other hand into a fist and rapped her knuckles against the scarred tabletop, beating out the rhythm for Gwoon Yum's song.

Together they chanted:

> "Look back on the way I have traveled
> And judge if a better be found.
> No husband to claim my devotion,
> No mother-in-law to control my every breath;
> No children to pull at my hands,

No fetters on the wings of my soul.
As free as the wind on the mountain,
Or the birds that soar up to the sun,
With jade and opals I deck me,
With the moon pearl I am crowned.
Who faithfully follows my footsteps
May share in my infinite gain;
And she who is brave enough to relinquish,
Will know what it is to attain."

With each line, it seemed to Mei Ju that their voices grew stronger, and she felt herself becoming less and less troubled by their families' anger, the wretched state of the hut, their uncertain future.

Shadow didn't feel drawn to the passion that happy husbands and wives—like Elder Brother and Elder Sister-in-law—shared. When choosing a life without a husband, however, Shadow had understood that she'd also be forgoing mother-hood. And unlike Rooster, who was afraid of dying in child-birth, and Mei Ju, who claimed she'd had her fill of babies from caring for her little brother and cousins, Shadow wanted children.

She'd told herself she could fulfill that desire by helping to raise her brother's sons and daughters. Now she wasn't sure, and at the words, "No children to pull at my hands," in Gwoon Yum's song, Shadow's eyes and throat flooded with tears for the babies she'd never birth, the possible loss of the babe growing in Elder Sister-in-law's belly. Neverthe-less, Shadow couldn't wish she and her friends had delayed their vows until Elder Sister-in-law's baby was safely deliv-ered; otherwise Rooster would have been trapped into mar-riage.

Thinking of the babe in Elder Sister-in-law's belly, Shadow became aware of the growling in her own, remem-bered she hadn't bought a cooking pot or rice, and as the song ended, she shot off the bench, forgetting Mei Ju had hold of one hand. Their arms pulled taut, and Mei Ju was jerked half to her feet before letting go.

Shadow, released, headed for the door.

Mei Ju ran after her. "Where are you going?"

"We've got nothing to cook with, nothing to eat."

"Never mind," Rooster said.

What? Shadow, spinning round, saw Rooster had lain the statue of Gwoon Yum flat on the dust-covered table and was smoothing down her loose-fitting tunic with her long, thin fingers. As the faded blue cotton flattened against Rooster, Mei Ju's eyes widened, Shadow became acutely embarrassed at how she filled her own tunic so completely that the seams threatened to split.

"We've become spinsters, not Goddesses," Shadow mut-tered.

Rooster, no less dramatic or amazing than a conjuror, lifted her tunic, plucked an egg from the pocket of her under-garment, and set it on the table at Gwoon Yum's feet.

Mei Ju applauded. Smiling, she demanded, "More! More!"

Shadow knew that had Mei Ju not seen something indicating there were additional hidden eggs, she wouldn't be calling for more. And, taken aback by her own blindness, Shadow wondered what else she'd failed to notice, who else she'd misjudged.

With great flourish, Rooster continued extracting eggs one by one, laying them on the table. Beautifully white, the eggs gleamed bright as the moon pearl on the Goddess's head. Indeed, they scarcely seemed less magical.

"Looks like our rooster is a hen," Shadow told Mei Ju.

Rooster grinned. "Since I know where Strongworm's more adventurous hens like to roam and nest, I decided to bring us some of their droppings. Too bad my pocket's not bigger."

Taking a pin from her hair, she pierced the top of the sixth and final egg. "Let's eat."

As Rooster carefully enlarged the pinprick into a hole through which she could drink, Shadow and Mei Ju returned to the table.

"Wah, none of them cracked," Mei Ju observed.

The eggs, without blemish, reminded Shadow more than ever of Gwoon Yum's moon pearl, the many difficulties she'd overcome before it became hers, and she felt ashamed at how easily she'd become dispirited.

Mei Ju handed Shadow an egg, took one for herself. Rooster propped up the statue of Gwoon Yum and raised her egg to the Goddess as an offering before draining it. Shadow, cradling her egg between her palms, savored its warmth, the warmth of her good friends.

New Lives

MEI JU recognized Rooster's ingenuity in suggesting they live in Strongworm's rain shelter. Not only was it free, but since it was situated on a strip of common land between the fields and the village proper, they couldn't be thrown out of the hut the way Grandmother had evicted the concubine from her little house.

Mei Ju also recognized Rooster's cunning in proposing they sell their embroidery through the water peddlers. Everybody in Strongworm relied on the peddlers for goods they couldn't grow or make themselves; and all the peddlers cared about was whether their customers had the cash to buy their goods. Old Bloodsucker wouldn't interfere. Even the clan elders wouldn't. Furthermore, if Rooster was as shrewd in business dealings as she was clever at planning, she'd drive a hard bargain with the peddlers for serving as middlemen.

Where the hut was at the north end of Strongworm, however, the water peddlers tied up their boats near the temple at the southern end. To reach them, then, required walking the entire length of the village, and the prospect filled Mei Ju with dismay.

By now, Rooster's parents would have told Old Bloodsucker that their daughter could not marry. Doubtless he'd have taken the news badly, and his roars would've been heard by his family and workers, who'd have gossiped to others with willing ears and busy tongues. Then, too, there'd been plenty of shouting in Shadow's family, her own.

While Mei Ju had been declaring her spinsterhood to Ma, Grandmother had rushed in from the outhouse, whooping, "You'll never guess what I just heard. That Shadow's gone and made vows of spinsterhood or some such nonsense, and those foolish Fungs are beside themselves. Hnnnh, what did they expect when they provided such poor home teaching? Didn't I always say that girl would come to no good?"

In her hurry, Grandmother had not finished knotting her pants, and with her head bent over as she'd tugged and pulled, she hadn't seen Mei Ju, who—aided by her mother—had escaped through the front door. Out on the street, Mei Ju had heard the shocked voices of the Fungs as well as Grandmother. Surely other neighbors had, too, and had since repeated every word many times over.

Mei Ju—fearful the gossips would scold as fiercely as their families—dreaded facing them.

Seeking delay, she suggested, "Let's tidy ourselves before we go."

In truth, Shadow and Rooster—with hair straggling over their faces and down their backs—*were* a mess, and bringing out the pow fa and combs from the tiered basket, Mei Ju advised, "You'd best start over."

Rooster tossed her head, shaking loose pins. "How were you able to comb your hair up so neatly?"

Shadow fussed with her collapsing bun. "And make everything stay in place?"

"Don't forget, I've braided my little cousins' and brother's hair for years. And before joining the girls' house, I used to watch my mother and aunts comb my grandmother's hair every morning."

Eager to perform a task that was comfortingly familiar, Mei Ju stepped behind Shadow and deftly finished unravelling the remnants of her bun. "Here, Rooster can watch me fix your hair. Then I'll do Rooster's and you can watch."

Carefully Mei Ju untangled the worst snarls with her fingers. Then she drew ever finer-toothed combs through the hair, stopping and straightening out each of the remaining snags strand by strand—not to protract the time it would take, but to keep from hurting Shadow, and because the concentration required helped ease the roiling in herself.

With surprising speed, the snags became fewer, the strokes longer and longer. And when Mei Ju could slide the comb repeatedly from scalp to ends in unbroken runs, she worked the pow fa into the sleek, silk-soft hair so that not even a wisp would stray.

Gathering up Shadow's hair for braiding, Mei Ju mused wistfully, "I wish all our difficulties could be overcome this simply."

"Don't!" Rooster barked.

Shadow flinched. Mei Ju sprang back as if she'd been bitten.

"Sorry. It's just that you can stop right there. See?" Rooster pointed at Gwoon Yum whose hair, peeking out from beneath her shawl at her forehead and shoulders, was as free of ties as the Goddess herself.

"We'd really be untidy then," Shadow said. "And we couldn't embroider properly, not with our hair falling over our faces and getting tangled in our thread."

Mei Ju pulled Shadow's gleaming hair back tightly, bound it at the nape. "Look, this is the secret to being neat. Tie the hair before braiding it, and then again at the end of the plait, before coiling it into a bun."

Rooster thrust out her chin stubbornly. "With buns, we could be mistaken for married women."

Mei Ju, dividing Shadow's bound hair for braiding, felt her stiffen.

"Maybe I didn't startle Elder Sister-in-law so much as I offended her."

Remembering Ma's outrage, Mei Ju shuddered, and as her fingers skillfully wove a five-strand plait, she searched for an alternative to the wifely bun. Leaving their hair loose was out of the question. Nor could they go back to girlish pigtails. Which left shaving their heads like nuns. No. Anything but that.

Mei Ju secured the end of the plait she was braiding and, having failed to come up with a replacement for the bun, began making one. Fear of what it might provoke, however, weighed down her arms and made her fingers thick and clumsy so that the plait tumbled out of her grasp.

She eyed the glistening black rope of hair swinging from Shadow's neck to her waist. "What about a single plait?"

Reaching back, Shadow fingered the uniform ridges of braiding approvingly. "This will set us apart from both wives and girls."

"Yes," Rooster agreed.

Mei Ju pulled out the pins from her bun, allowing the plait to unfurl down her back and hang free. "Good."

The hut had a door facing Strongworm's flagstone road. Its window looked out onto a small open space skirted by a dense bamboo grove. At Mei Ju's urging, the three set out for the water peddlers through the window. "That way no one will know we've moved in here until we've had a chance to secure it."

Climbing out one by one, they dashed across the open space and ducked into the bamboo. Rooster led the way. Behind her, Shadow cradled their little bundle of embroidery samples. Mei Ju, forcing one leg after the other, brought up the rear.

Thorny undergrowth crackled beneath their feet, scratching their ankles, snagging their pants. Slender branches scraped against their widebrimmed hats, slapping their shoulders and legs, stinging. Still they pushed on.

Mei Ju, swallowing the yelps that leaped to her throat, peered anxiously at the sky. To her relief, the slivers and patches she caught through the breaks in the canopy of green remained clear of rainclouds, so the chances of passersby stopping in the hut and finding their tiered basket were slim. And by the time they had to quit the grove for the road, the sun was high, meaning morning rice was over, most people already back at work in their fields or wormhouses.

For a while, the road *was* clear. As they approached the village proper, though, Young Chow and his father emerged from behind the rows of houses, headed in their direction.

Deep in coversation, the Chows didn't seem aware of them. Even so, Mei Ju wedged herself between Shadow and Rooster, tucking her arms through theirs.

Shadow clutched the bundle to her chest. "Perhaps they'll pass without noticing us."

"What are you two afraid of? The Chows can't beat us like they do Yun Yun," Rooster said.

At the sound of her voice, father and son looked up, halted abruptly.

"You dare show your faces?" Old Man Chow spat. "What gall!"

Young Chow leered cruelly. "We should smear their faces with mud. That'll teach them some humility."

At the first lash of their tongues, Mei Ju wanted to run. She felt Rooster tense, Shadow freeze as if turned to stone.

"Let's go back," Mei Ju whispered.

"No," Rooster blazed, quickening her step.

Shadow dug in her heels, and Mei Ju, stretched awkwardly between the two, tugged at Rooster's arm, trying to pull her back.

Rooster slowed but did not stop. "How will we ever get to the water peddlers if we let bullies run us indoors with their threats?"

"You're right." Shadow, coming back to life, lunged forward, forcing Mei Ju to continue walking too.

As though she could hide from the Chows by studying the ground, Mei Ju bowed her head.

"That's better," Young Chow sneered.

Under her breath, Mei Ju begged Rooster and Shadow to lower their heads as well.

"Why should we?" Rooster protested, but softly. "We've done nothing wrong."

Shadow, bobbing down her own head, reminded, "With Empress, we got away with more when we pretended to listen."

As Rooster bent her neck, the Chows broke into raucous guffaws. Afraid she'd rear her head up again, Mei Ju crooked her elbow so that it squeezed Rooster's arm. "Please."

Unlike the Chows who'd stopped walking altogether, Shadow and Mei Ju had paused for scarcely more than a moment or two, Rooster not at all. And out of the corner of her eyes, Mei Ju suddenly saw the men's dirty sandaled feet. "We're passing them."

Indeed, the feet soon disappeared from sight. "They're behind us now."

"Look at that!" Young Chow bellowed. "Those sluts have gone and combed their hair into men's queues! What nerve! We should cut them off."

"Ai," Mei Ju quavered beneath his roar. "I never thought . . ."

"Don't pay them any mind," Rooster hissed.

"Those aren't queues," Old Man Chow jeered. "They're fox tails."

Young Chow snorted. "Those whores are sly as foxes alright."

Mei Ju shivered. "What should we do?"

"Keep walking." Rooster veered towards the river. "They're not going to come after us."

The Chows didn't. But their loud taunting had brought people out of the closest houses, and more than a few of these took up where the Chows had left off.

"They're going to drown themselves."

"That's what they should have done in the first place."

"Well said! Whoever heard of girls choosing for themselves?"

"Only wantons would act so boldly."

"And now that they've disgraced their families with their shamelessness, what can they do *except* kill themselves?"

Mei Ju had thought Rooster's decision to avoid going through the village wise. But the longer they walked along the riverbank without hurling themselves in, the worse the heckling became. With her head bowed, Mei Ju couldn't see their abusers, and the voices were so distorted with hate that they were unrecognizable. Or perhaps she was too frightened to make them out.

Finally, they reached the water peddlers. Pulling her arm free, Rooster leaped onto the nearest boat. Mei Ju and Shadow followed, giving rise to derisive cries, roars of disapproval.

Mei Ju, wishing she could make their abusers disappear, rubbed the palms of her hand over her eyes, her ears.

"We've come to buy," Rooster calmly told Shorty, whose boat they'd boarded.

"And sell," Shadow said, unwrapping their small bundle of embroidery.

As she unfurled her most recent achievement—a golden phoenix rising in a night sky—Shorty's eyes gleamed bright as his two silver teeth.

Turning to the people ashore who were shouting, "Jump!" "Jump now!" he blubbered, "You don't mean that! What'll I do for customers? For trade?"

Scabby Woo, the peddler tied up beside Shorty, picked at his scaly skin and mock-wailed shrilly, "Ai yah! Take pity on us! Ai yah!"

A few people snickered. Others continued to hurl insults, and the most boisterous among these climbed on board the boats, crowding the small decks so terribly that Mei Ju feared she and Rooster and Shadow would be forced into the water.

Throwing his arms up to Heaven, Shorty thanked the Gods for his windfall of customers while insinuating himself protectively between the spinsters and their abusers. Scabby

Woo placed his right hand over his left fist and comically jerked his head and hands up and down in welcome to those who'd boarded his floating store.

"Wai, what about me?" Big Mouth, whose boat was on the other side of Scabby Woo's, shouted. "I have goods to sell too."

Several people teetering over the gunnel of Scabby Woo's boat flung themselves, laughing, onto Big Mouth's deck.

Big Mouth slapped his paunch. "This belly of mine thanks you."

Little by little, the three water peddlers managed to diffuse the crowd's anger, to create a space for conducting business—coming to terms with Rooster over cooking pots, rice, and other necessities; examining the samples of embroidery Shadow showed them, negotiating agreements for marketing future work. The terms, though, were so much to the peddlers' advantage that Mei Ju didn't know how they'd be able to fill their rice bowls.

Only One Heaven

In Shadow's memory, thieves had stolen fish from Strongworm's outlying ponds and stripped the leaves from entire fields of mulberry; bandits had successfully kidnapped Old Bloodsucker's eldest son for a large ransom and robbed those foolish enough to risk taking to the road alone and unarmed. But the village itself had never been attacked, and the hut, despite its considerable distance from the closest house, was within the boundaries of the area patrolled by the nightwatch. During the first nights of their spinsterhood, Shadow nevertheless jumped at every sound, including the nightwatch's gong, his shouted assurance that all was well.

So did Mei Ju, who fretted the nightwatch would turn a blind eye should bullies like Young Chow attempt an assault. Indeed, Mei Ju insisted on shuttering the window and securing it, as well as the door, with makeshift crossbars of bamboo from the grove, then taking their cleaver to bed.

But Rooster, declaring they were under Gwoon Yum's protection, slept soundly from the start despite the suffocating heat, bedboards warped from damp, the irritating whine of mosquitoes trapped inside. She didn't even fully wake when slapping at the mosquitoes or scratching the welts from their bites, the sharp stings of spiders, bugs that continued to crawl out of the porous mud walls no matter how much the three scoured and scrubbed.

After a dozen or so uneventful nights, Rooster convinced Mei Ju to leave their window unshuttered. A few more, and Mei Ju's anxious tossing stopped, the bedmat beneath her became as quiet as the section under Rooster. Shadow, however, couldn't settle into sleep, not with Elder Brother still angry at her.

Twice now they had passed in the street and he'd turned from her, refusing to return her greeting. Yet Elder Sister-in-law seemed to have recovered from the shock of her near fall. Why else would she be squatting on the river bank washing the family's clothes?

Of course, had Shadow not vowed spinsterhood, she'd be in the wormhouse and Mama could be doing the wash. Was that why Elder Brother remained angry? Didn't he realize that she, Shadow, would gladly help at home *and* somehow make up for the loss of her bride price if he and their parents would let her?

Since she couldn't tell him directly, Shadow considered writing him a letter—rejected the idea. She did not want to remind him of their previous quarrel, and should her letter be seen by their father, it would not only fuel their parents' condemnation of her but engulf Elder Brother in their anger as well.

So Shadow began work on a meh dai, baby carrier, that would show Elder Brother her true heart feelings. Because she had to devote her days to embroidering for her livelihood, she made the carrier at night while Rooster and Mei Ju slept. And since there was no spare cash to buy fabric, Shadow cut up the least worn of her three tunics and pants for the carrier's central square, the four long strips of cloth that extended from each corner as ties.

At the top center of the square, she sewed a triangle of cloth five layers thick to represent the five blessings: riches, long life, peace, virtue, good health. Directly below, she embroidered a pair of mandarin ducks to signify her hope for her brother's marital happiness. Under the ducks, she stitched blue ripples for a lake; two pink lotus blooms on a single stem to express her further hope that they could return to sharing harmony. Finally, Shadow tripled the usual number of reinforcing stitches on the joins for each tie so her concern for the baby's safety would be clear.

Placing the completed carrier in the top tier of the basket she'd borrowed from home, Shadow carefully lowered the crossbar from the door, stole out of the hut and through the village, hoisted all over her family's courtyard wall.

Since newly hatched silkworms require almost constant feeding, Yun Yun's mother-in-law had ordered her to quit her marriage bed for the wormhouse at the start of each new generation. Seven times, then, during the past season, Yun Yun—disguising her enthusiasm as learned obedience—had hurried to make up a pallet for herself on the floor between the shelves of hungry worms.

These periods of incessant chopping, feeding, and cleaning exhausted Yun Yun. But her nights in the wormhouse were undisturbed except by the tiny creatures in her care. And, her heart aflutter, Yun Yun could snatch moments when she'd slip into her pallet and quietly sing:

> "I lie waiting for my sister, my friend,
> Waiting for my Lucky.
> My Lucky whose body is soft and warm,
> Whose breath is sweet.
> My Lucky who pledged friendship forever,
> Who vowed she'd come to me in my dreams."

Soon, very soon, Yun Yun would smell Lucky's distinctive musky scent, see her generously wide mouth spread in a smile bright as her own. Damp and feverish with excitement, Yun Yun would stretch out her arms and embrace Lucky. Then, slowly, tantalizingly slowly, they'd unbutton each other's tunics, revealing milky skin kissed by moonlight. Next off were their tight undershirts, so their breasts, smooth and tasty as almond cream, could spring free. Then their pants would fall, exposing their downy gateways to hidden treasure. Skin to skin at last, they'd rekindle the joy they'd found in the girls' house from coming together as one.

Of course, Old Granny in the girls' house had taught them, "Once you're married, you must honor your husband as if he were Heaven itself. You'd also do well to remember that there's only one Heaven, and to seek more than one in this mortal life is to invite disaster." But Yun Yun's need for Lucky was greater than her fear. Nor did Lucky ever refuse Yun Yun's call. Not so long as Yun Yun was alone in the wormhouse.

With the end of the silk season, however, came the end of Yun Yun's stolen happiness, any chance of escape from Young Chow. And when he invaded her, as he did night after night, often more than once, Yun Yun would silently cry:

> "You're the mountain dog
> That bites me as I pass,
> Tearing off my skin,
> Drinking my blood."

Mei Ju couldn't remember a day when her grandmother had not reminded the family, "Grandfather was chosen to serve as an elder on both the clan and the village councils because of his upright character. So it's important for every one of you, no matter how young, to watch yourselves in all you do and say. You must be especially careful not to bring shame on our family in any way." And during Mei Ju's final month at home, Grandmother had frequently added, "Grandchildren, take Bak Ju as your example. She understood that just as there's only one Heaven, we each have only one family, and family, like Heaven, is paramount, more important than self. That's why she sacrificed herself."

Mei Ju, then, had realized her grandmother and parents and aunts and uncles wouldn't soon forgive her for raising her own desires above theirs. Never for a moment, however, had Mei Ju imagined Shadow's easygoing brother and parents would suddenly turn unyielding as Grandmother. Nor had Mei Ju ever guessed Rooster's parents would openly condemn her for shaming their family.

To Mei Ju's further surprise, Rooster defended her parents. "How else can they placate Old Bloodsucker? Or convince my brother's patron in the clan school that the blame for my behavior doesn't lie with them, that they're giving Laureate good family teaching?"

"I wish we could somehow prove ourselves," Shadow sighed.

"We already are," Rooster said, throwing wide her arms to encompass the hut clean of dust, cobwebs, and debris; the neat piles of embroidery ready for delivery to the water peddlers; the vegetables they were growing in the patch of ground just outside the window.

Mei Ju beamed proudly at what they'd accomplished. "People are beginning to recognize we're capable. Respectable, too. The talk against us isn't anywhere as strong as it was three months ago."

Shadow's eyes puddled. "Only because everyone's talking about Yun Yun's father and brother coming all the way from Twin Hills for her." Tears streamed down her cheeks. "*Our* fathers and brothers won't even return our greetings when they see us in the street, and I have yet to catch so much as a glimpse of my niece."

"You know the weather's turned too cool to safely bring a baby outdoors," Mei Ju soothed. "But . . ."

"But other people can—and do—see her *indoors*." Shadow's stream of tears turned into a sea. "I've heard them say she's tiny and sickly."

Mei Ju had, too. Moreover, they placed the blame for the puny babe on Shadow for frightening her sister-in-law. But Mei Ju dismissed these assessments as gossip. "And gossips like nothing better than to exaggerate."

Sniffing hard, Shadow smeared her face dry with her sleeves. "Don't you see? I thought vowing independent spinsterhood would let us keep our families, everything that was good in our lives. Instead, we've become outcasts."

"Not entirely. Strongworm's Council of Elders has the power to expel us from the village the way it did the Tankas." Rooster bowed in the direction of the niche she'd made into an altar for Gwoon Yum. "But thanks to the Goddess, no one has hauled us before the Council, and the elders haven't ordered us to come before them either."

Mei Ju thought of the Tankas who, their usefulness ended, had been driven from the hut now sheltering her friends and herself. Grandfather's concubine had also been driven out when her usefulness ended. Why hadn't her friends and herself?

Mei Ju understood why no one in the village spoke up for them though. After her failed attempt to prevent Second Uncle from carrying his daughter out into the open to die, she'd never again spoken up for another person either at home or in the girls' house. Nor had she ever seen Shadow confront anyone openly. Only Rooster had.

She'd been especially vigorous in challenging Empress's

mistreatment of Lightning and Thunder. These girls, born within a month of each other, had been inseparable from the time they were small children, and they went in and out of each other's houses as though they were one. Yet Empress would order them to sit apart.

"Why should they?" Rooster would challenge.

"Haven't you learned unquestioning obedience yet?" Empress would screech.

Rooster would bravely shout back, and she'd persist for as long as was necessary to safeguard Lightning and Thunder from Empress's spite.

Rooster's championship of the pair ended when she began studying, however. "I still sympathize with Lightning and Thunder, I just can't jeopardize my one chance to acquire book learning," she'd confided.

Was it possible that Rooster, Shadow, and herself also had silent sympathizers, Mei Ju wondered.

A Lick
of Hope

FEW DAYS passed that Yun Yun didn't mistake a man working the oar of a skiff in the river or stooped over in a field for her father; a woman fetching water from the village well or stepping out of a house or into the temple for her mother. Or Yun Yun might suddenly catch the particular odor of her grandfather's tobacco, hear her grandmother urging her to take another bowl of rice, one of her brothers reciting a lesson, laughing, asking her for a story or a lullaby. And for the brief moment before Yun Yun reminded herself that she was in Strongworm not Twin Hills, that the distance between the two villages was too great for visiting, she'd feel a sharp lick of hope.

So when Yun Yun, responding to a steady rapping, threw open the Chows' front door and saw her father and youngest brother, she wasn't unduly surprised, and she quickly extinguished the hope flickering in her chest with a fit of blinking, a stern, "You're dreaming again."

Shrieking, "Elder Sister," Third Brother hurled himself at

Yun Yun, wrapped his little arms around her hips, and buried his baby face into her belly, unwittingly pressing against raw bruises inflicted by Young Chow the night before.

Yun Yun winced. The muscles in her father's jaw tightened, the cords of veins in his neck and forehead pulsed so violently they threatened to burst out of his skin, and Yun Yun realized the bridal guide, when taking her gifts to her family after her wedding, must have told all.

Heedless of her many hurts, Yun Yun scooped up Third Brother and hugged him close, hiding her face in the thick tuft of hair springing over his forehead, nuzzling his chubby cheeks and neck, breathing in his milky scent. Behind them, Old Lady Chow swept into the common room like a chill winter wind.

Her skin prickling with gooseflesh, Yun Yun raised her head from her brother's and stammered, "Mother-in-law, my father and Third Brother have come."

Her father bowed, handed Old Lady Chow a basket of choice dried red dates. Her voice stony as her face, she accepted, invited him in, ordered Yun Yun to pour tea.

As her father and mother-in-law settled into the pair of blackwood chairs adjacent to the family altar, Yun Yun—still hugging her baby brother tight—walked to the table under the window on the wall opposite. Reluctantly, she loosened her hold just enough so she could perch him on a hip and reach for the teapot in the padded basket.

Straddled across Yun Yun's hip, Third Brother bounced up and down, squealing, "You're coming home!" whenever he got even remotely close to her ear. And with every bounce, his knees and feet struck Yun Yun's many hurts anew. But her heart beat so wildly at the prospect of home that she scarcely noticed. Fearful his flailing would knock over the teapot or break a cup and bring down her mother-in-law's wrath, however, Yun Yun set Third Brother down.

"Yun Yun *is* home," Old Lady Chow said tartly.

"No," Third Brother howled, rolling on the floor and thrashing the air with his arms and legs as if he were having a fit. "No."

Yun Yun, hurrying over to the corner by the altar where Third Brother had rolled, felt their father's hand on her arm, restraining.

"Your little brother is too young to understand."

Old Lady Chow scowled. "He isn't too young to learn."

Yun Yun understood her mother-in-law meant for her father to scold Third Brother. But her father merely furrowed his brow and pursed his lips as though he were in deep thought, and Third Brother's clamoring continued unabated.

Old Lady Chow's scowl deepened. Yun Yun, uncertain whether she should try and appease her mother-in-law by reprimanding Third Brother on their father's behalf, rubbed one foot against the other.

"Stop that at once!" Old Lady Chow shouted.

Yun Yun froze. Third Brother screamed louder.

Their father shrugged helplessly. "You see the problem."

Like a petitioner unburdening himself before a magistrate, he continued, "The poor boy's been crying since Yun Yun left us. That's why we're here. To ask your permission for Yun Yun to come back to Twin Hills for a visit. Their mother wanted me to come months ago. I did too." He pointedly surveyed the room's plain furnishings, Yun Yun's work clogs. "We know from the matchmaker that *you're* sufficently well off to do without Yun Yun's labor throughout the year. But every hand in our household is needed except in late autumn and winter, so we couldn't come until now."

At his thinly veiled accusation, Old Lady Chow bristled, and Yun Yun braced herself against her father's chair, hoping against hope her mother-in-law wouldn't take vengeance by refusing to release her.

"We cannot spare Yun Yun," Old Lady Chow snapped.

Third Brother, who'd quieted while their father was speaking, burst into loud sobs. Yun Yun gulped down sobs of her own. Their father shook his head sadly.

Suddenly Third Brother shot out of the corner, doubled over in front of Old Lady Chow, and knocked his head against the floor in wordless supplication. Ignoring Third Brother, Old Lady Chow sternly reminded Yun Yun she hadn't yet served tea.

Yun Yun, stuttering apologies, stumbled back to the table.

Third Brother seized Old Lady Chow's legs and began thumping his head on her feet, wailing, "I want my sister."

Old Lady Chow whirled up from her chair. But with Third Brother wrapped round her legs, she lost her balance and sank back onto the seat.

Curious neighbors and passersby—who'd been poking their heads in the doorway and then lingering at the threshold since Third Brother began his tantrum—gaped in amazement; and there were scattered sniggers, gasps of "Ai yah!", more than a few sympathetic mutterings on his behalf.

Yun Yun, having somehow managed to pour the tea, wondered whether she should try and serve it, whether her mother-in-law—sputtering like a bead of water in a wok of hot oil—would strike her on account of her unruly brother if she came within reach.

Her father shifted in his chair so he faced the crowd gathered at the threshold. "As you see, the little one is desperate for his sister. So I asked permission for Yun Yun to come back to Twin Hills for a visit. Maybe some of you heard us talking. Maybe you already know. Yun Yun can't be spared."

Apparently taking his appeal to them as an invitation, many in the crowd eased into the common room and pleaded with Old Lady Chow.

"Have a heart!"

"Even your buffalo has this season for rest."

"Look at that poor boy. He'll do himself an injury."

Third Brother's face had become so swollen and red that Yun Yun did fear for him, and although she now recognized her father's ploy and longed for its success, she had to dig her toes into the soles of her shoes to keep from running to her brother and cradling him in her arms.

More and more people spilled in, addressed Old Lady Chow.

"Take pity on the boy."

"Do you mean to say your daughter-in-law isn't a useless rice bucket after all?"

"Obviously the little one values her."

"And now her mother-in-law, too."

White with anger, Old Lady Chow balled her hands into fists, slammed them down onto the arms of her chair. "Five days!"

Springing to his feet, Yun Yun's father confirmed, "Five days."

Their father's boat was still some distance from Twin Hills when Yun Yun heard First and Second Brother calling, "Elder Sister!" "Elder Sister!"

Looking up from Third Brother, asleep on her lap, Yun Yun scanned the riverbank, found the two boys on a large flat rock that jutted out into the water. Naked to their waists as though it were hot summer instead of cool autumn, they were swinging their jackets back and forth like flags while they jumped up and down, whooping and hollering.

So as not to disturb Third Brother, Yun Yun didn't shout back. But she waved with such enthusiasm that Third Brother woke anyway.

Sitting up, he confided proudly, "They wanted to come fetch you, but I cry better."

At the stern, their father steered the boat towards shore. "Don't you get any ideas about pitching more fits."

That her family had plotted together to bring her home

touched Yun Yun to the core, and when she called out to First and Second Brother, her voice cracked with emotion.

"We'll race you," First Brother shouted, waving their father off.

Leaping up from Yun Yun's lap, Third Brother urged her to help their father row. Yun Yun, glad for the chance to release her feelings through energetic rowing, scrambled to her knees, her feet.

"Third Brother," their father cautioned.

"I forgot." Quickly Third Brother seized Yun Yun's hands, pulled her back down, rocking the boat crazily. "I have to let you rest."

Spreading his own legs wide for balance, he recrossed Yun Yun's, restoring her lap, snuggled down in it. Yun Yun, pinned to the deck by her sweet burden, rested her chin on the top of her baby brother's head and closed her eyes.

Glare from the setting sun warmed her eyelids, and as the golden glow penetrated the darkness within, Yun Yun thought of the day she'd stared up at the sky looking for buffalo with her father. Reminded of the story he'd told of the buffaloes' fall, she understood that just as the blind Earth God, Day Jong Wong, and the Community Grandfather, Seh Gung, had tried to show their remorse and prove their integrity to the animals they'd betrayed, so too was her father attempting to redeem his mistake.

On those rare occasions when gentry came through Twin Hills and Strongworm, they sent runners ahead of their pa-

lanquins to open the road for them by blowing bugles or
hitting gongs, bellowing, "Make way!" And it seemed to
Yun Yun that her brothers, racing ahead of their father's
skiff, yelling, "Elder Sister's coming!" were not unlike these
runners, that all her family—with the exception of Third
Brother—treated her with the deference reserved for an
honored guest rather than a familiar member of the household.

There was meat at every meal, and her parents and grandparents heaped her bowl with the best pieces. Nor would her
mother allow Yun Yun to assist with either the preparation of
the meals or the washing up. If she so much as picked up a
broom or a bit of mending, it was snatched out of her hand,
and she'd be urged to sit, offered a bowl of steaming tea, a
tasty snack. If she was caught playing with Third Brother or
helping him with some small task, she'd be pulled away and
he'd be sternly reminded, "Let your sister rest."

Over and over Yun Yun begged her parents to let her resume her old chores.

"We only have you for five days," they'd say. "Let us spoil
you."

Finally, realizing her pleas upset them, she gave in.

With their houses side by side, Yun Yun saw Lucky daily.
But Yun Yun didn't seek Lucky out. And when Lucky visited,
Yun Yun evaded any prolonged talk by fussing over Third
Brother or feigning a headache, a sudden need to use the out-

house. For Yun Yun, having been as close to Lucky as if they were wearing one pair of pants, found restricting their exchanges to idle chatter unbearable. Nor would she disturb Lucky—betrothed to be married that winter—with unhappy tales of the Chows' cruelty. Most of all, Yun Yun did not want to torment Lucky, as she herself was tortured, with the knowledge that in Strongworm three girls had accomplished what the two of them hadn't dared imagine: seizing control of their own lives, refusing marriage, and vowing lifelong spinsterhood, so they could remain together.

Outcasts

ON HER WAY to Strongworm in the wedding sedan, Yun Yun's grief over leaving everyone she loved had been tempered by her mother's promise that her husband would be as gentle, kind, and affectionate as her father. Returning to the Chows on her father's boat after her five-day visit, Yun Yun recognized that all the rivers and streams in the world would run dry before her husband or in-laws would become what she and her parents had wanted for her. In truth, she felt like an outcast who'd been granted a brief reprieve and was now returning to exile. Yet Yun Yun still harbored hope of happiness. Indeed, she had happiness growing in her belly.

Seated cross-legged on the deck and warmed by the winter sun, she could already feel her babe's sweet weight in her arms, his lips sucking at her left breast, then her right. Satisfied, he gurgled, gave Yun Yun a wet, bubbly grin. And Yun Yun, her own hungers eased, brushed the tip of her nose, her cheek against his silky skin, burrowed her face into the firm flesh of his belly and breathed in his special fragrance. . . .

A brisk river wind swept Yun Yun from her imaginings back to the cold, hard deck. Above her, dark clouds had rolled in, hiding the sun. On the bank to her right loomed the towering eucalyptus trees that marked the approach to Strongworm, and the air was soon permeated with their bitter scent.

Shivering, Yun Yun scrunched her chin down into her tunic's high collar, squeezed her eyes shut, and resolutely restored her babe to her arms.

A husband was not supposed to impose on his wife while she had a baby in her belly or at her breast. When Yun Yun told Young Chow she was with child, however, he refused to release her from pleasuring him.

Shielding her belly with both hands, Yun Yun attempted to reason with her husband. Young Chow, his face twisted with rage, slapped her into silence and fell on her.

Desperately she tried to push him off. Tearing off her sleeping clothes, he bellowed, "Refusing your husband is a sign of immorality." And his attack, always brutal, was so vicious that Yun Yun's spirit fled her body.

How long her spirit was gone, Yun Yun didn't know. But she dimly became aware of Young Chow cruelly pinching her lips, the soft flesh of her inner thighs, the sound of her own voice whimpering pleas for mercy—not for herself, but for their unborn son.

In answer, Young Chow roughly forced her to turn over

onto her belly, then attacked her again, this time from behind.

Under his pitiless battering, the baby died.

With their first new year as spinsters approaching, Mei Ju felt the familiar excitement of her favorite festival heightened by the prospect of reconciliation.

At home, Grandmother was doubtless marshalling the entire household into scouring walls, stove, and furnishings so they shone. And under her direction, Ma and Second and Third Aunt would be preparing special treats—fried dumplings stuffed with sweet red bean paste, several varieties of steamed cakes, crispy gok filled with crushed peanuts, sesame, and sugar—to serve to family, friends and acquaintances who came to offer New Year wishes. Just recalling the wonderful mix of sweet saltiness melting on her tongue made Mei Ju's mouth water. But buying a winter quilt had used up too much of their savings for her and her friends to consider such indulgences for themselves, and they had no reason to expect callers.

"I do want to give lucky money to my little brother and cousins when I call on my family, though," Mei Ju said.

Shadow picked at a loose thread on the hem of her pants. "If I give a red envelope to my niece, it's likely to upset Elder Sister-in-law the way my matronly bun did."

Rooster reached over, snapped the thread. "We're not married, but we're not girls either, and as independent spinsters, we have the right, if not the obligation, to assume the responsibility of giving out red envelopes."

"We could take gifts of steamed cake, *goh*, to express our hopes that our families, like the cakes, will rise," Shadow, already fussing with another thread, suggested.

Hoping to ease Shadow's fretting, Mei Ju hurriedly agreed. "Grandmother will like that, and I won't have to spend as much as I would if I handed out lucky money."

"You don't have to put more than one copper in each red envelope," Rooster said. "Let's give lucky money *and* cakes."

Astonished, Mei Ju pointed at Shadow's frayed hem, the worn elbows and odd lumpiness of their tunics, which they'd padded against the winter chill with silk batting from their quilt. "Do we look like people who can afford both?"

"Being generous although we're in tatters will show our families how high we hold them," Rooster came back.

"And return us to favor," Shadow murmured, tucking a stray tuft of silk batting into the sleeve of her tunic.

Their families, like every household in Strongworm, had paper images of the Kitchen God above their stoves, and while setting up housekeeping in the rain shelter with Rooster and Shadow, Mei Ju had pasted one above theirs. To prevent soot from soiling their embroidery, however, they always dragged their small, clay stove outside when they cooked.

When the time came for the Kitchen God to make his year end report to Heaven, then, Mei Ju—having smeared his mouth with honey so he'd say only good things—carried his image outside to burn. Rooster and Shadow followed with a lighted taper, and in the cold light of the moon, they appeared almost spectral.

"Look." Shadow pointed to the thin threads of smoke above Strongworm's houses. "Our families, every family in the village is doing the same thing."

Rooster lit the paper Mei Ju held. In one brilliant, searing flash, the Kitchen God's image crackled into flame, and as it ascended to Heaven in a spiral of sooty smoke, it seemed to Mei Ju that the smell of burning sugar was as bittersweet and powerful as her feelings about her family.

Mei Ju had valued her sister too much herself to ever begrudge Bak Ju her position as family favorite. But Mei Ju had often felt unjustly criticized by her family, including her sister, and on these occasions she would comfort herself with thoughts of New Year.

Back to sharing a bed with Bak Ju and Grandmother for the duration of the festival, Mei Ju would waken long before they or anyone else in the house stirred. Soon as her eyes became accustomed to the dark, she'd slip out from under the thick quilt and, shivering despite the layers of undergarments she wore to ward off the winter cold, she'd carefully feel her way to the stool where Ma would have left her a new suit of clothes.

As Mei Ju pulled on the tunic and pants, the crispness of

the unwashed cloth would make her bits of exposed skin itch deliciously, the intensity of the indigo dye would tickle her nose, and to keep from giggling or sneezing, she'd gulp great swallows of chill air. Ma of course made everything extra long to allow for growth through as many years as the cloth would endure, and Mei Ju would have to fold back the sleeves, hike up the pants, and stuff handkerchiefs into the shoes. These adjustments completed, she'd stand absolutely still to savor the clothes' stiff newness. Then she'd pad out to the kitchen, start a fire in the stove, and put water on to make Grandmother her tea.

Waiting for the kettle to spout steam, Mei Ju would rake her fingers through her hair to unravel her pigtails, hurriedly comb and rebraid them. She'd pace the length and breadth of the small kitchen once, twice, become sure she'd burst if she lingered another moment, and whether the water was boiling or not, she'd make the tea.

Almost at a run, she'd carry it into Grandmother with a glad shout of New Year wishes for wealth, health, and long life, confident that Grandmother—although wakened abruptly and presented with a bowl of tepid water thick with leaves—wouldn't glower or snap, "Nuisance child." Instead, she'd smile, hand Mei Ju a red envelope of lucky money.

Bak Ju, also wakened by Mei Ju's loud greetings, would silently slip out of the bed, the room. Their little brother and cousins would come tumbling in, ply Grandmother with their good wishes, and eagerly accept their red envelopes before running out to wash and dress.

By then, Bak Ju would be back with her face washed, her hair neatly combed, a perfectly brewed pot of Grandmother's favorite Iron Goddess tea. And after offering Grandmother New Year greetings and accepting her red envelope, Bak Ju—laughing at the mess Mei Ju, in her impatience, had made of her hair—would comb and braid it for her.

There were more red envelopes to collect from their parents, aunts, and uncles, then gambling games to play with their lucky money. There were also firecrackers to set off, treats to eat. Better than the tasty treats, lucky money, and joyous play, however, was the knowledge that for fifteen wonderful days she, Mei Ju, did not have to brace herself against criticism from her grandmother, parents, uncles, aunts, and sister.

Now, steaming cakes and preparing envelopes of lucky money for New Year calls, Mei Ju was confident that she and her friends would be free from censure for the length of the festival. What she and Shadow and Rooster were hoping for, though, were lasting reconciliations.

Mei Ju arrived home just as her family was gathering before the altar in the common room to make offerings to their ancestors. And, as she'd expected, their faces were wreathed in New Year smiles.

The moment they noticed her stepping over the threshold, however, her grandmother's, father's, and uncles' faces turned stern, her mother's and aunts' shocked, her brother's and cousins' fearful. Stammering out New Year wishes to each member of the family, beginning with Grandmother, Mei Ju couldn't hide her own shock and fear.

Grandmother's acknowledgment was terse, her tone harsh. Mei Ju's parents, uncles, and aunts were likewise cold and hard, her brother and cousins only slightly warmer. And when Mei Ju offered them the bundle of cakes with additional good wishes, no one reached out to take it. When she tried to give lucky money to her brother and cousins, they backed away from her.

"Better set off firecrackers to drive away evil spirits," Grandmother told Ba.

Her meaning was unmistakable, and Mei Ju, dropping her gifts on the table, dashed out of the house. Almost immediately, firecrackers exploded behind her, and it seemed to Mei Ju that her heart, too, was bursting.

On New Year's eve, Rooster had written, "Sweep out strife, Bring in peace," on a strip of red paper that she'd pasted on the wall beside the door, and Mei Ju had marvelled at how simply yet clearly the couplet expressed their shared hope. Hurrying back to the hut after her visit to her family, Mei Ju found the words a mockery. Even so, she was appalled to find Rooster attacking the paper with a knife.

"My father accused me of deliberately adding insult to injury by bringing home cakes." Spitting out each word as if it were a hurtful stone, Rooster repeated her father's tirade.

"Your brother might have risen like these cakes and carried us with him. But you've shamed our family too deeply for Laureate to have any chance of rising now. The Low elder whose patronage has been protecting him from Old Bloodsucker has all but abandoned him, and Laureate will be lucky if he's allowed to continue in school."

Mei Ju searched frantically for words of comfort, found none. And for a long time, the only sound in the hut came from Rooster scraping the couplet off the wall.

Opposite
Sides

During Shadow's New Year visit with her family, she'd been treated like an unwelcome guest. But in her dreams that night, her parents received her warmly, and when she asked to hold her little niece, Elder Brother smiled, Elder Sister-in-law handed her the baby.

Just as Shadow was about to embrace the tiny bundle, she was wakened by loud squawking. Horribly disappointed, she opened her eyes—saw a hen stretching its neck, flapping its wings, straining to break free of Rooster's grasp.

According to Rooster, this hen—which she'd found outside their door—was a gift from Gwoon Yum to give them heart. But Shadow believed her brother had left it to show her his true heart.

The next time she passed Elder Brother in the street, then, Shadow thanked him.

"It wasn't me," he told her.

And so unyielding was his tone that Shadow was instantly carried back to a steamy hot day in her fourth year.

. . .

On that hot summer's day, Elder Brother had piggybacked her to a little stream south of Strongworm's rice fields so they could cool themselves splashing, paddling about in the shallows, and long before they'd reached the stream, he'd been dripping with perspiration, which had acted like glue, sticking her chest and arms to his back, his neck.

Peeling herself off Elder Brother, Shadow asked, "Why didn't you go to the river? It's much closer."

"Because this stream is magical," Elder Brother said, stripping off his shorts.

He helped Shadow off with hers, took her hand, walked her into the cool water. "Can't you see that?"

The water around them glittered gold in the sun's glare. Below the surface, fish—large and small, colorful and drab—swam past, some so close their scaly skins and spiky fins and tails brushed her thighs, her brother's calves. One fish nibbled her fingers, tickling. Soft silt oozed deliciously between her toes, and even when she clouded the water by poking her feet deeper to increase her pleasure, the stream was clearer than the river where Mama did the family wash and water peddlers tied up their boats. Prettier, too, since the grass on the banks was untrampled. With only their two voices, birdsong, the faint whirring of dragonflies' iridescent wings, quieter as well. But magical?

"It's an ordinary stream," Shadow decided.

"Wait till I tell you what happened here in olden times— after buffaloes came down to earth but before they lost their ability to talk. You'll change your mind then."

Always eager for a story, Shadow gazed up expectantly. Elder Brother settled on a mossy rock in the shallows, drew her onto his lap.

"In those faraway days, the seven daughters of the Sun God used to come down from the sky to bathe in this very stream." He pointed at their shorts lying in the grass where they'd dropped them. "And those seven sisters would leave their clothes on the bank just like we do."

Folding Shadow's right hand in his, Elder Brother directed it at a buffalo grazing upstream in the shade of some willows.

"One day, a Cowherd was minding his buffalo under those same trees, and he was so hot and tired and bored that he fell asleep."

Elder Brother released her hand. "Now what do you think happened while the Cowherd was napping?"

"The seven sisters came down to bathe?"

"Right! And when the Cowherd woke and saw them, he fell in love."

Shadow's eyes widened. "With all seven?"

Elder Brother laughed. "Just the prettiest—the Weaving Maid, who made cloth out of cloud-silk for the other six sisters to stitch into robes for the Gods.

"Anyway, the Cowherd's buffalo, who could see into his master's heart, said, 'Don't just stand there gawping at the Weaving Maid. Go steal her robe.'

"'Which one is it?' the Cowherd asked.

"'The prettiest, of course.'

"The Cowherd set out, stopped. 'I'm not sure I should.'

"The buffalo pawed impatiently at the grass beneath his hooves. 'You want the Weaving Maid, don't you?'

"The Cowherd gave a lovesick moan. 'Oh, yes.'

"'Then you'd best be quick about it or you'll lose your chance.'

"Lickety-split, the Cowherd raced over to the sisters' robes, snatched the prettiest, dashed back to his buffalo. And when the Weaving Maid couldn't find her dress, she couldn't go back to the sky with her sisters, she had to go to the Cowherd. Not just to get her robe, but to marry him since he'd seen her naked."

Shadow looked down at her nakedness, her brother's, threw her arms around his chest. "Like we will."

Gently he lowered her arms back onto her lap. "No, you silly melon. Not like us. Brothers and sisters can't marry. And nakedness doesn't matter until you're big."

Shadow pouted. "But I want . . ."

"The rest of the story?" Elder Brother asked, scooping up a handful of water and pouring it over her head.

The water streamed down Shadow's forehead and nose, her cheeks in cool rivulets, trickled inside her ears, down her neck and chest and back, tickling.

"Yes," she giggled.

"Well, the Cowherd and the Weaving Maid were very happy. But the Gods were furious because without the Weaving Maid, they had no new robes. The Weaving Maid's sisters couldn't help either, since they were needlewomen, not weavers.

"After three years, the Gods' robes were in tatters.

"'Enough!' the Queen of Heaven screeched down to the Weaving Maid. 'Get back to your loom.'

"By then, the Weaving Maid and the Cowherd had two babies, and she loved her husband more than ever. But she was too afraid of the Queen of Heaven to disobey. So the Weaving Maid bid the Cowherd a tearful farewell and returned to the sky with their babies."

Tears of sympathy rolled down Shadow's cheeks. "Can't the buffalo help them?"

"You'll have to wait and see," Elder Brother admonished, tapping the tip of her nose with a finger.

"The Weaving Maid went back to her loom, and while she worked, the six sisters took turns caring for her children like I take care of you for Mama.

"Busy as the Weaving Maid was, she missed her husband terribly. The Cowherd missed her too. Saddest of all was the buffalo, who cried for them just like you.

"'Kill me,' the buffalo told the Cowherd. 'Use my skin to ride up into the sky.'"

"No," Shadow yelped.

"That's what the Cowherd said. When the buffalo insisted, however, the Cowherd gave in."

Shadow's yelp turned into a wail. "No."

"Yes." Elder Brother squeezed her in a comforting hug. "The Cowherd killed his buffalo, skinned it, and flew up to his wife's home in the sky.

"Directly before he reached her, though, the Queen of

Heaven saw him. Wah, she was angry! Shouting, 'I'm never going to wear shabby clothes again,' she snatched out a long hairpin and swept her arm across the sky.

"That one stroke created the Silver Stream of Heaven, with the Cowherd on one side, the Weaving Maid on the other. And the two are still on opposite sides—close enough to see each other, but unable to touch."

"That's not fair," Shadow sobbed.

"I'm not finished."

Relieved, Shadow swallowed her tears, nestled against her brother's chest.

"Husband and wife begged the Jade Emperor for mercy, and he decreed that once a year, on the seventh day of the seventh moon, all the crows and magpies in the world should come together and make a bridge with their wings and bodies so the Weaving Maid can cross the Silver Stream to meet the Cowherd."

Shadow waited for Elder Brother to continue. When he didn't, she cried, "That's it?"

"That's it," he told her firmly.

And although she renewed her sobbing, Elder Brother refused to relent, insisting, "You can't change what is."

Yun Yun, mourning her dead baby, had counted the days until spring, the start of the silk season, the moment the first generation of eggs would hatch and she could return to sleeping in the wormhouse, Lucky's comforting embrace.

When at last Yun Yun slid into her makeshift pallet on the wormhouse floor and called for Lucky, however, she didn't come.

Hastily Yun Yun tried again.

> "Lucky, the sun has traveled to the west
> And disappeared behind the hills.
> Lucky, the birds have flown away
> And are snug in their nests.
> Ai, Lucky, my Lucky,
> Fly to me now."

Waiting for the musky scent and gentle warmth that would signal Lucky's arrival, the cold hardness of the earth floor penetrated Yun Yun's thin pallet. She became aware of the worms' crunching, the fetid odor of their accumulating waste.

Feeling as if her husband's ever-hungry worm had somehow multiplied into the thousands, and with it, his habit of creating a stink wherever he went by deliberately breaking wind, Yun Yun slid deeper into her pallet, covered her head, smothering everything except her grief for her dead baby, her need for Lucky.

Night after night, Yun Yun called for her friend. And when Lucky failed to come, Yun Yun began stumbling over stools and buckets, sweeping the same spot and washing the same garment or bowl many times over.

Then she forgot to shut the door to the wormhouse. The worms, blasted by a cold draft, caught the thief-wind sickness, turning very red, so stiff they could no longer crawl. Those few that survived produced undersized, discolored cocoons.

Old Man Chow took one look at the sampling Yun Yun brought him and roared, "They're not worth reeling."

Snatching a mulberry branch from the kitchen, he swung at her. "This'll teach you a lesson you won't soon forget."

Instinctively Yun Yun ducked, and the branch struck the side of the family altar, snapped in two. Hurling down the broken wood, Old Man Chow punched her with his bare fists.

Knocked off balance, Yun Yun staggered, fell, curled into a ball, and rolled towards the door. Young Chow, coming in, kicked her back to his father.

Begging for mercy, she dodged his foot, crawled under the altar. Her husband dragged her out, held her down for her father-in-law, who seized a broom and beat her with the handle.

Silent now, Yun Yun escaped by going inside herself.

FOUR

1838

Mountain
Pines

BENT OVER her embroidery frame, Mei Ju manipulated her needle as skillfully as the long chopsticks and reel she used for unwinding silk from cocoons. But she felt little of the pleasure and none of the peace that reeling brought her. Her friends knew no peace either.

Rooster, accepting her father's blame for her brother's troubles, had purchased a string of prayer beads from a pair of itinerant monks who'd told her that repeating the Bo-dhivistic chant for overcoming disasters would help Laureate regain his patron's favor. And it seemed to Mei Ju that except for when Rooster was at her embroidery frame or doing chores, she was pushing the wooden beads through her fingers while murmuring, "Nam-mo-oh-neh-toh-fu." Even in her sleep, Rooster's fingers twitched.

Shadow lay perfectly still in bed at night. Nevertheless, her eyes were ringed black. She ate so little that her tunic and pants—which had all but burst at the seams when they'd made their vows—hung loose. Mei Ju didn't have to ask why. At the boisterous talk, grunts, and sighs of men passing their hut on their way to or from the fields, Shadow would cock her head toward their door, and when the sounds faded without anyone leaving the road for the short path to the hut, her head and shoulders would sag with a sharp little catch of breath.

Not wanting to add to her friends' worries, Mei Ju said nothing when she noticed the mud walls weeping from the spring rains. Nor did she remark on the clamminess of their bedding, their clothes, the dank smell of mold, the moss that was creeping up the legs of their tables and stools, the squish and slide of their clogs on the damp floor. Even when one section of wall, bulging under the weight of water, finally sagged and slid to the floor, leaving a gaping hole, she told them cheerily, "If we turn the table on its side and push it against the hole, that'll keep most of the rain out, and I'll fix it as soon as the sun comes out again."

Shadow, her face ashen, sank to her knees and plunged her hands into the mound of soggy fallen dirt.

Rooster stared at the water streaming through the hole, puddling around Shadow's knees, Mei Ju's feet, her own. "This is why the Council of Elders hasn't bothered to banish us from Strongworm. They knew the rains would do it."

More upset by her friends' reactions than the damage, Mei Ju reminded, "Our first day in the hut, the two of you showed me how mixing straw and dried grass into the mud turns it into a strong plaster, and we patched almost a dozen holes. This one's bigger, but I can take care of it."

Shadow held up two handfuls of mud. "You can't."

She spread her fingers, and Mei Ju, watching the wet dirt slump and fall back onto the mound in soft plops, suddenly remembered her grandmother saying, "Dozens of huts were built for the Tankas, but most washed away after a season or two of big winds." Refusing to give in to her friends' gloom, however, Mei Ju assured Shadow and Rooster that the rain they were experiencing wasn't serious. Moreover, since the big wind in which her sister had drowned, there had been no storms.

"I can fix this," she repeated. "We'll be fine."

Shadow, her muddied hands empty, pointed at the hole. "Look at it. Only the bamboo frame is left. That's why the wall caved in. There's no wattle to hold a patch."

Mei Ju could see that. But every fall, the men in Strong-worm cut down mulberry and spread it out to dry for weaving into chicken pens and wind baffles, and it seemed to Mei Ju that she should be able to likewise weave more wattle for their wall.

Tipping the table on its side and shoving it against the hole, she said as much.

"How?" Rooster demanded. "We have no mulberry stems and no way to get any."

She was right, Mei Ju realized. Although there was such an abundance of dried mulberry that it was also used for fuel, no one was going to risk censure by giving—or even selling—any to outcasts.

"Can't our clever rooster produce mulberry stems for us the way she did eggs?" Mei Ju asked hopefully.

Rooster shook her head. "Not the amount we're going to need."

"Come on," Mei Ju coaxed. "The hole's not that big."

"But the wall is," Shadow said. "And we have four that need fixing, because you can bet the mulberry has rotted all the way around."

Full understanding hit Mei Ju with the force of a hard fist. The Tanka huts that remained were those the Council of Elders had decided to keep in repair as rain shelters. This winter, the Council—knowing full well that she and Rooster and Shadow had neither the access to mulberry nor the skills to fix any large-scale damage—had sent no one to make the annual repairs. And with one wall already caving in from light spring rains, the hut clearly wouldn't survive the heavier summer downpours even if there were no big wind.

Sinking onto the edge of the bed, Mei Ju surrendered. "I can't fix this. We'll have to hire someone."

Rooster clicked her tongue impatiently. "We earn barely enough to buy rice and oil and salt fish. Can you remember the last time we tasted meat? So if by some miracle we did find someone willing to work for us, what would we pay them with?"

"We can produce more embroidery for the water peddlers to sell, and they can bring in someone from another village and advance the person's pay and the cost of materials for us. . . ."

Rooster sliced a hand across the air. "No! That would bind us to the water peddlers the way my father is bound to Old Bloodsucker."

"I know that, but what else can we do?"

"Use young, thin bamboo instead of mulberry and try to rebuild the walls our . . ." Breaking off in midword, Shadow knocked her forehead with the heel of her palm, smudging it with mud. "Ai yah! Even if we work on a small section of wall at a time, how will we protect our embroidery silks from water damage when it rains?"

The answer seemed obvious to Mei Ju. During the summer months, many men and women wore clothes made from black gummed silk because it was waterproof, and the inside of their hut could likewise be kept dry by hanging this cloth across the rafters and between the bamboo frames empty of wall. About to give this idea voice, however, she realized that inexpensive as black gummed silk was, they couldn't afford to buy the many lengths they'd need.

Finally, with a confidence she didn't feel, Mei Ju said, "We'll find a solution while we're cutting the bamboo."

Except for picking mulberry leaves, Shadow had never worked in the fields. But from her years of following Elder Brother around Strongworm, she'd become as familiar with outdoor labor as in. And when she'd seen Mei Ju about to throw away a broken hoe while cleaning out the hut, Shadow had snatched it from her, exclaiming, "We can use this to break ground for a vegetable patch." She'd then designed a vegetable patch for the back of the hut with the same careful attention to detail that she applied to her embroidery.

To minimize the area for cultivation, Shadow alternated

vegetables that grew underground with those on the ground and in the air; she calculated the number of plants necessary to support three people, also the exact distance between each plant so there'd be no waste of space, seeds, or labor. Plan in hand, she walked the space between hut and grove a dozen times in the course of a day, studying the sun in the sky, the placement and length of shadows on the ground. Finally, she marked out a plot four feet by nine where light fell earliest in the morning and lingered the longest in the afternoon.

So their hands wouldn't form callouses that would snag silk and spoil their embroidery, Shadow cut her shabbiest pair of pants into narrow strips which she and her friends wrapped around their palms and fingers. So as to save their strength, Shadow shared what her father had told her brother: "Begin work from the center of the plot. Pull out the wild grasses by the roots and remove all rocks and stones before attacking the hardpacked dirt with the hoe. After turning over each layer of soil, let the sun dry out the large clods of earth for easier crumbling."

Shadow, though, could only bend her back to the hoe for short stretches. Nor did Mei Ju—whose grandmother assigned all heavy labor to the men in their family—bear up any better. Both had improved with time. But neither had ever matched the endurance of Rooster, who'd been forced from childhood by Old Bloodsucker to labor long and hard in the fields.

Compared to hacking down bamboo, it seemed to Mei Ju that breaking ground for their vegetable patch had been child's play. And knowing every family in the village had mulberry stems to spare made the sweaty, backbreaking work of harvesting the bamboo even more burdensome for her.

But Shadow said, "The bamboo will save us work in the long run because it's stronger than mulberry and won't rot."

"At last we have something to use our cleaver for," Rooster joked.

Shadow giggled. "From now on, I'm going to pretend the bamboo is really a juicy suckling pig."

Amazed but relieved at her friends' apparent rise in spirits, Mei Ju laughed when next she thrust their cleaver into a bamboo, "I'm chopping a chicken."

Rooster, taking the cleaver for her turn, smacked her lips. "Duck for me."

They were, in truth, needful of meat to boost their strength, and Mei Ju wished another chicken or a slab of pork would arrive on their doorstep.

What appeared was a bolt of black gummed silk. Rooster attributed this gift to Gwoon Yum too. And Mei Ju agreed, as she had before with the hen. Where Rooster claimed Gwoon Yum had personally brought them the chicken and cloth, however, Mei Ju believed the Goddess had gifted them with an earthly benefactor who shared her merciful heart.

. . .

The wall around the gaping hole was so weak that Mei Ju knocked it down with a few sharp taps of their broken hoe. But removing the dirt so she and Shadow and Rooster could weave the wattle into the frame was harder: they had to fill their two baskets bowl by bowl, then haul the filled baskets across the clearing to empty.

Together they slashed through huge swathes of grass in the hills, lashed what they'd cut into sheaves that they strung onto lengths of sturdy bamboo and carried back to their hut. They spread the grass out to dry, then dragged the felled bamboo out of the grove for splicing into narrow strips that they wove through the hut's frame.

The wattle completed, they made countless trips to the river to fetch water for turning the dirt back into mud. They mixed dried grass into the mud to form a plaster and covered the wattle handful by handful.

They worked on only one section of the wall at a time. And between each section, they returned to their embroidery for a few days so they'd have a break from their labor, something to sell. But after just one wall was rebuilt, even Rooster admitted exhaustion.

Rubbing liniment on each other, they tried to ease their hurts. Nevertheless, jagged streaks of pain ripped up and down their arms and across their backs each time they lifted a bucket of water, a basket of dirt, or shouldered the yoke. Then their necks and backs became so stiff that they had difficulty bending over their embroidery frames. The joints in their fingers swelled until they could scarcely hold their needles. The muscles in their legs knotted and cramped whether they were walking or at rest. In truth, it seemed to Mei Ju that they moved more like they were seventy than seventeen and eighteen.

Yet Mei Ju was certain that she and her friends would persist until all four walls were rebuilt. What she fretted over was whether this success would be enough to win them back their families, a place in Strongworm, and with it, a return to reeling silk.

Yun Yun's mother-in-law, claiming the family had to make up the losses she'd caused, rationed her food, allowing her only watery gruel made from the scrapings of the rice pot.

Yun Yun, already slender, soon became so thin her belly sank against her spine. Dark shadows circled her eyes. Her hair came out in her comb.

No one in the village spoke up for her. Not even those who, drawn by her baby brother's loud wails, had crowded at the Chows' door, then spilled into the common room and pleaded with Old Lady Chow to take pity on the boy and release Yun Yun for a visit home.

More than once, though, she heard someone mutter, "It's people like the Chows that make girls afraid of marriage."

The Chows had widely proclaimed their disapproval of the spinsters from the day Shadow, Mei Ju, and Rooster had made their vows, and Yun Yun noticed that every time the talk against the women started to lose its intensity, her in-laws and husband would stir it up again the way she stirred the buckets of nightsoil before fertilizing the fields. She also frequently saw them among the men and women crowding round the mud hut, scoffing at the spinsters' toil.

"You're going to fail anyway, so you might as well save yourselves this effort."

"Yeah, give it up."

"Give it up now!"

Nor did the nay-saying stop when the spinsters completed the repairs.

"Just wait. A few heavy downpours, and those walls will wash away."

"They'll collapse in a big wind."

"Hnnnh, a small wind will do."

The hut withstood the first summer storms, however. And when Yun Yun saw the spinsters wearing clothes made out of black gummed silk, she thought of the mountain pines that endure despite roots sunk into rocky ground, assaults of bitter cold and wind.

Dead
Useless

YUN YUN's father had long ago taught her, "Each plant has its very own character and needs. Just like a person. Plants also think about the next generation like we do."

"How do you know?" she'd asked.

In answer he'd pointed to a broccoli and two bak choy that were struggling to stay alive although they'd sprouted from stray seeds beyond their field and were therefore neither regularly watered nor ever fertilized.

"Look how undersized they are. Yet they already have little yellow flowers. Why? Because the plants are suffering and know they're dying, so they're rushing to make seeds in spite of being young and puny."

The malnourished broccoli and bak choy had indeed made seeds long before the carefully tended plants in the field had even flowered. And Yun Yun, starved for affection and weak from her mother-in-law's meagre rations, was consumed by desire for a baby, fear that while her husband was young and healthy, he'd continue to overlook his obligation to ensure descendants for his parents and insist on taking his pleasure regardless of whether she was with child.

She considered seeking her mother-in-law's help since Old Lady Chow called her dead useless for failing to produce a grandson. If Yun Yun told her the reason, though, Young Chow was bound to refute it, and who would Old Lady Chow believe?

So Yun Yun sold a gold ring from her few pieces of wedding jewelry, and soon as she realized she again had life in her, she gave her husband the necessary cash to go to a house of pleasure. He forced her to serve him in bed anyway, killing their second baby as he had their first. Then he used the money to lease another field for growing mulberry, adding to her work; and his glee over tricking her was as vicious as his assaults on her body.

That her husband's appetite was not for pleasure but suffering, especially her suffering, Yun Yun now understood. If she couldn't protect life in her from her husband, however, she couldn't bear a child. And if she didn't have at least one child to love, to soften the harshness of her life, she didn't see how she could endure.

Of course, she could release herself from her suffering *and* show who had caused it simply by looping her husband's red wedding sash around her neck, then hanging herself from their bedpost. No one would dispute such a damning accusation. She'd be justly avenged. But her suicide would also be a

condemnation of her father for agreeing to the match, and
Yun Yun would not heap her own blame onto the burden of
regret that so clearly weighed on him and her mother already.

Last year, when Mei Ju had been new to weeding, she'd
heard her grandmother snapping, "You really are dead
useless," each time she slowly, clumsily worked her way
through the leafy tops of sweet potatoes, turnips, and peanuts. Now Grandmother was silent. Not because Mei Ju's
fingers plucked weeds from the warm, moist soil with prac-
tised ease, but because Grandmother had been crowded out
by other voices.

"What right do those three upstarts have to wear sober
black?"

"They'll learn it takes more than dressing in black
gummed silk to make a body old and wise."

"Hnnnh, those spinsters aren't capable of learning!"

"Looks like that Rooster's brother isn't either."

"The want-to-be laureate?"

"Yeah. He'll be in the fields before the summer's over."

That gossip was as inevitable and persistent as weeds Mei
Ju had realized since childhood. Mei Ju had even expected
that making clothes for themselves out of the black gummed
silk would spawn exactly this kind of criticism. But their cotton tunics and pants had turned into rags, and they'd had no
money to buy cotton, no other use for the black gummed
silk. Moreover, Mei Ju hadn't anticipated this new round of

reproof would propel the ill will against Shadow, Rooster, and herself onto Laureate.

Of course, she'd known since Rooster's New Year visit home that Laureate had fallen out of favor with his patron on their account. Ever since this Low elder had first shown an interest in Laureate, however, people had acknowledged the boy was aptly named. Indeed, his brilliance had been the talk of the village.

"See how flat our foreheads are? Laureate's bulges out with brains."

"That boy learns as easily as other boys spit."

"Mark my words, when he's old enough for the district examinations, he'll bring honor to the Low clan."

"To all of Strongworm."

So Mei Ju had thought popular sentiment for Laureate would hold strong despite the loss of the patron's favor. She'd also thought it would protect Laureate from Old Bloodsucker. Now she wasn't sure. And Rooster clearly shared her doubts. When reaching for her prayer beads the night before, she'd muttered bleakly, "If my brother is banished from the clan school, I'll never forgive myself."

Mei Ju understood: she would certainly forever hold herself responsible for the part she'd played in her sister's death.

Yun Yun felt as dead as the brush her mother-in-law was ordering her to go gather from the hills for fuel. But with no hope of deliverance, Yun Yun didn't waste spittle pleading for release. She put on her wide-brimmed straw hat, hung a basket from each end of the carrying pole, shouldered it, and headed for the uncultivated slopes beyond Strongworm's fields.

Even before Yun Yun left the village proper, she was panting. Moreover, the carrying pole was rubbing her bony shoulder raw, and the morning sun was burning through her hat, piercing her skull. But going back to her mother-in-law with empty baskets was impossible. So Yun Yun staggered on, forcing her right leg up, setting it down; then her left; then her right.

By the time she reached the road between village and fields, sweat was seeping through her every pore, drenching her tunic and pants so that the wet cloth clung and twisted round her arms and legs like shackles. Still Yun Yun dragged one foot after the other, stirring up clouds of dry dirt that caked her sweaty sandaled feet, stung her eyes, and clogged her nose, her throat.

Each step demanded more effort than the last. Soon her heart was pounding so fiercely she feared it would leap from her chest. Then the fields in the distance, the bamboo grove, the very road she was walking blurred into darkness. Yet she felt no cooling clouds coming between her and the sun's white heat.

Stumbling to a confused halt, Yun Yun stooped to lower her shoulder pole for a moment's rest—pitched forward and careened off the road, toppling into a shallow gully, her shoulder pole clattering after her, the baskets hurtling in, bouncing back out.

Through it all, she uttered no sound. At first because she was too startled. And then because her spirit had flown.

Mei Ju, weeding in their vegetable patch behind the hut, heard the rasp of small stones and dirt, the sharp snap of breaking branches. In the grip of the voices in her head, she didn't even glance up. Then, the weeding completed, Mei Ju tossed what she'd pulled into the mound of wood ashes, leaf mold, and decaying vegetable scraps at the far end of the clearing. Instantly flies and gnats spiraled up in a noisy buzz, and Mei Ju, jumping back to avoid them, caught a flash of blue in the shallow gully between the road and bamboo grove. A trick of the eye?

Standing on tiptoe, she stretched her neck. The wild honeysuckle and grasses around the gully were too thick for her to actually see in. But between the varying shades of green and flecks of white, there was definitely blue. Duck-egg blue.

A magpie roosting on the hut's roof cawed, and through the window floated Rooster's steadfast chanting, "Nam-mo-oh-neh-toh-fu," the clang of their wok. Mei Ju chuckled. What fun it would be to surprise Rooster and Shadow with duck eggs for their morning rice! Laughing out loud, she strode out of their clearing into knee-deep grass.

The gully was twenty, thirty feet distant, and Mei Ju had covered about half of it when she realized she was looking at clothing, not eggs. And since no one in Strongworm would be so wasteful as to throw away clothing that, however worn, could be used as rags, the duck-egg-blue tunic or pants she was looking at was *on* someone. Someone who was crouched or lying absolutely still. Halting abruptly, she wondered whether she should go any further.

Neither a child at play nor a bandit would choose such a poor hiding place, Mei Ju reasoned. So the person in the gully was likely injured. Should she take the time to go back to the hut for Shadow and Rooster? Or should she try shouting for help? Ai, what if she was blamed for whatever had happened? Anyway, what she could see of the road was empty. Everybody must have already gone to their homes for morning rice. When they returned to the fields afterwards, though, someone would notice the blue, as she had, and stop. Or ignore it, as she was tempted to. Or find it was too late to help. Maybe it was too late already.

Overwhelmed, Mei Ju sagged onto a nearby rock, sprang back up from its heat, the memory of all the times she'd failed to help others—and plunged on through the thick tangle of her confusions and fears, the grass.

As she approached the gully, Mei Ju recognized Yun Yun, although her hat was skewed and covered much of her face. And Mei Ju guessed from the empty baskets and shoulder pole that Yun Yun had been on the road to the fields.

The slope between road and gully wasn't either steep or long, but it was strewn with sharp stones, and Yun Yun's visible cheek was grazed, her hands had several small wounds, one leg of her pants had a long tear from knee to hem, and the exposed skin was covered with blood. Blood and flies.

Ants and other bugs were crawling over Yun Yun too. Yet not an eyelid fluttered open. Not a finger twitched. Most worrying, Mei Ju, squinting unblinkingly at Yun Yun's chest, couldn't detect the slightest rise and fall.

Reluctant to climb down to a corpse, Mei Ju squeaked, "Yun Yun," from above. Yun Yun did not stir. But then Mei Ju could hardly hear herself.

Taking a deep breath, she tried to squeeze something louder out of her throat, couldn't. Again and again she tried, failed. Finally, she sank into the grass and edged into the gully.

During Grandfather's last months, Mei Ju had heard her mother talk about how she'd restored his spirit with white flower oil. Now, in imitation, she picked a handful of fragrant honeysuckle, crushed the petals to intensify their scent, then crouched, trembling, beside Yun Yun's face and held the broken blossoms under her nose.

Freedom

As though from a great distance, Yun Yun smelled Lucky's distinctive musky scent.

"Lucky?" she breathed.

"Mei Ju."

Mei Ju the spinster? Yun Yun's eyes flew open, blinked up at a halo of blinding light surrounding a hat, a face, Mei Ju's face.

"You fell."

Memory returned to Yun Yun in a rush, and with it, sharp pricks of pain, a flood of panic over her unfilled baskets.

"I've got to go."

Over Mei Ju's protests and with her considerable help, Yun Yun crawled out of the gully, her lips folded tight so she wouldn't leak the howls that were roaring in her head at the tiniest movement, the gentlest touch.

At least the cut in her leg seemed to have stopped bleeding, Yun Yun told herself. Nothing was broken either. But every inch of her hurt down to her bones. And even greater than the torment of her wounds and the exhaustion that had led to her fall was her terror that someone would see her and Mei Ju from the road.

When at last they reached the top, then, Yun Yun forced herself to stand alone, and through her tortured breathing, gasped, "Thank you, I'll be alright now."

Her lips unfolded, she could not hold back a groan. Mei Ju, pulling the carrying pole out of the gully, dropped it.

"Let me ask your father-in-law and husband to bring a chair to carry you home," she urged.

"No."

Fear made Yun Yun's tone harsher than she intended, and Mei Ju flinched.

Remorse swept through Yun Yun, stripping away pretense. "You're very kind. But I'd just get punished for being with you and failing to bring back the brush I was sent for. As it is, I'll be scolded for being slow. Probably for falling, too."

"Don't worry." Mei Ju pointed up at the sun high in the sky, the dark smoke rising from the houses in the village, the spinsters' hut. "There won't be any prying eyes until morning rice is over. And we have plenty of brush. Enough to fill both your baskets."

She smiled warmly. "So come to our hut for a wash, something to eat, and a proper rest."

Listening to Mei Ju, Yun Yun recalled Shadow's mother urging her to take shelter from the rain in the hut. She, too, had claimed there was no need for worry, and Yun Yun, in accepting that invitation, had earned a beating.

Already, though, Yun Yun's shoulders had slumped, her legs were sagging at the knees, and the prospect of washing, eating, and resting, however high the risk, was enticing. Too enticing to refuse.

Returning Mei Ju's smile, Yun Yun murmured a fervent, "Thank you."

Mei Ju insisted on returning for the pole and baskets later so she could brace Yun Yun for the short walk to the hut. And Yun Yun, leaning heavily on her, realized Mei Ju's wisdom, her own foolishness in claiming she could walk unassisted. Yun Yun also appreciated Mei Ju's thoughtfulness in distracting her with a steady stream of chatter. Nor were Shadow and Rooster any less kind, quickly smothering their astonishment with a hearty welcome, a basin of water for washing, even a temporary change of clothes.

The hut itself had been transformed from when Yun Yun had last been inside. Still small and bare and dim, it was spotlessly clean and neatly arranged, made rich by the skeins of colorful threads and the shawls, robes, and lengths of brightly dyed silks; the fragrance of sandalwood incense burning before the Goddess Gwoon Yum; the pungent smells of vinegar, garlic, and ginger from dishes of pickled cabbage, salt fish, long beans, and pea shoots on the table.

Yun Yun, her tongue and throat excited, sat down readily on the stool Shadow pulled out for her, fixed her eyes on Rooster, who had lifted the lid from the pot of rice and started scooping it into bowls.

She was, Yun Yun soon noticed, holding back, not filling

the bowls completely because they wouldn't otherwise have enough rice for four.

Embarrassed, Yun Yun stammered, "I'm not hungry."

Mei Ju, making no pretense of plenty, said out loud what Yun Yun had already observed. "We don't have much. But by holding back a few spoonfuls from each of our bowls, Rooster has filled one for you. This way we all eat."

Yun Yun's belly growled loudly.

Mei Ju smiled. "That's settled then."

In Yun Yun concern for the spinsters' bellies vied with the yearning in her own.

"Anyway, we're more hungry for a visitor than we are for rice," Shadow encouraged.

With a grateful sigh, Yun Yun accepted the bowl Rooster handed her. Mei Ju picked up pea shoots with her chopsticks, dropped them in Yun Yun's bowl. Shadow added a bit of salt fish, Rooster some beans.

"Sik faan, eat rice," they chorused.

Echoing their invitation to begin, Yun Yun fell on the food, and as the spinsters took up their own bowls, Shadow reminded Yun Yun that they'd once been neighbors.

"You probably don't recognize me." Playfully Shadow pinched her once plump cheeks. "Look, there's no flesh left."

Yun Yun flushed, set her chopsticks down guiltily.

"No, no," Shadow protested. "You mustn't stop."

"She's just boasting about how hard she's been working," Mei Ju teased.

Shadow giggled. "You're lucky you weren't here for one of our early meals."

Mei Ju laughed. "None of us had ever cooked on a movable clay stove before, and our fires were either too big or too small."

"A couple times we almost set the roof on fire," Rooster said. "And we were always covered in soot long before the meal was cooked. Now you know why we cook outside."

Their playfulness, generosity, and kindness made Yun Yun feel like a girl with her own family, free of fear or tension, and she savored this freedom even more than the tastes pleasuring her tongue, the warm fullness in her belly. In truth, she wished she never had to leave.

To safeguard Yun Yun from would-be tattlers, Mei Ju and Shadow posted themselves at the two bends in the road from which they could signal Rooster, who was standing in the doorway of their hut. And from her post, Mei Ju saw Rooster wait for the all clear from them both before ushering Yun Yun out. Watching her totter under the load of brush, however, Mei Ju recognized Yun Yun wasn't in the least safe. In truth, Mei Ju felt that in sending Yun Yun back to the Chows, she and her friends were not unlike Second Uncle carrying Eldest Cousin out of the house to die.

For a long time Mei Ju was too discouraged to move, and when at last she returned to the hut, Shadow was already bent over her embroidery frame, Rooster was working her beads, murmuring, "Nam-mo-oh-neh-toh-fu."

Reminded of their own troubles as outcasts, Mei Ju closed her eyes and breathed deeply. Like a balm, the fragrance from the incense burning before the Goddess entered her, and Mei Ju was reminded of the comfort that chanting Gwoon Yum's song together had offered the day they'd made their vows of spinsterhood.

Impulsively she rapped her knuckles against the tabletop, beating out the rhythm. Shadow looked up from her embroidery, Rooster from her beads, and Mei Ju, warmed by her friends' swift response, nodded at Rooster to lead the chant.

Smiling acknowledgement, Rooster did. Not from the beginning of the song, as Mei Ju had expected, but near the end.

> "With jade and opals I deck me,
> With the moon pearl I am crowned.
> Who faithfully follows my footsteps
> May share in my infinite gain;
> And she who is brave enough to relinquish,
> Will know what it is to attain."

Confused, Mei Ju didn't join in. Shadow, too, was silent until Rooster finished.

"We have nothing left to relinquish," Shadow cried then. "Nothing."

"Yes we do." Rooster's voice pulsed with excitement. "We have ourselves."

"Ourselves?" Mei Ju echoed stupidly.

"Yes, we can surrender ourselves to the Lord Buddha by becoming nuns."

Mei Ju, struck speechless, wondered if she'd misheard.

"What are you talking about?" Shadow spluttered.

"When we chose to comb up our hair, we thought only of ourselves. Now, through my prayers, I see that's why we're outcasts, why my brother lost his patron's favor. But it's not too late for us to take the road we should have walked from the start. Then all that's been lost will be restored."

"We'll be in a nunnery, you mean."

Mei Ju, aghast at Rooster's proposal, was grateful for Shadow's sharp retort, hopeful it would act like a slap on a hysteric and return Rooster to her senses.

Rooster, however, beamed. "Yes." Worse, she declared she already had a nunnery picked out, a large one in the market town downriver, and she proceeded to pour out what she'd learned from itinerant monks about Ten Thousand Mercies Hall.

"Naturally none of these monks have been within Ten Thousand Mercies' walls. Men aren't allowed. But they say the nunnery has a fine reputation that goes well beyond its gates. The town's very best families send for Ten Thousand Mercies' nuns to chant at the deathbeds of female relations and dispel evil influences in the streets surrounding their houses. There are also plenty of visitors, supplicants and pilgrims who describe the grounds as extensive, the buildings beautifully decorated.

"The main building houses an immense figure of the Lord Buddha as well as smaller images of Gwoon Yum and other lesser Gods. Then there are four or five smaller buildings, where the nuns sleep and sew and spin. Obviously I couldn't ask outright, but it sounds as if a few of the nuns have book learning, and my guess, my hope is that they pass their time studying the sutras."

Nothing Rooster was saying attracted Mei Ju. Rooster, though, was radiant, crackling with wonder and joy as she paced back and forth declaiming the virtues of Ten Thousand Mercies Hall. Nor was Shadow, tracking Rooster with her eyes, making any further effort to quench Rooster's fire. Had Shadow become snared by Rooster's zeal?

At the possibility that she might be abandoned by both her friends, cold terror seized Mei Ju, and she ground her teeth together to keep from crying out while Rooster continued to exhort.

"What's certain is that Ten Thousand Mercies is governed by an abbess whose holiness is indisputable. Her rule isn't rigid either. Of course every nun has to chant liturgies three times a day before Buddha. But they can pray as often as they wish before the Goddess of Mercy or any of the other Gods. The nuns also take turns going out to beg for rice and fruit and vegetables. . . ."

"You said you'd had your fill of begging," Mei Ju, unable to stay quiet another moment, reminded.

"That's my point. I was too proud." Rooster pulled her long thick braid from behind her back, held it up with both hands as though it were an offering. "In becoming independent spinsters and refusing to cut off our hair or beg, we were all three too proud. We have to be like Gwoon Yum, willing to give up not just our hair but our very lives. Only then will we gain true freedom. Do you see?"

Mei Ju turned anxiously to Shadow for her response.

"No, I don't."

Relief flooded Mei Ju. But Rooster's face drained of joy, and her pallor reminded Mei Ju of Grandfather's concubine walking out of Strongworm alone.

"I'll go with you," Mei Ju blurted.

Shadow gasped. Rooster grabbed Mei Ju's hand.

"Can you help Shadow see the light?"

"No," Mei Ju said, reproaching herself for misleading her friends. "I just mean to keep you company for the journey."

Dropping Mei Ju's hand, Rooster bowed her head and began working her beads. "There's no need. Gwoon Yum will be with me."

Mei Ju, searching for something she could say or do to make amends, chewed her lips, fidgeted with her collar, the buttons of her tunic. Suddenly, Shadow pushed aside her embroidery frame, rose, walked towards the altar, and as she passed Mei Ju, gave her elbow a squeeze.

Grateful for the comfort, Mei Ju watched Shadow retrieve their last earnings from behind the statue of Gwoon Yum, tilt the sack towards Rooster, bowed over her beads. The coins within the little sack jingled like temple bells, and when Shadow raised her eyebrows questioningly, Mei Ju nodded a vigorous yes.

Shadow held the sack out to Rooster. "Let this be our farewell gift to you."

Rooster looked up, stared at the sack, folded both her hands around her prayer beads.

"At least take your share," Shadow urged.

Rooster's fingers tightened around her beads. "I don't need money."

"What about your journey?" Mei Ju said.

"Nuns beg, remember? Hnnnh, with what the water peddlers have made off of us in commissions, it won't really *be* begging no matter which one of them I convince to take me."

"Then give the money to your parents and brother," Shadow pressed.

"I won't see them before I leave. It would only upset them. Anyway, once I'm a nun, Laureate will be restored to his patron's favor and my family's future will be secure, so they really don't need these few coins. You will."

Magpies Cry
and Caw

MEI JU usually woke to birdsong, the rich scent of freshly lighted sandalwood incense overpowering the stink of their honeybucket, the sharp click of Rooster's prayer beads, her soft, steady chanting of "Nam-mo-oh-neh-toh-fu."

Sometimes, though, Mei Ju would waken from the faint rustle and tug of their sleeping mat as Rooster slid her legs over the side of the bed and reached for her clogs with her feet. Knowing Rooster cherished her time alone, Mei Ju never opened her eyes or spoke on these occasions, but continued to lie quietly with Shadow, always the last to stir, deep in sleep beside her.

Their hen wasn't as considerate. Caged inside for safety at night, it would squawk and peck at the bamboo bars the moment Rooster's clogs began tapping across the hard dirt floor.

"Shush, now. Shush," Rooster would implore, quickening her pace.

Soon Mei Ju would hear her flick open the cage, the scritch-scratch of the hen's claws as it hopped out, the muffled sounds of Rooster carefully raising the crossbar and unfastening the latch, the creak of the door easing open, the two quitting the hut for their vegetable patch.

According to Rooster, the hen trailed her as she ladled water onto the base of each plant. "I tell you, our hen is as merciful as the Goddess who gave it to us. It only eats the bugs that get stunned by the cool water, the ones that'll sicken and die anyway."

Now, watching Shadow return the small sack of coins that Rooster had refused to their hiding place behind Gwoon Yum, Mei Ju recalled the many times she'd seen their hen stalking, chasing, and snapping up many a healthy insect and worm; and she hoped Rooster, in her determination to shave her head and become a charity spinster, wasn't likewise blinding herself. Certain Rooster couldn't be dissuaded from her course in any case, Mei Ju didn't try, but threw herself into preparing their evening rice. Nor did Shadow and Rooster talk further about Ten Thousand Mercies or anything else. Not then. Not while eating their evening rice. Not after they returned to their embroidery.

Seeking escape from this uncomfortable silence, Mei Ju climbed into bed early. Shadow and Rooster soon followed, doubtless for the same reason, and Mei Ju, lying between her friends, felt them seething, tossing, and roiling with an intensity that matched her own, knew they were as unsuccessful in courting sleep as herself.

How could it be otherwise? Although it was not unusual for men to go to the market town to sell cocoons or skeins of reeled silk, Mei Ju knew of no woman who'd been. As a small girl, she'd been entranced by her grandfather's, father's, and uncles' talk of amazing sights: jugglers and trained monkeys that performed in the streets; lavishly decorated temples; stores crammed with bolts of cloth, furnishings, crockery, mats, clothing, and adornments of every color, shape, and size. When she'd asked permission to accompany Ba to market, however, Grandmother had snapped, "Modest girls like modest women stay close to home."

Now Rooster would be going. Alone. Offering herself to the Lord Buddha as a sacrifice to save her brother and family. How would that be different from her sacrificing herself in marriage? Or from Bak Ju sacrificing herself to the River Dragon?

Some time during the watch before dawn, Mei Ju at last tumbled into troubled dreams—from which she was pulled by birdsong, Shadow's even breathing. Dimly aware of hot sun on the soles of her feet, Mei Ju realized the air was not only fetid from their hen's waste, their own, but moist and heavy, with none of the freshness of dawn, no sandalwood smoke either. Indeed, rubbing away the crust sealing her eyelids, Mei Ju found herself squinting at golden light blazing through the window left unshuttered because of the summer heat. Then why hadn't Rooster come in from watering yet? And if she was still watering, why was there no sound of ladle knocking against waterbucket?

Groggily Mei Ju propped herself up on her elbows, surveyed the hut. The hen was gone from its cage. There was no new incense burning before the Goddess. The crossbar from their door was propped against the wall. Beside it were their two waterbuckets and shoulder yoke. On the table was the red lacquer box in which Rooster kept her inkstick, stone, brush, and paper.

Of course! That was why Rooster hadn't started watering yet, why she wasn't cleaning Gwoon Yum's altar or praying. She'd been writing. Practicing her calligraphy in search of calm, perhaps. Or composing a couplet to commemorate her decision. Or trying her hand at an essay like Laureate.

Curiosity jolted Mei Ju fully awake, and she leaped out of bed and ran barefoot to see—halted in midstep, wondering where Rooster could be. Fearful now of what Rooster's writing might reveal, Mei Ju slowly backtracked for her clogs. And when she set out again, she moved at a crawl.

But the hut was too small for Mei Ju to delay reaching the table for long, to avoid finding and reading Rooster's note in which she explained her intent to leave Strongworm while the village slept: "This way, I can spare us the misery of a prolonged leavetaking, and my departure will be as inconspicuous as I can make it."

Stumbling over to their small altar, Mei Ju emptied cold ash from the incense burner, lit new. And as fragrant smoke rose and surrounded the Goddess, Mei Ju prayed for smooth winds to carry Rooster to Ten Thousand Mercies and the peace she sought.

At the end of Yun Yun's stop in the spinsters' hut, Rooster had cautioned her to walk with care, Mei Ju and Shadow had told her, "Don't be a stranger." "Come back soon." That her visit had escaped notice, however, Yun Yun considered a rare stroke of good fortune, and she didn't dare risk another.

Inside her head, though, Yun Yun returned over and over to the time they'd passed together. And, recalling the spinsters' kindnesses, large and small, she'd chant soundlessly to them:

> "You swaddled me with your concern,
> You suckled me with your goodwill.
> True sympathy is more valuable than gold,
> I will remember yours forever."

The spinsters didn't always leave their hut together. So Yun Yun, like the rest of the village, didn't realize Rooster was gone until Shorty tied up in Strongworm again.

It was common practice for the water peddlers to attract customers with news from other villages, the market town, sometimes even the provincial capital. Shorty—his silver teeth flashing, his caterpillar eyebrows leaping—declared he had information about one of Strongworm's own, and he dropped teasing hints for almost a day to an ever growing crowd of patrons before revealing he'd taken Rooster to Ten Thousand Mercies Hall, a large nunnery in the market town downriver.

Yun Yun, burdened with chores in the Chows' fields and wormhouse, didn't hear him directly but through her in-laws and husband, who chewed on Shorty's every word, pause, expression, and gesture like dogs thrown particularly meaty bones. In truth, much the village acted the same, and Yun Yun continued to hear talk of Rooster long after Shorty left Strongworm.

"Too bad she didn't shave her head from the start, before she shamed her family and destroyed her brother's future."

"Maybe that's what shamed her into doing right."

"Could be. Then again, who knows whether she *is* doing right."

"What do you mean?"

"How do we know she isn't in a house of pleasure rather than a nunnery?"

"Hnnnh, you got a point there."

"That Shorty claims he didn't take any fare from her. Maybe not in cash. But what do you want to bet he had a taste of her?"

"Not much to eat on that chicken!"

"Never mind, there's that plump one for him to look forward to."

"She's not plump anymore."

"Yeah, Shorty had better hope she gives up this spinster business soon."

"She will. The other one, too."

"No!" Yun Yun wanted to shout at them. "No!"

But she didn't dare. Instead, she lamented silently:

"Beware, sisters,
Magpies cry and caw at your door.
Close your ears to them, sisters,
Sisters, stay strong."

Mei Ju noticed that Shadow still cooked rice for three. In bed, they each lay down in their usual space. Even in sleep, neither stretched their limbs beyond their usual boundaries. And Mei Ju, on waking, inevitably listened for Rooster before remembering she was gone.

Jarred anew, Mei Ju would bolt from the bed and busy herself with chores. But the first tasks of the day had been Rooster's, and Mei Ju, feeling her absence sharply, would hurry to get past them, to settle into her own work where familiar routine allowed her to pretend for a little while that nothing had changed, that the village wasn't afire with vicious gossip.

Every time they left their hut, Mei Ju found the talk against them had grown wilder, more slanderous, and she feared Laureate's place in the Low clan's school was in greater peril than ever. As she told Shadow, "Rooster's parents certainly think so. I just heard them accusing her of smashing their rice bowl forever."

"Me too." Shadow, untying the bundle of new commissions they'd gone to fetch, sighed. "If only I'd been quicker, or if Rooster hadn't left before I wakened with the idea, we could have worked together on a letter to Laureate's patron explaining why she decided to be a charity spinster, and she could have sent it from the market town so people would think she'd gone to a letter writer. Better still, she could have given it to her abbess to add a few words. Then Laureate's patron would be praising Rooster's parents for good family teaching, the gossips wouldn't have dared start this vile talk, and Laureate's place in school and the family's future would be secure."

"Rooster's a clever planner. Most likely she'll come up with that idea herself after she's had a chance to settle into her new life at Ten Thousand Mercies," Mei Ju said hopefully.

"A letter might yet help Laureate. But the talk has become too poisonous for people to believe anything except the worst about us."

A Miracle

MEI JU was now the first to rise, and while she was raising the crossbar, the hen danced around her feet. The moment the door cracked open, it squeezed through with a happy squawk, and as the door swung wide, Mei Ju started to follow.

Something struck her head, her shoulder, her feet. The blows were glancing, but shocking, and Mei Ju jumped back with a piercing shriek. The hen shot into the air, flapping its wings and squawking furiously. Had it also been hit?

Shadow sprang off the bed, bounded across the hut, crying, "What is it? Are you hurt?"

Her heart thrashing around in her chest and her belly leaping up to meet it, Mei Ju slammed the door, dove for the crossbar. Fumbling in her haste and panic, she dropped it.

In one swift movement, Shadow seized the bar, fixed it in place, slipped a stool under Mei Ju. "Here, sit down."

With Shadow steadying her, Mei Ju sank onto the stool, fretting over whether the crossbar was enough to secure them from her attacker, whether there was more than one attacker, why the hen had stopped squawking. . . . Through this tangled whirl, she vaguely felt Shadow's hands move down her back, rubbing in broad, soothing strokes. And slowly, the spinning of head and heart and belly quieted under Shadow's touch until Mei Ju became calm enough to speak.

"Something or several things, I don't know what, hit me. Maybe our hen too."

"Did you see anyone?"

"No. But I was looking down at the hen so I wouldn't trip over it."

Shadow stepped around Mei Ju to the door, pressed an ear against the rough wood planks.

"I can't hear anything. But that doesn't mean there's no one out there."

Turning from the door to face Mei Ju, Shadow stopped, grabbed her head with both hands.

"Ai!"

Alarmed, Mei Ju half rose.

"Look!" Giggling now, Shadow pointed to the wall opposite the door.

Thoroughly confused, Mei Ju twisted round. At the sight of their unshuttered window, she crimsoned bright as the streaks in the dawn sky. What a woodenhead she was to have thought them secure because their door was barred! Or herself under attack, when anyone wanting to harm them could have come through the window while she and Shadow slept.

"But I *was* hit." Mei Ju tapped the left side of her head, her shoulder, and foot. "Here and here and here."

Shadow sobered. "Everybody's been predicting our repairs wouldn't hold up. Maybe part of the roof came down on you."

As though they were one, Mei Ju and Shadow spun around, examined the ceiling above the door.

"It seems alright, but we'd better check outside," Shadow said.

Reason told Mei Ju nobody was lurking on the other side of the door. Even so, her intestines clenched as Shadow raised the crossbar and threw open the door.

Peering fearfully through half-closed eyes, Mei Ju saw no one. But littering the path were short, slender, reddish-brown sticks that resembled nothing from their roof. Mei Ju gasped. Firecrackers? No, these sticks, unlike firecrackers, were linked together in pairs with string. Moreover, their hen was pecking contentedly at one stick, then another, and another.

"Sausages?" Shadow swooped up the closest pair. "They *are* sausages! Lap cheung, preserved sausages."

Shouting, "Scat," Shadow rushed at their hen, which fled, squawking, beating its wings, leaving a trail of down and feathers in its wake.

Mei Ju wanted to help Shadow gather up the sausages. Awed that Rooster might have been right in insisting their hen and black gummed silk had come directly from Heaven, however, Mei Ju remained glued to the stool.

Shadow, gaily swinging sausages from both hands, returned to the hut. "Someone must have hooked these above the door to keep them out of reach of animals."

She spread the sausages out on their table. "Then you must have dislodged them when you opened the door."

"Yes," Mei Ju murmured.

Even so, their appearance seemed a miracle.

The previous summer, Yun Yun had carried the stools for her husband and in-laws out to the street in a single trip. Now she'd become so weak, she had to go back and forth three times, and when she returned to the kitchen for the food she'd cooked, she was as breathless as if she'd walked the length of Strongworm.

At the savory smells, Yun Yun's nose, chest, and belly seized with desire. In truth, were it not for her mother-in-law's habit of counting every vegetable stalk and measure of rice and meat, Yun Yun would have snatched a few swallows for herself as she heaped three large bowls with steaming mounds of rice, mustard greens, and ju yuk beng, pork cakes. That being impossible, she pretended she was eating by scraping her tongue and the insides of her cheeks with her teeth.

Since early afternoon, the air indoors had been thick and heavy as cotton wadding. And while Yun Yun was serving her in-laws and husband their evening rice, more families spilled out of their houses to eat in the street, then linger, gossiping, smoking, and stirring up breezes with palmleaf fans until the need to sleep drove them inside to their beds.

In Twin Hills, Yun Yun had enjoyed these summer nights,

when the whole street seemed to turn into one big family. Indeed, Lucky had always had to take her firmly by the hand and all but drag her to their girls' house. Here, for fear of being accused brazen, Yun Yun felt compelled to keep her head bowed. Nor did she dare acknowledge the neighborly greetings she received from women and children with anything more than a slight nod, an unintelligible mumble. So she was relieved when, having delivered the last tantalizing bowl of rice and greens and pork, she could escape into the wormhouse to shred mulberry for the worms, pilfer some of the coarse, bitter-tasting leaves for herself.

The one small window, set high in the back wall, had to be left open for air, and over the chopping of her cleaver, the worms' noisy crunching, and her own determined chewing, Yun Yun—listening for her mother-in-law's shouted commands—caught the faint clatter of chopsticks against bowls, snatches of convivial chatter. Each time Old Lady Chow called, Yun Yun dropped what she was doing, forced down the shard of bitter pulp in her mouth, shuffled out as quickly as she could to refill bowls, to bring tea, pipe, fans. And so frequent were these interruptions and so tough the leaves that Yun Yun never managed to sneak more than a half-dozen. Her pinched belly, then, continued to grouse and cramp. Finally, however, she finished feeding the worms, and with her mother-in-law's grudging permission, went to ease the worst of her hunger with the meager leavings in the kitchen.

Yun Yun poured a bowl of water into the bottom of the rice pot, scraped what she could off the bottom. Forbidden from starting a fire in the stove for herself, she was in any case too tired, too starved to hold back from instantly gulping down the tepid, rice-flecked water. But she forced herself to pro-long the rest of her meal, trailing each of the three stalks of mustard greens through the dab of congealed fat, all that was left of the pork cakes, then biting off no more than a quarter-inch at a time and chewing slowly.

As she often did when eating, Yun Yun recalled her fa-ther's long-ago counsel, "A properly cared for plant must be fertilized before flowering and after bearing fruit." Surely a woman needed no less. Was that why no child grew in her despite her husband's repeated assaults? What, though, could she do?

The spinsters had generously hidden dried peanuts from their vegetable patch under the fuel they'd given her. But Old Lady Chow had come into the kitchen while Yun Yun was unloading the baskets and confiscated the peanuts, claiming they were from the family's harvest. Yun Yun couldn't admit she'd had contact with the spinsters. Moreover, arguing would have earned her a beating. So Yun Yun had said noth-ing. Neither did she make any attempt to buy herself food from her own small store of cash since it would have no better chance of reaching her belly than the spinsters' peanuts.

The last shred of greens swallowed, Yun Yun licked the wok in which she'd cooked them, her husband's and in-laws' bowls, carried them out to the courtyard to wash. On the other side of the wall, the members of the girls' house were chanting a weeping song, repeating each line after Widow

Low called it out. Sinking onto the stool in front of the wash-bucket, Yun Yun silently joined the girls.

> "I strain my eyes looking for my dear ones,
> But my dear ones do not appear.
> I strain my ears listening for my loved ones,
> But I do not hear their steps.
> No, never do my loved ones come."

The widow's voice, quavering with old age, and Yun Yun's own longing for her family and Lucky in Twin Hills added to the emotion of the words. After only five lines, Yun Yun burst into loud, wracking sobs that drowned out Widow Low, the girls, everything except her misery.

How long she wept, Yun Yun did not know. But by the time she recovered herself sufficently to resume the washing, the singing was over and Widow Low was telling the girls:

"There was once a pious wife who begged permission from her husband to enter a nunnery. He refused her. So she entreated her in-laws. But they, too, refused her.

"Then the wife stopped serving her husband in bed. She also stopped making offerings to the family's ancestors, saying, 'I'll serve no one except the Lord Buddha.'

"Her husband and in-laws didn't want the trouble and expense of getting another wife. So they beat her in hopes of forcing her to surrender. Still the pious wife insisted, 'I'll serve no one except the Lord Buddha.'

"Furious, husband, mother-in-law, and father-in-law attacked the woman together. But before their hands could touch her, the Lord Buddha magically transported the pious wife to a mountain nunnery.

"Even then, husband, mother-in-law, and father-in-law did not repent. Only after many years did they come to recognize their wickedness, and they went to the mountain nunnery to seek forgiveness."

"Daughter-in-law!"

From Old Lady Chow's high-pitched fury, Yun Yun realized her mother-in-law must have shouted for her before. Absorbed in Widow Low's story, however, Yun Yun had failed to hear her.

Calling, "Coming," she dropped the lid she was washing back into the water with a splash.

"Coming are you?" Old Lady Chow sneered from the kitchen doorway.

"I'm sorry. I . . ."

Old Lady Chow cut her off with a stinging slap. "Sorry, hah! Stubborn, you mean! Slow, too! And stupid! Too stupid to learn!"

She kicked Yun Yun off the low stool.

"Now get inside, ladle out three bowls of almond cream, and bring it out to us!"

Yun Yun, picked herself off the ground where she'd fallen, felt Old Lady Chow's razor-like nails cut into her right ear, her head jerked back, her mother-in-law's hot breath blasting the side of her face.

"Now!" Old Lady Chow screeched directly into Yun Yun's ear. "Not tomorrow! Now!"

Thrown off balance, Yun Yun would have fallen again. But one outstretched hand caught hold of the bucket's edge, another gripped the side of the overturned stool, and these offered just enough support so she could haul herself upright, stumble into the kitchen.

While serving the almond cream, Yun Yun heard Old Lady Chow declare that Rooster, in shaving her head and becoming a charity spinster, was betraying the vow of independence she'd made when combing up her own hair. But it seemed to Yun Yun that if the pious wife in Widow Low's story could win praise for becoming a nun, a pious spinster like Rooster should too. And when Yun Yun returned to the courtyard to finish the washing up, she defiantly reimagined Widow Low's story with Rooster as the heroine.

In Yun Yun's pious spinster story, Rooster made her own miracle, as she had in life, by convincing Shorty to take her to the nunnery. But Rooster's parents and little brother were not alone in begging her for forgiveness at the end: the naysayers in Strongworm—with the exception of the Chows—did as well. Moreover, Mei Ju and Shadow were embraced as independent spinsters by their families and all of Strongworm—again, except for the Chows.

"Even the Lord Buddha couldn't move them," Yun Yun muttered bitterly.

Pouring out the dirty water from the bucket, however, Yun Yun thought of how her baby brother's unrelenting wailing had spurred the Chows' neighbors to speak up for her, how they'd then pressed Old Lady Chow into acting justly. Could that miracle be repeated? Not with Third Brother, of course, since he was in Twin Hills, but with the members of the girls' house next door?

Tongues
as Swords

YUN YUN, having suffered many a beating for no good reason, was certainly willing to risk a thrashing to get enough food so she could grow a baby. The very next evening, then, she butted her washbucket and stool directly against the wall separating the Chows' courtyard from the girls' house, pressed a cheek against the rough, sun-baked bricks, and in a voice breathy with terror, desperation, and hope, chanted the plea she'd composed:

> "Listen, sisters, I beg you,
> To this sad person;
> This sad person,
> Who has met with misfortune;
> This sad person,
> Cut off from parents and brothers;
> This sad person,
> Who can do nothing except entrust her sorrow to
>   you."

Her heart pounding in her ears, Yun Yun couldn't tell whether the girls were still chattering and playing as they had been when she'd begun her appeal, and she fretted over whether she'd caught the attention of at least one. Yet she didn't dare chant any louder for fear she'd ruin her plan. And, concerned her mother-in-law would interrupt with some demand before the song's end, Yun Yun started rushing a little.

> "Listen, sisters, I beg you,
> I am dying.
> You can't untie the knot around my neck,
> But you can loosen it with your songs.
> Listen, sisters, I beg you,
> Hunger eats at me.
> Already it has swallowed all my flesh.
> Now it is gnawing on my bones.
> Listen, sisters, I beg you,
> Sing of this suffering in your songs,
> And if I cannot repay you in this life,
> I will in my next."

Mei Ju, lifting the lid from the rice pot, released a cloud of steam redolent with sausage. "Wah, I'd forgotten how wonderful lap cheung smells."

"I haven't."

Shadow, coming out of the hut, set down the bench she was carrying, reached over Mei Ju's shoulder, snared a piece gleaming with lovely pearls of fat.

"Thief!" Mei Ju laughed, rapping Shadow's arm lightly with the rice scoop.

Shadow popped the sausage into her mouth. "Where?"

Laughing even harder, Mei Ju filled two bowls with rice and sausage while Shadow swooped up the bench, carried it around to the back of the hut. Mei Ju covered the pot and followed her to their usual spot just left of the window—chosen so they had the hut's mud wall for a backrest and could climb in through the window for anything they'd forgotten.

In the purple light of dusk, Mei Ju could barely make out the shapes of the bamboo and trees on the edge of their clearing, the hills beyond. From the village came snatches of laughter, weeping songs. Closer, crickets chirped, cicadas shrilled. Shadow, taking her bowl from Mei Ju, swiftly snapped up another piece of sausage.

"You're like a silkworm with hands," Mei Ju teased.

More tired than hungry, she sagged against the wall, wishing yet again that she could earn her rice by reeling silk instead of bending all day over her embroidery frame, and as the wall's hard heat penetrated her tunic, easing the knots in her shoulders, Mei Ju recalled her long ago wish for Shadow to join the girls' house, to become her friend.

Shadow, grinning, clicked her chopsticks against Mei Ju's bowl. "Better get started, or I'll be eating yours too."

Returning Shadow's grin, Mei Ju bit into a sausage, felt the fat spurt thick, warm, and delicious onto her tongue.

Compelled to obey her mother-in-law, Yun Yun had never spoken to any member of the girls' house. But piecing together her observations of the girls as they came and left with what she heard when eavesdropping, Yun Yun not only knew all the members' names, faces, and voices, she was confident of their sympathy. A senior, Lightning, had even slipped her a piece of beef jerky once in passing, accomplishing this feat so smoothly that Yun Yun hadn't truly believed she held something in her hand until, hidden in the stink of the Chows' outhouse, she'd uncurled her fingers and seen the treasure, stuffed it into her mouth, tasted its honeyed richness, and licked every trace of sweet saltiness from her skin.

When the girls failed to respond to her plea for help, then, Yun Yun worried that no one had heard her. She also worried that if she became too weak, she'd be beyond help when it came. So after waiting six long nights, she decided to repeat her lament, this time chanting louder.

That afternoon, though, the worms woke from their great sleep. Nearly full grown, they were long as Yun Yun's thumb, thick as her little finger, and struggling to cast off their skins for the last time. They always ate the most after they finished shedding, and Yun Yun knew she'd be feeding them late into the night.

"Tomorrow," she vowed. "I'll make my appeal to the girls again tomorrow evening."

· · ·

She was bringing in a third basket of leaves when she saw the worms, having wriggled free, were rearing up, opening their jaws wide, and swaying back and forth, demanding to be fed. Swiftly Yun Yun began searching the trays for worms trapped in their old skins. These worms, whether they were still squirming or had given up the struggle to break free, were sure to die before morning, and Yun Yun plucked them out, spread mulberry over the rest.

She was, of course, supposed to save the dead and dying worms for the fish in the Chows' ponds, and since there'd be questions if the bucket held an unusually small number, Yun Yun was careful not to eat too many. Months ago, when she'd started sneaking some for herself, she'd been unable to eat these worms unless she knocked them dead with the cleaver and pretended they were cooked chrysalides. Now she thrust the dying worms into her mouth the moment she picked them up from the trays, and her only concern was to avoid getting caught.

She worked methodically, tray by tray, shelf by shelf, and as more and more jaws clamped down on the leaves and ground them into pulp, the noise from their munching swelled. Midway through the shelves of worms, Yun Yun thought she heard the members of the girls' house chanting, and her skin tingling with hope, she headed for the window, positioned herself directly under it.

"Mother-in-law,
At cock's crow, Daughter-in-law leaps out of bed,

At the second crow, her face is washed, her hair
    combed.
At the third crow, she serves you tea.
Yet you do not value her."

Although the verse could apply to any daughter-in-law, ordinary weeping songs were always directed at a bride's family
members, not her mother-in-law, and Yun Yun, excited,
clutched the rough-hewn shelf in front of her.

"Father-in-law,
You have so many fields,
You have so many ponds,
Daughter-in-law labors in them all,
Yet you do not value her."

This verse was a little closer to the mark, but still rather
general. Willing the lament to become more specific, Yun
Yun tightened her grip, heedless of the splinters piercing
her palms.

"Husband,
Your wife came to you lovely as a peach blossom,
Yet you did not value her.
With her hair clutched in your hands,
You attacked her,
Now the blossom looks like a dead person.
Who will take pity on her?"

Yun Yun's blood quickened: certainly those lines hit home.

"Neighbors,
Open your eyes and you will see
Daughter-in-law does more than any other.
Yet Husband eats the best in the pot.
Mother-in-law and Father-in-law eat the rest.
Neighbors,
Open your ears and you will hear
Voices scold, sticks strike.
Neighbors,
This person who is dying could be your daughter,
Won't you save her?"

The girls *were* singing about her. Since she and her husband and in-laws weren't actually named, however, would the
people relaxing outside recognize that, understand the girls
were calling on them to act?

"This person who could be your daughter
Suffers days that are worse than prison
Nights that are worse than being caged.
Let us wield our tongues as swords
And restore this person to light."

Old Lady Chow's shrill command, "Daughter-in-law!
Tea!," pierced the chant, and Yun Yun, stepping out of the
wormhouse, could hear the girls loud and clear out in the
street. She could also see no one was paying them any mind.

True, Yun Yun had recognized from the start her plan was
a gamble. Nor was she ready yet to give up hope. Deeply dis-

couraged, however, she could hardly find the strength to fill the hefty green glazed teapot with boiling water, carry it out of the kitchen, the house.

Steadying the pot so she could pour tea into her father-in-law's bowl without spilling, Yun Yun sucked in her breath as the pot's heat seared one hand and the straw handle ground against the splinters in the other, driving them deeper. Despite her best efforts, she could not keep a firm hold.

The teapot swayed, splashed hot tea onto Old Lady Chow, who whipped out her hand and slapped Yun Yun soundly. Staggering, Yun Yun hugged the teapot to her chest for fear of dropping it—toppled backwards. As she landed, the back of her head cracked against the sharp edge of a raised flagstone. The lid flew, and hot tea gushed out, scalding her hands, her neck, soaking through her thin cotton tunic and undergarment, burning. Screaming, she dropped the teapot, which rolled a moment or two, hit she knew not what, shattered.

Stunned from the fall, exhausted and frightened, Yun Yun tried to rise. But a thickening black cloud weighed her down.

"Chicken hands, duck feet!" Old Lady Chow shrieked.

"You really are worthless," her father-in-law bellowed.

Still Yun Yun couldn't summon sufficient strength to move. Not even when her in-laws kicked her thighs, her shoulders, her head, demanding she get up and clear her mess.

"Wai, have a care," a woman cautioned.

"She won't be any use to you dead."

Through the deepening darkness, Yun Yun was aware of footsteps, grunts, as people gathered round her, squatted; and there were shocked expressions, gasps, cries of "Ai yah!" as if the familiar faces hovering above were seeing her for the first time.

"She looks half dead already."

"Starved more like."

"You miserly fools, can't you see you're killing her?"

Then the darkness became complete, and Yun Yun saw and heard no more.

Tipping
the Scales

SHADOW'S FATHER, like most men in Strongworm, leased the land he cultivated, and for days before an auction of tenancy contracts in which he planned to make a bid, he'd snap and snarl over small irritations that he usually overlooked or dismissed with a laugh. This change had frightened Shadow when she was little, and she'd run to Elder Brother for shelter.

"Baba is worried, not angry," Elder Brother had explained. "You see, if Baba bids too low, he won't get the land, and without land, we'll have no harvest, nothing to eat. If he bids too high, he'll get the land, but lose so much of the harvest to the landlord that we still won't be able to fill our rice bowls."

Whether Baba won or lost a lease he was bidding on, he'd come home dark with gloom. "The landlords are the only ones who come out ahead in this game. All I can do is try and lose as little as possible."

To improve his odds, Baba juggled his five-year leases so they came up for renewal at different times. He rented from landlords in their own clan so he could use their kinship as a plea for payment delays when they suffered a poor harvest or sustained losses in a big wind or flood.

Similarly, from their earliest transactions with the water peddlers, Shadow and her friends had tried to better their odds by working through several instead of one. But there'd been no kinship ties, no ties of any kind that she or Rooster or Mei Ju had been able to call on. Moreover, the hostility they faced in Strongworm as spinsters and their reliance on the peddlers was abundantly clear.

Commissioned work paid the most, and since Shadow was the only one whose embroidery was of a high enough quality for commissions, she stretched the number of pieces she could complete by having Mei Ju and Rooster take over the time-consuming tasks of outlining the complicated designs by dusting ground oyster shells through stencils, stitching seams and hems and trim. Shadow also left all negotiating to Rooster, whose tongue was sharper than her own or Mei Ju's.

The peddlers always heaved and clucked over Rooster's demands.

"I wish I could give you more, but I can't wring another copper out of the store owners, so I have to turn you down."

"I'm close to taking a loss myself."

"I'd give you double if it was mine to give. No, triple."

The peddlers spoke with conviction, and Shadow could see the admiration in their eyes when they examined her work. But the landlords had sounded no less sincere when telling her father, "I'd like to give you an extension on your rent. I'd forgive it if I didn't have obligations of my own to meet. Really, I would."

Indeed, the peddlers possessed the same sleek look, the same air of confidence and command as Strongworm's landlords, and Shadow suspected they were as greedy. Then she fell on proof of her suspicions.

They were entering their second year as spinsters. Rooster and Mei Ju were on the small deck in the stern of Scabby Woo's boat, unwrapping their bundle of embroidery for his inspection. But Shadow, having caught sight of Elder Brother loading their father's boat for market, was lingering on shore, hoping he'd notice her and return her smile.

When at last he did see her, his lips tightened into a line thin and sharp as the edge of a knife. Cut to the quick, Shadow whirled around, leaped onto the boat. Then, realizing she'd jumped onto the foredeck instead of the aft, she started to swing one leg back onto the river bank, somehow lost her balance and dove under the awning arched between the two decks, landing on Scabby Woo's stock of fabric, sliding off as the boat rocked and the neat piles collapsed under her, knocking over a basket, spilling papers in every direction.

More distressed over Elder Brother's grimace and the mess she'd made than the jolt she'd taken, Shadow scrambled to her knees in the tiny cabin and shouted reassurances that she hoped would keep Scabby Woo from looking in.

"Good thing you're not clumsy with your needle like you are with your feet," Scabby Woo shouted back.

Shadow, relieved he seemed amused rather than annoyed or concerned, poked her head through the oilcloth flaps separating cabin and deck so her friends could see she was alright.

"I really am clumsy." Shadow smiled winningly at Scabby Woo. "And with your permission, I'll just stay here and catch my breath while you finish looking over our work."

Ducking back in before he could refuse her, Shadow began gathering the scattered papers. She never thought to read them, only to get everything back in place as quickly as she could. Even so, her eyes registered on a character here, another there, and she soon realized that the papers were receipts, some of them for her commissions. Furthermore, the store owners were paying Scabby Woo five, six times more for the embroidery than he claimed.

Furious, she was about to burst out and confront him, when Mei Ju stuck her head in.

"Are you truly alright?"

Shaking her fistful of receipts at Mei Ju, Shadow hissed, "Scabby Woo *is* taking more than his fair share. Look!"

Mei Ju scooted in, took the papers from Shadow, laid them down without reading them. "We can't force Scabby Woo or any of the other peddlers to deal fairly with us any more than we can our families."

Shadow, straining to keep her voice low like Mei Ju, seethed, "Why not?"

"You know the answer as well as I do. We can't confront

the peddlers without admitting we have book learning. And proving we're being cheated won't help us anyway since we've no way to fetch our own work or to sell it except through the peddlers. Then, too, they've made it clear they know we've been refused employment as reelers in all the neighboring villages as well as Strongworm. So we have no choice but to accept their terms, however unjust."

What Rooster had pried out of the water peddlers had covered their expenses. For as long as they'd been spinsters, though, Shadow couldn't remember having had so much as a copper to spare, and she worried that without Rooster's sharp tongue, she and Mei Ju would be paid even less for their work. They'd certainly have to take on fewer commissions. How would they manage?

The question pounded in Shadow's head until, blinded by the pain, she couldn't embroider. She couldn't rest either. Pacing back and forth, she searched for an answer—suddenly saw that Rooster's departure could have tipped the bargaining scales in their favor.

As Shadow explained to Mei Ju, "Before, the peddlers would never have believed us if we'd said that unless they paid us more, we'd move to town and deal directly with the merchants ourselves. Now that Rooster's there, though, the peddlers might."

Mei Ju's eyes, her entire face brightened with desire. "Even if you do manage to get more out of the peddlers, you won't make as much as you would by dealing directly with the merchants, and if we moved to town, I could get work reeling at the filatures, and we'd be able to visit Rooster at Ten Thousand Mercies."

Shadow's chest burned as though her heart were frying in oil. "I combed up my hair so I could stay in Strongworm. . . ."

"I know that," Mei Ju interrupted. "But . . ."

"I'll never leave. Never." The words spilled out of Shadow hot as live coals.

"Then I won't either," Mei Ju said quietly.

From the figures in Scabby Woo's receipts, Shadow calculated how much she could reduce the water peddlers' share of her commissions and still leave the business too profitable for them to abandon. During negotiations with the peddlers, Mei Ju responded to initial offers by telling Shadow, "We can't live on that. Let's move to town where we can deal directly with the merchants." And when the peddlers protested, as they inevitably did, that town was no place for women without the protection of a family or nunnery, Shadow, imitating Rooster's fixed stare and sharp tongue, demanded more money. Protesting that they were taking money out of their own pockets to help the spinsters stay in Strongworm, every one of the peddlers eventually gave in, and Shadow and Mei Ju were finally able to set aside coins instead of spending all.

. . .

When calling on her family at New Year, Shadow carried a tiered basket filled with gifts. Still thinking of the house as home, she threw open the door and stepped into their common room without knocking. Seeing no one, she was about to call out New Year greetings when she noticed her niece crawling from under the table.

Dressed in New Year red, the baby's tiny fingers and pinched cheeks were red, too, doubtless from the red envelopes in her fists. Shadow's heart seized. Was it the thick padding in the child's little jacket and pants that made her neck and wrists and ankles look so thin, the red stains on her skin that made her seem so pale?

Catching sight of Shadow, the babe dropped the red envelopes, wrapped her hands around the closest table leg, and pulled herself onto her feet. Then, crowing over her success, she tottered unsteadily towards Shadow with both arms raised.

Swiftly setting down her basket, Shadow stooped to pick the child up. But before Shadow could embrace her, Elder Brother appeared from nowhere, snatched his daughter, and stalked out of the room without uttering a single word.

Shadow, staring down at her empty hands, felt like the dragon that failed to grasp the moon pearl no matter how cleverly it danced, how high it leaped. And, like the dragon, she couldn't stop trying.

Yun Yun's father-in-law accused her of deliberately falling in front of their neighbors.

"Don't you dare throw mud in our face like that again," her mother-in-law warned.

But they didn't beat Yun Yun for it. Nor did Young Chow. Moreover, Old Lady Chow increased the food she allotted for each meal so there was again enough for four.

Day by day, month by month, Yun Yun gained flesh and strength. Her hair stopped falling out.

The seeds her husband planted in her didn't grow, however.

By spring Yun Yun's mother-in-law was calling her a broken pot.

Yun Yun herself was beginning to worry that her husband's assaults might have harmed her as well as their babies. Or perhaps she'd been damaged by her in-laws' brutal beatings, the long months of starvation.

In truth, she feared her belly might never again swell with child.

Mercies

WHETHER ROOSTER had prompted the abbess of Ten Thousand Mercies to write her parents, Mei Ju did not know. The very same day Big Mouth delivered the letter, though, she knew its contents from the gossips.

The abbess praised Rooster's parents for the good family teaching that had led their daughter to renounce marriage and choose spinsterhood. Moreover, the abbess claimed Rooster's intelligence and devotion had already proven a blessing to Ten Thousand Mercies Hall. In closing, the abbess predicted that Rooster's prayers would raise her brother high, and Laureate would bring honor, power, and wealth to his family, his clan, the entire village.

Happily, this prophecy—and Rooster's role in it—restored not only Laureate but his sister to favor. A few people even lauded Rooster for the commitment she'd made to a life of chastity before shaving her head to become a charity spinster. And it seemed to Mei Ju that, in time, this praise for Rooster's spinsterhood softened the talk against Shadow and herself a little.

The talk didn't stop, though, and when they began shoring up the hut against the spring rains, more than one heckler suggested they would do better to shave their heads and join Rooster at Ten Thousand Mercies.

"If only *they* would show more mercy," Mei Ju sighed. "I'd hoped we'd get hired as reelers when the new silk season begins, but feelings against us are obviously still too strong."

Shadow tossed her head. "Now that our earnings from embroidery have increased, we don't need to go back to reeling. Not this season. Not ever."

"I *want* to."

Instantly Shadow dipped her head in remorse. "I know. I'm sorry."

Mei Ju wanted to soothe Shadow's distress by murmuring, "It's alright." But her tongue, heavy as her heart, refused to utter the lie.

Yet Mei Ju didn't begrudge Shadow her determination to remain in Strongworm. Mei Ju just wished Shadow's family—at least her brother—would stop her suffering by reconciling with her.

Since Shadow could not speak to her family directly, she searched for news of them like a fisherman trawling the river for fish, dragging her feet when she walked past gossips, sometimes even pretending she was tired and had to rest a moment.

She knew, then, that Elder Brother—claiming, "Our family is growing, our income must grow too"—had persuaded

Baba to lease three more fields so they could increase the number of silkworms they raised. And Elder Sister-in-law had weaned the baby so she could return to working in the wormhouse, reeling silk.

"Let me feed and wash and dress and comfort and teach your baby like you fed, washed, dressed, comforted, and taught me," Shadow wanted to ask Elder Brother. From the way he'd snatched his daughter from her at New Year, however, Shadow already knew what his answer would be.

Less than two months into the silk season, Elder Sister-in-law, her belly swelling with a new baby, was forced to quit the wormhouse.

"My family has to accept my help now," Shadow said.

Mei Ju chewed her lip worriedly.

"I won't ask to take care of my niece," Shadow assured her. "Not yet. I'll offer to reel their cocoons and work in the wormhouse."

But when she saw her family's front door closed tight despite the late spring heat, Shadow fretted that they'd seen her coming and shut it against her. Only her hope—nay, her need—for a reconciliation kept her from running.

As she came closer, Shadow heard her niece crying, realized the door was more likely closed to keep out drafts that might harm her. Even so, Shadow decided to go in without knocking, as she had at New Year. That way, she couldn't be refused entry.

Opening the door and stepping from bright sunlight into

the common room, she was blinded by the darkness, and while she was still blinking and straining to see, it seemed to Shadow she could smell sickness, hear it in the baby's whining and crying, in Elder Sister-in-law's desperate attempts to quiet her.

"Isn't it enough that you marked your niece while she was in her mother's belly and made your brother ill?" Mama demanded.

Squinting through the dimness at the room's disorder, Shadow found her mother seated alone at the table in front of a half empty bowl of rice, her hair frazzled, her eyes smudged black, her face shiny with sweat.

"Elder Brother's ill?"

"He's burning with fever. What worse trouble have you brought us?"

"I've come to help," Shadow stammered.

"Help, hah!" Mama threw down her chopsticks so hard they bounced off the table and clattered onto the floor. "Before you turned Heaven and earth upside down, we enjoyed good fortune. Then our grandchild came out a sickly girl. Next thing we know, your brother is sick too. And if the baby doesn't stop that racket, the worms will sicken as well. Get out before you do us more harm."

As Mama railed, Shadow crossed the room, started stacking the dirty bowls and dishes to demonstrate her goodwill.

"Are you deaf?" Mama stormed, pushing herself up from the table. "Out! Get out!"

. . .

Back with Mei Ju, Shadow sobbed, "I didn't want to go. But Mama was shaking, she was so upset, and I was afraid I'd do more harm by staying. So I did leave. I had to."

Her throat choked with distress, Shadow could say no more. Mei Ju pulled her close, stroked her hair, her back.

But Shadow couldn't be comforted. "I didn't harm my family knowingly."

"You *didn't* harm them."

"Mama . . ."

"Your mother's tired and frightened. But your brother will be well again in a day or two, and once your mother gets a chance to rest and realize the family hasn't overreached itself with the additional fields and trays of worms, she'll regret what she's said. She probably regrets it already."

Shadow wanted to believe Mei Ju. But anxious over Elder Brother and the strain his illness must be placing on their parents, Shadow made a large pot of red date tea that was good for building up blood and strength, took it to them.

This time it was Baba who met her at the door, and he refused to let her in. Nor would he accept the clay pot Shadow held out to him.

Without any other means of getting information about Elder Brother's illness or how the rest of the family was faring, Shadow listened even more carefully to the gossips.

Most people seemed to think Elder Brother's illness— whether from Heaven's displeasure over her unfilial behavior or some other cause—was mild, that the family's greater problem was picking and preparing sufficient mulberry leaves to feed the worms, keeping their trays clean, expanding the number of trays as the worms grew so they wouldn't become overcrowded and suffocate.

"Hiring a laborer for the wormhouse and fields would ease the burden."

"But eat up any chance of a profit."

"Trying to continue without help can lead to worse trouble."

"Yes. Sickness in the old man or the old lady from overwork."

"I tell you, they'd best accept they've lost their gamble for more money."

"I agree."

Mei Ju dismissed such talk as exaggerations. "I distinctly heard the herbalist himself say the diagnosis is a mild but recurring fever. Your brother will be up and working again soon."

"Elder Brother hasn't been out of the house—perhaps not even out of bed—for over a month now, and there've been times when the fever's heat has affected his senses and he's shouted wildly. We've both heard him. Hnnnh, is there anyone in the village who hasn't? Surely that's serious, not mild."

"Surely when it comes to your brother, you're so soft you make bean curd seem hard," Mei Ju came back.

"Don't be angry," Shadow pleaded. "I want to send for Master Choy."

Mei Ju stared at Shadow as though she'd lost her reason.

"The herbalist in the market town that came and cured the district magistrate's son?"

Shadow nodded.

"How do you expect to pay for him?"

"I can't," Shadow admitted, her voice so low she could scarcely hear it herself. "Not alone. But if we use all our savings, we should have enough to cover one visit and a prescription."

"Your father wouldn't accept the red date tea you made for Elder Brother," Mei Ju reminded.

"I've thought about that. But neither Baba nor Mama will turn Master Choy away. Not if he's already at their door. And if I write Master Choy, they won't know he's coming until he *is* at their door."

"After he comes to us for payment, your parents will realize you sent for him, and everyone will know you have book learning," Mei Ju warned. "Elder Brother's part in your learning is bound to come out, and then he'll be in trouble with your parents too."

"But he'll be alive."

"He'd be alive anyway, and if you think your family is angry with you now . . ."

"I'd rather risk their added anger than Elder Brother's death."

Mei Ju fetched brush, inkstone, and paper, laid them on the table. "Then let's get started on the letter."

Quickly Shadow poured water onto the inkstone, ground ink. "If we hurry, we can get a water peddler who'll take our letter to Master Choy today."

A Stranger

THE LOCAL HERBALIST insisted Shadow's brother had never been in danger. "Even his delirium was nothing more than the fever taking its natural course. There was never any doubt that he'd make a full recovery."

But Master Choy claimed he'd saved Elder Brother from certain death. "Another day's delay and I couldn't have helped him either."

The gossips' tongues wagged long and hard, speculating on which claim was the more accurate, how Shadow had learned to write, whether Mei Ju had book learning too, the exact cost of Master Choy. What mattered to Shadow, however, was that Elder Brother was no longer ill. Moreover, once he returned to work, their parents' burden would lighten, and if there was no big wind or sudden contagion, Elder Brother could yet win his gamble to increase the family's income.

Hoping to catch a glimpse of Elder Brother on his way to the fields, Shadow set her stool and embroidery frame just in-

side the door. But with every copper gone to pay Master
Choy, she felt pressed to complete the commissions in hand,
and unable to embroider with only one eye on the frame,
Shadow's surveys of the road were neither frequent nor prolonged. Indeed, she might have missed Elder Brother had he
not come to the door.

She'd waited nineteen long months for this moment, and
soon as she recognized his tread on the path, Shadow leaped
from her stool, intending to run out and greet him. Suddenly,
strangely shy, however, she stopped at the threshold.

"What is it?" Mei Ju, outlining a pattern at the table,
asked.

"Elder Brother."

At Shadow's salutation, Elder Brother's sallow cheeks col-
ored, and when she invited him in to rest, drink a bowl of tea,
he refused awkwardly. Dismayed at his discomfort and her
own, Shadow searched for something she could say that
would ease them both.

"I won't ever forget what you did," Elder Brother added in
a voice thick with emotion. "Neither will our parents. Mama's expecting you to come for evening rice, so she and Baba
and Elder Sister-in-law can thank you as well."

Had she heard correctly? Quickly, before he could say anything different, Shadow accepted. "I'll come early and help."

"Good."

She turned, drew Mei Ju into the doorway beside her.
"Without Mei Ju's contribution, I couldn't have paid Master Choy."

"Then I owe you . . ." Elder Brother began.

"Nothing," Mei Ju finished for him. "If not for you, we wouldn't have been able to write Master Choy."

At the word "we," Elder Brother's eyes flashed fire. But when he spoke, his tone was so cold it chilled Shadow to the marrow.

"You did teach your friends."

"I'm sorry," Mei Ju breathed, shrinking close to Shadow.

Shadow, her throat squeezed tight at the speed and intensity with which Mei Ju's slip had refueled her brother's anger, willed herself to force out, "I'm not."

Elder Brother's nostrils flared. His fingers curled into fists. Abruptly, however, he raised both arms and, his knuckles cracking, locked his hands together in the traditional expression of gratitude to Mei Ju. "I will ask Baba to invite you and your family to a banquet to celebrate my recovery."

Dizzy with relief, Shadow thanked her brother.

"You really don't need to go to such expense," Mei Ju told him.

"On the contrary," Elder Brother said. "My parents and wife and I have an obligation to meet, and you may rest assured we will."

Shadow recognized that Elder Brother's attempt to effect a reconciliation between Mei Ju and her family was, at heart, a peace offering to herself. But when Shadow, arriving home for evening rice, found the front door wide open, the memory of her previous visits was still too raw for her to consider going in without announcing her presence.

Timorously she called, "Mama. Elder Sister-in-law."

Inside the common room, Elder Sister-in-law didn't look up from untying her meh dai, lowering her daughter onto the floor. Nor did Mama, who was helping Elder Sister-in-law, respond.

Hadn't they heard? Or were they deliberately ignoring her? More anxious than ever, Shadow tried again.

"Mama. Elder Sister-in-law."

This time they both returned her greeting. Yet Shadow feared she'd somehow upset them, for Elder Sister-in-law was unaccountably bundling up the meh dai she'd been using, passing it to Mama, who slipped it behind the family altar. Then Shadow, stepping inside, noticed the meh dai she'd embroidered for them on the table, understood Elder Sister-in-law and Mama had been about to switch.

"I'm too early," Shadow apologized.

Mama, despite eyebrows crossed in consternation, protested otherwise. Little hands tugged at the hems of Shadow's pants. Looking down, she saw her niece pulling herself up with a strength that belied her spindly arms.

"Wah," Elder Sister-in-law exclaimed. "She doesn't usually take to stran . . ."

The unfinished word pierced Shadow's heart all the more for being true. She *was* a stranger to her niece. She didn't even know the child's name since she'd never heard anyone use it. Nor could Shadow think of the right words to ask for the name now.

Having hoisted herself upright, the baby hugged Shadow's left leg. And at the tender warmth of the child's touch,

Shadow's hands ached to reach for her. Still mindful of how Elder Brother had snatched his daughter from her, however, Shadow didn't even dare smile at the girl without some sort of signal from Elder Sister-in-law or Mama that they wouldn't do likewise.

"Didn't I say you'd marked your niece while she was in her mother's belly?" Mama laughed.

Uncertain of her mother's meaning but emboldened by her laughter, Shadow swooped up her niece—was pierced anew by the child's bony frame. Holding the babe so they were face to face, Shadow nuzzled the pinched cheeks, the sparse, downy hair. The baby, crowing with pleasure, blew wet bubbles, clumsily clasped Shadow's long braid, which had fallen forward when she'd leaned down, pulling loose strands of hair.

"Don't make a mess of Auntie," Elder Sister-in-law scolded.

"I don't mind," Shadow said. "I'm glad of the chance to carry her."

Elder Sister-in-law picked up the meh dai on the table. "Here, use this."

Shadow, preferring to cradle the child, shook her head.

"Your arms will get tired," Mama warned.

"I don't mind," Shadow repeated.

Indeed, her only regret was when she had to return her niece to Elder Sister-in-law at the evening's end.

Although Shadow's family had been cordial to her during her visit home, the only heartfelt affection had come from the baby, and at the end of the evening, no one had asked her back. Nor had any of them responded to her parting offer, "Please, come visit Mei Ju and I when you have time." They did acknowledge both Mei Ju and herself when they passed in the street, however. And when Elder Brother stopped by to report Mei Ju's family had refused the invitation to the celebration banquet, he seemed genuinely sorry.

Shadow and her brother were standing at the threshold of the hut, Mei Ju watering the vegetables in the back. Taking advantage of her absence, Shadow asked Elder Brother to invite Mei Ju's former employer, Master Low, to the celebration banquet.

"Have you taken leave of your senses? Why would a big landlord like Master Low come when Mei Ju's own family won't?"

At her brother's harsh tone, Shadow's heart quailed, but she forged on. "If Mei Ju hadn't sacrificed her desire to work as a reeler for mine to remain in Strongworm near you, we would have moved to town after Rooster left. Then we wouldn't have been here when you fell ill. And you did say you wanted to repay Mei Ju for saving your life. So, since you used to play with Master Low's son, I thought you could get Young Low to convince his father."

"Say I can. Don't you think it would be a little obvious to have Master Low and his wife as our only guests?"

"You must have other friends who can persuade their fathers to come. And if these fathers also employ silk reelers, that would improve Mei Ju's chances of returning to the work she loves."

Sisters

SHADOW had been uncertain whether anyone would accept her brother's invitations to the celebration banquet. But the two tables in their family courtyard included Master Low and two minor landholders and their wives, and Mei Ju, seated beside Shadow, shone with hope. Worried whether that hope would be realized, Shadow was glad of her little niece's cheerful presence on her lap.

Baba presided over the men's table, Mama the women's, and both heaped their guests' rice bowls with choice pieces from each dish. Elder Brother and Elder Sister-in-law were no less gracious, plying the six with special attention, honeyed words. In response, the guests sweetened their own speech.

"Shadow has true family loyalty."

"She's a filial daughter indeed."

"Capable, too."

Mashing her rice with tasty lotus soup and feeding it to her niece, Shadow was relieved when the tributes to her spilled over to Mei Ju.

"Both daughters are filial."

"Modest and respectable."

"Also hardworking."

"Thanks to good family teaching."

Shadow teased open the baby's mouth, popped in another morsel. If Mei Ju's family on the other side of the wall was listening, wasn't it possible her mother or father might be persuaded to reconcile with her in spite of fierce Grandmother Wong?

"Mei Ju, you always were a dependable worker," Mama said. "You must come and help us reel our cocoons."

Bobbing her head in assent, Mei Ju whispered in Shadow's ear, "How can your parents afford to hire me?"

Shadow, tipping her chin, directed Mei Ju's eyes towards the men's table, where Baba was pouring wine for Master Low.

"Won't you drink to my good luck in securing such an excellent worker?"

"Certainly." Master Low drank deeply. "But you must let Mei Ju return to me when she's finished with your cocoons. You know, I'm the one who recognized she'd be a skilled reeler while she was still an apprentice."

"In that case, she should come to you immediately," Baba said, pouring more wine for Master Low.

Bending over and tickling the baby, Mei Ju breathed, "Your grandparents are working their guests as skillfully as duck herders driving their flocks home."

The baby chortled. Shadow giggled softly.

"Don't forget me," one of the minor landholders said. "I'm always on the lookout for skillful reelers."

"What about Shadow?" his wife suggested.

"You're too generous," Shadow demurred.

"Shadow is as modest as she is talented," Mei Ju boasted on her behalf. "The fact is, though, her embroidery commissions pay too well for her to return to reeling."

There was a chorus of praise from both tables for Shadow, and she basked in her parents' obvious pleasure, their pride.

Master Low, his face flushed with drink, said, "If you ask me, raising girls no longer has to be a loss. Not if you're lucky enough to have a daughter who's capable and has a nonmarrying fate."

Baba, beaming, slapped Elder Brother on the back. "Here's proof of our daughter's worth."

That her father didn't value her for herself, Shadow had understood for some time. But hearing him declare it, and proudly, she had to hug the baby tight against her chest to keep her heart from shattering.

Going back to reeling after more than a season's absence, Mei Ju suffered almost as much from the fire's heat as when she'd been an apprentice. Oozing sweat from every pore, she wrinkled her nose at the stench of boiling cocoons, fumbled when manipulating strands of silk through the thick haze of steam, scalded her fingers while adding fresh cocoons and removing the dregs. Even so, reeling excited her as much as ever. And as the day progressed, she became more deft. Her awareness of the discomforts receded. Peace returned.

"Now if I could just figure out a way to get to Master Low's without walking through the village," Mei Ju joked during evening rice. "The gossips' tongues are going full force over what he said at the banquet. That bit about, 'Raising girls no longer has to be a loss. Not if you're lucky enough to have a daughter who's capable and has a nonmarrying fate.' Let's hope no one who was actually at the banquet reveals Master Low was drunk when he said it."

Laughing, Shadow scooped more spicy bean curd on top of Mei Ju's rice, her own. "Isn't walking past the worst gossip easier than sitting down to eat with the other reelers—girls and women who've talked endlessly *about* you yet not one word *to* you for over a year-and-a-half?"

"I did feel trapped," Mei Ju admitted. "Especially after I realized several of the older reelers are Strongworm's worst gossips."

Indeed, although a morning meal was part of a reeler's earnings, Mei Ju would gladly have come back to the hut to eat had she not recognized that would provide more fodder for the women's sharp tongues.

"Luckily, Lightning and Thunder also work for Master Low, and when his cook struck the gong for us to stop reeling and eat, the two girls came up on either side of me and shielded me from the gossips while we walked to the table. During the meal as well."

"Lightning and Thunder didn't sit together?"

Mei Ju understood Shadow's astonishment. Despite Empress's storms of temper and heavy fines, the pair had never surrendered to her spiteful attempts to split them by demanding they sit apart.

"Lightning and Thunder each took one of my elbows and steered me onto a stool between them," Mei Ju explained. "They also kept my bowl filled and included me in the conversation without making me talk."

Shadow set down her bowl. "How did they accomplish that?"

"I know it sounds impossible, but they did."

Picking up the grains of rice that had dropped on the table, Shadow said, "To be honest, there were moments when I didn't think my family would ever reconcile with me."

"I can tell you mine never will. And for all Master Low called us capable women, I'm sure Grandmother still thinks of me as dead useless—if she thinks of me at all."

"You heard how Baba calculates my worth." Shadow swallowed hard. "Probably Elder Brother, too." She reached over, covered Mei Ju's hands with her own. "But you've supported me even when we've disagreed, and with no thought of personal gain. In truth, as happy as I am that my family and I have made up, I feel more strongly bound to you. So why shouldn't we be family for each other?"

Too deeply moved to speak, Mei Ju nodded.

Shadow squeezed her hands. "Sisters, then?"

"Sisters."

The talk that bothered Mei Ju the most was what people said about book learning.

That Shadow's ability to write Master Choy had been crucial in saving her brother, all the gossips acknowledged. But a few of the most vicious would furrow their brows with false concern and question Shadow's chastity since "a virtuous woman has no learning."

No one guessed Shadow had learned to read and write from her brother. He didn't even seem under suspicion. Instead people speculated whether Shadow had shared her learning with Mei Ju or whether Mei Ju had taught her. Then Mei Ju's virtue would come under attack by the same vicious tongues that questioned Shadow's chastity.

When one of the reelers at Master Low's, a crony of Old Lady Chow's, attempted to bait Mei Ju by bringing up learning during morning rice, Lightning said, "Have you forgotten the abbess of Ten Thousand Mercies wrote Rooster's parents?"

"You're not suggesting the abbess is lacking in virtue, are you?" Thunder asked.

The other reelers smirked, snickered, laughed outright. Old Lady Chow's crony squirmed like an ant on a hot stove. Just then Master Low's cook brought out a basin of ripe lychee, the first of the season, and the woman, visibly relieved at the distraction, gushed over the fruit—its large size and beautiful color, the generous amount. Others joined in. And as hands all around the table grabbed up the lychee, Mei Ju wondered which was more cruel: a gossip's wicked tongue or watching others eat her favorite fruit.

Sorely tempted to risk a nasty, prickly rash by delving in and peeling some for herself, she clasped her hands together on her lap. Then, unable to hold back, she reached out.

As her fingers closed over the lychees' scaly skin, Mei Ju

realized that if her hands roughened even a little, she would have to stop reeling. Torn, Mei Ju could neither release the lychees nor pick them up.

Lightning jogged her elbow. "Here, I've peeled one for you."

As Mei Ju abandoned the fruit at the center of the table, Thunder also dropped a peeled lychee in front of her.

"How did you know?" Mei Ju gasped.

Lightning flashed a smile. "We remember from the girls' house."

True, her sister or Shadow or Rooster had always skinned the fruit for her. But for Lightning and Thunder to have noticed such a small thing, and then for them to have remembered and acted on it, Mei Ju found remarkable, and that night, she told Shadow, "I think Lightning and Thunder might be our mystery benefactors."

Shadow tapped her chin doubtfully. "They could have given us the hen, I suppose. But the bolt of black gummed silk and all those sausages, too? Where would they get that kind of money?"

Mei Ju, having thought of little else since morning rice, was ready with the answer. "Lightning and Thunder have been reeling for Master Low since they completed their apprenticeships three years ago, and they always hire out to him for the whole season, since both their families have daughters-in-law to do their reeling. Of course, the gifts were still extraordinarily generous. Carefully considered as well. But those are the very qualities that make me believe Lightning and Thunder are our benefactors."

"They've certainly gone out of their way to be kind to you at Master Low's," Shadow agreed. "Why haven't they spoken up though?"

"They're probably afraid someone will overhear them."

"Why would they mind when they've shown their support for you over and over?"

"You're right. But if Lightning and Thunder didn't bring us the gifts, who did?"

Changing
Luck

AFTER YUN YUN's betrothal, her mother had told her, "You'll know you're with child when your little red sister fails to come." The two times Yun Yun had happiness in her, however, she'd realized it from a sense of well-being deep in her bones. The subsequent absence of her little red sister had merely confirmed what she'd already felt. And just before the fourth generation of worms for the season hatched, Yun Yun once again recognized she had life in her.

To avoid polluting the eggs about to hatch, she knew she should immediately quit working in the wormhouse. But it was more important to her to protect her unborn child by avoiding her husband. So Yun Yun put into action the plan she'd conceived during her long months of waiting, and under the pretext of fetching mulberry leaves, she set off for the spinsters' hut.

In the months since Shadow had saved her brother by sending for Master Choy, Yun Yun had noticed many people greeting the spinsters when they passed in the street. But she knew of no one outside of Shadow's own family that had extended an invitation for them to call. In any case, few people had time during the silk season for visiting. And since Shadow had not returned to reeling, Yun Yun was almost certain she'd find her at home.

Wary of prying eyes, Yun Yun left the main road and approached the spinsters' hut from the rear. The grasses, moist from an earlier shower, dampened Yun Yun's pants, and as the cloth soaked through and stuck to her legs, she recalled the morning she'd toppled into the gully, the musky scent of the crushed honeysuckle blossoms Mei Ju had used to restore her spirit.

Neither Mei Ju nor Shadow had spoken more than a dozen words to her since that day. But the generosity and kindness they'd shown her then warmed her still, and Yun Yun was sure that Mei Ju and Shadow held back from engaging her in conversation only because they understood it would cause her problems with her in-laws and husband.

"Yun Yun."

Startled from her reverie, Yun Yun found herself already in the spinsters' clearing.

Shadow poked her head through the window and beckoned cheerily. "Climb in. That's what Mei Ju and I do when we're too lazy to walk around to the door."

Buoyed by Shadow's warmth, Yun Yun halted, bent her knees, and soon as she felt the baskets on either end of her carrying pole touch the ground, she shrugged. With a barely perceptible swish, the pole slid off her shoulders, down her back, settling on top of the baskets, and Yun Yun, freed from her yoke, ran the last few steps to the window.

Careful of her unborn baby, though, she didn't swing her legs over the sill. Instead, she perched on it. Then, steadying herself with one hand and cradling her flat belly with the other, she eased each foot up and in.

"You're with child, aren't you?" Shadow said, drawing Yun Yun over to the bench and dropping down beside her.

Shadow's understanding loosened Yun Yun's tongue, and she confided in a single, seamless rush that the child she was carrying was not her first, that if she was to hold this baby in her arms, she'd have to avoid her husband in bed by going back to her parents in Twin Hills.

"Will you write what I've told you to my father and ask him to come for me?"

Shadow's response was instant. "Gladly."

Awash with relief, Yun Yun poured out her thanks.

"If anyone notices you or Mei Ju or I giving the water peddlers a letter for your father, though, there'll be talk," Shadow interrupted, her eyebrows knitted together in a concerned frown.

Yun Yun's hands flew to shield her unborn child. "Ai yah! I didn't think! My husband and in-laws are bound to question me with their fists and sticks."

"But no one will question my sending a letter to Rooster," Shadow said slowly, as if she were thinking out loud. "And she could write your father."

Bowing, Yun Yun whispered joyfully to her baby, "Listen to your clever auntie. She's a capable woman, alright."

"Better not celebrate yet," Shadow warned. "Rooster's abbess may not allow her to write your father. Hnnnh, the abbess might not even give Rooster my letter."

Yun Yun jerked her head up. "The nunnery is called Ten Thousand Mercies. How could the abbess refuse?"

"Let's hope she doesn't. But Ten Thousand Mercies is in the opposite direction of Twin Hills. It'll be days before your father can possibly know you need help. How will you manage?"

"I'll be safe for a while. I'm expecting a new generation of worms to hatch later today, and my mother-in-law will want me to pass the next eight, nine nights in the wormhouse."

Shadow blanched. "You'll pollute the worms."

"I have to protect my baby," Yun Yun said firmly.

Just as resolutely, she pushed aside the doubts Shadow had raised, smiled. "Will you be my child's godmother?"

Shadow returned the smile. "With pleasure."

In her letter to Rooster, Shadow expressed her fear that Yun Yun's father might not come. "But I know that if anyone can convince him, it's you."

Shadow also wrote at length about Mei Ju's return to reeling and Elder Brother's daughter:

"I finally discovered my niece's name when I chanced upon Elder Sister-in-law chasing her, shouting, 'Woon Choi, Change Luck, get back here.'

"I could see Elder Sister-in-law—lumbering on account of her swollen belly—would never catch the babe. So I ran after her and swooped her into my arms just as she was about to stick a rusty nail into her mouth.

"When I returned her to Elder Sister-in-law, I noticed Woon Choi's shoes were worn, and I made her a new pair with big black eyes that would see evil and thereby avoid it."

Clutching the tiny pair of shoes, Shadow had waited for someone in her family to respond to her knock. Through the closed door, she'd heard a cleaver striking wood in short, rapid strokes, Woon Choi's broken, exhausted sobbing. Should she risk entering uninvited, leave, or knock again, Shadow had fretted.

Glad of the generous eaves that staved off the sun's fierce glare, she tapped the shoes indecisively against the wood.

"Come in," Elder Sister-in-law called.

Shadow, hugely relieved, swung open the door—was struck by a blast of ovenlike heat. Lurching back, she waved her gift at Elder Sister-in-law, who was hunched over the table with Woon Choi strapped to her back.

"I made Woon Choi a pair of shoes."

At the sound of Shadow's voice, Woon Choi squirmed, writhed, kicked, and wailed with renewed vigor. Wrenched by the child's distress, Shadow longed to run to her, but was afraid of offending Elder Sister-in-law.

Without breaking the rhythm of her chopping, Elder Sister-in-law bounced the baby by jiggling her shoulders. "Come in and shut the door quick."

Obeying, Shadow silently berated herself for forgetting her niece was susceptible to drafts, all the while assuring her sister-in-law that the day was airless, without the whisper of a breeze.

"I know," Elder Sister-in-law cut her off. "We keep the door shut to muffle the baby's crying. Otherwise the sound carries into the wormhouse and the worms lose their appetite."

Hoping she didn't sound critical, Shadow asked, "Why's she crying?"

Elder Sister-in-law stopped chopping, soaked up the perspiration coursing down her face with her sleeves. "She wants out of the meh dai. But if I give in to her, she'll get into mischief. You saw what happened the other day."

With her cleaver, Elder Sister-in-law swept the sliced turnips from the chopping block into a large earthenware crock, added a handful of salt. Then, bending clumsily on account of her big belly, she scooped up more turnips from the basket by the table, dropped them onto the chopping block, brought the cleaver down hard and fast.

Woon Choi, shrieking her unhappiness, flailed her arms and legs.

"I'll watch her for you," Shadow blurted, throwing her hat and Woon Choi's little shoes onto a chair.

"Wah, that would be wonderful."

As Elder Sister-in-law unknotted the meh dai, Woon Choi's cries diminished, and she tumbled into Shadow's arms in a steaming, redhot heap.

Elder Sister-in-law blotted the baby dry with the meh dai. "Now that she's got what she wants, she won't cry, so you can go out into the courtyard where it's cooler."

"What about you?"

"I can't stop working." Elder Sister-in-law peeled her soaked tunic from her back and rubbed the small. "Anyway, it's too much trouble to drag everything outside. Soon as you leave, I'll have to put Woon Choi in the meh dai again. That's bound to start her crying, and I'll have to bring everything back inside. Just open the door for me, will you?"

"Why don't I stay until you're finished?" Shadow offered.

Elder Sister-in-law took up her cleaver. "I'm never finished."

Shadow had relieved Elder Sister-in-law of Woon Choi's care for a stretch every day since.

"The baby calls, 'Auntie,' and reaches out her arms for me the moment I come through the door," Shadow wrote Rooster. "And Elder Sister-in-law says Woon Choi continues to call for me long after I leave. In my heart, I call for her too."

Capable Women

MEI JU anticipated biting into the sweet, pearly flesh of lychee with the same eagerness that her grandfather used to await the lychee wine Grandmother made for him.

Each year Grandmother would personally select the best of the crop, peel off the lychees' rough coats, their inner gauzy skins, pit them, then drop their shimmering flesh into a large earthenware container of good quality wine, which she'd seal for six months. Grandfather always marked the date the wine would be ready on the calendar. But long before the actual day, he'd tell Grandmother to bring it out to the common room, and night after night, his knobby fingers would caress the smooth glazed surface of the earthenware jar, toy with the seal until, suddenly, he'd snap it open, filling the whole house with a delicious fragrance.

His narrow, wrinkled face alight with desire, Grandfather would inhale deeply while Grandmother poured him the first bowl. Placing it in his hands, their fingers would touch, and it seemed to Mei Ju that in that fleeting moment, Grandmother's fierce black eyes would mist, her permanent scowl and downturned corners of her mouth would quiver. But Grandfather's eyes and nostrils would pinch tight, and he'd pull away so swiftly the wine would slosh to the bowl's rim.

At the first sip, Grandfather's eyes and nostrils would relax. Having drunk long and deeply, his thin lips would spread in a satisfied smile. Once, after downing several bowls in a row, he'd even broken into song, quavering, "As the lychee follows its own nature, so must I follow mine."

White with anger, Grandmother had snapped, "Help your father to bed," and Ba, together with Third Uncle, had each draped one of Grandfather's rail-thin arms over their burly shoulders, and carried him out the door to the concubine's.

At the time, Mei Ju had thought it was her grandfather's drunken state that had infuriated Grandmother. After two years as an independent spinster, however, Mei Ju recognized the root of her grandmother's anger and her grandfather's— and her own—happiness lay in the sentiment he'd expressed.

Of course there were times when Mei Ju wished the life she shared with Shadow was as carefree as the one they'd dream-talked in the girls' house with Rooster. Nevertheless, Mei Ju was happy. And on the last day of reeling for Master Low, Mei Ju—determined not to slight anyone the way she and her friends had been—told all the reelers, even Old Lady Chow's crony, "Now that the silk season's over and you have more time, please come visit."

That night, as Mei Ju and Shadow were washing up from their evening rice, there was—for the first time since they'd claimed the hut for their own—a knock on the door. Without taking time to dry her hands, Mei Ju ran to answer it.

Before she reached the door, it swung open, and Lightning, fairly crackling with excitement, darted in. "We'll be late for the girls' house, but we couldn't wait until tomorrow to come."

Thunder, as usual, followed just behind her. "We'll be fined, but we don't care. We've been waiting forever to talk to you. Really talk, I mean."

Lightning nodded. "Because we want to comb up our own hair and make vows to live as independent spinsters too."

The girls' revelations had never occurred to Mei Ju. Yet they seemed a natural unfolding. Shadow, still standing by the wash up bucket, was clearly astonished, however.

Mei Ju had questions as well. "Did you give us the hen and silk and sausages?"

Lightning's eyes sparkled. "You guessed."

"Why didn't you tell me? Why didn't you come visit long ago?"

"We didn't want to impose ourselves on you," Thunder explained. "Since you invited . . ."

"*I* didn't want to impose on *you* any more than I was already," Mei Ju broke in.

Walking toward them, Shadow said, "Without your help, we might not have succeeded. How can we ever thank you?"

"There's no need." Lightning slid her right arm around Thunder's slender waist. "We were helping ourselves as much as you."

Thunder leaned into Lightning. "Because if you succeeded as independent spinsters, then we could join you."

Abruptly, the sparkle in Lightning's eyes dimmed and anx-
iety flickered across her face, then Thunder's.

"Can we?"

"Join you?"

Confident that Shadow, smiling beside her, would agree,
Mei Ju answered for them both. "My sister and I welcome
you."

Busy in the wormhouse, Yun Yun hadn't heard what passed
between her father and in-laws when he'd come to Strongworm in response to her plea for help. But on their way to
Twin Hills, he'd seethed, "I claimed I'd come to warn them
that the ghosts of your dead sons were threatening to avenge
their deaths from starvation and brutal assaults, and those
cowardly bullies were so frightened they didn't even try to
deny their abuse. They just wanted to know how they could
avoid punishment. So I told them they'd have to make
amends, and they should start by releasing you into my care
until the birth of the child you're carrying."

Yun Yun understood then why her husband hadn't scolded
when he'd called her in from the wormhouse, why he hadn't
questioned her about how her father had known she was with
child. Indeed, so powerful was the impact of her father's
threat that when Yun Yun returned to Strongworm ten
months later with a daughter, Old Lady Chow grudgingly al-

lowed, "The baby is a small brightness. You're apparently not a broken pot, and a girl can lead in a son."

For Yun Yun, however, her daughter was a large brightness. And although the babe was too young to understand, Yun Yun would softly croon when they were alone:

"In a hut built for outcasts
Live women who combed up their own hair.
Independent spinsters strong as mountain pines,
Capable women merciful as Gwoon Yum.
Talk to them and you will know
That for daughters with courage and vision,
Old laws can be swept aside,
New laws can be made."

Bright afternoon sunshine poured through the hut's window. Hoisting Woon Choi—as sturdy now at thirty months as she'd been frail at birth—up in her arms, Shadow showed her the dragon she'd embroidered.

"See, it has the head of a camel, the horns of a deer, the eyes of a rabbit, the ears of a cow, the neck of a snake, the belly of a frog, the scales of a carp, and the claws of a hawk. That's why the dragon is magical and can prance and leap in the sky."

As Shadow spoke, Woon Choi's head drooped, heavy with sleep. Fighting to stay awake, she rubbed her eyes with her small fists, pointed to the luminous moon pearl hovering just beyond the dragon's reach. "Can't magic dragon catch pearl?"

Recalling her own frustrated attempts to seize the moon pearl, Shadow explained what she'd finally come to understand, "Catching the pearl would take away the dragon's reason for dancing."

Apparently satisfied, Woon Choi burrowed her head against the curve of Shadow's neck and surrendered to exhaustion. Savoring the child's soapy scent, her small puffs of hot, moist breath, Shadow was reluctant to put her to bed. Only when Woon Choi napped, however, could Shadow work uninterrupted, and she gently laid the child down on the cool matting.

Woon Choi's eyes fluttered open. "Mama."

Shadow brushed the child's eyes shut, caressed her silk-smooth cheeks.

"Mama's here," she said, sitting down beside her.

Watching Woon Choi sink trustingly back into sleep, Shadow thought of what Rooster had sent in response to her letter: a picture of the Goddess Gwoon Yum crowned with the moon pearl, and written in Rooster's precise hand, "May you know the peace I've found here at Ten Thousand Mercies Hall." But Woon Choi was what Shadow wanted, not peace. And she was grateful that Heaven had answered her father's and brother's cry for a boy and her family had soon after given in to Woon Choi's cries to stay with her.

Gossips immediately claimed the baby had been aptly named Woon Choi, Change Luck.

"Certainly she changed her family's luck by bringing them a boy."

"And now Shadow's relieved them of the girl's care."

"By saving the family the expense of raising a daughter, Shadow's more than made up for the loss of her bride price."

"Have you forgotten Shadow saved her brother too?"

"Master Low is right. Having an independent spinster for a daughter really is lucky."

Not everybody agreed. But Lightning and Thunder won the approval of their families for their choice, and when the two combed up their hair and made vows of spinsterhood, scarcely any of the talk was condemning.

Yun Yun, stopping to offer her congratulations, said people in Twin Hills knew about independent spinsterhood from water peddlers, and since the district's network of rivers spilled into the sea, Shadow liked to imagine that little by little, daughters everywhere would come to understand that they could control their own lives.

Acknowledgments

In researching and writing this novel, I had the help of many people, and I am grateful to them all.

At the heart of the book are my mother, Bo Jun, and the many spinsters, concubines, widows, and wives who used to gather at our house in Hong Kong. Even when I was very young, these women allowed me to sit among them as they unburdened their sorrows or shared their joy, and what I learned from listening to them has informed every aspect of my life, especially my work.

As Janice E. Stockard points out in *Daughters of the Canton Delta: Marriage Patterns and Economic Strategies in South China, 1860–1930*, accurate recovery of the past frequently rests on constructing the right questions. Her book and the work of Marjorie Topley and Andrea Sankar—in particular their dissertations *The Organization and Social Function of Women's Chai T'ang in Singapore* and *The Evolution of the Sisterhood in Traditional Chinese Society: From Village Girls' Houses to Chai T'angs in Hong Kong*—were invaluable in providing the foundation from which I constructed my questions about nineteenth-century Sun Duk. So were diverse works in Chinese from the archives of Him Mark Lai and Judy Yung, ably translated by Ellen Lai-shan Yeung.

Tsoi Nu Liang and Hu Jie made it possible for me to meet with four elderly self-combers in Shiqiao—Lee Moon, Leung Chat Mui, Tam Ngan Bing, and Yiu Lau Fong—to whom I posed my questions. In answer, these women spoke frankly of their own experiences and those of their sisters and friends. They showed us their spinster house and described others from their youth. When I asked whether they would make the same choice again, their responses were an immediate yes.

Joseph S. P. Ting and Rosa Yau, curators at the Hong Kong Museum of History, and Pauline Phua at the National Archives of Singapore gave me access to interviews of independent spinsters in their collections. Phoebe Lam transcribed and translated tapes in Hong Kong. Ellen Lai-shan Yeung translated transcripts from Singapore.

Tsoi Nu Liang and Tsoi Hoi Yat located Cheung Ching Ping's collection of over sixty weeping songs, *Hok Goh Gee Tse*, which Ellen Lai-shan Yeung translated. Other sources include: Yang Pi-Wang's "Ancient Bridal Laments" in *China Reconstructs* (October 1963, vol. 12, no. 4) and C. Fred Blake's "Death and Abuse in Marriage Laments: The Curse of Chinese Brides" in *Asian Folklore Studies* no. 37. All the collectors noted the extemporaneous nature of the songs, and I could see for myself that the same stock phrases were used repeatedly. From these recurring expressions, I composed some of the weeping songs in this novel. The rest of the weeping songs appear as they were recorded or with minor changes. Gwoon Yum's song is drawn from "Some Popular Religious

Literature of the Chinese" by Mrs. E. T. Williams, *Journal of the China Branch of the Royal Asiatic Society 1900–1901*, vol. 33. The muk yu, wooden fish song, that Rooster sings in praise of Shadow's embroidery was adapted from Ellen Lai-shan Yeung's translation of Ng Sheung-chi's "Traditional Embroidery Song" in the Chinese Culture Center of San Francisco's April 6, 1996, program for "Traditional Toishan Muk-'yu Singing."

Most of the myriad articles, dissertations, and books I sought were obtained through the perseverance of the staff at the San Francisco Public Library's interlibrary loan department. Lourdes Fortunado, Roberta Greifer, and Carol Small at my local branch in Noe Valley were helpful too, and during the months I could neither go to the library nor read what I'd already requested, Miriam Locke acted as my legs and eyes. Judy Yung could almost always find what eluded everyone else, and *The South China Silk District: Local Historical Transformation and World-System Theory*, by Alvin Y. So, which she brought to my attention, proved crucial in deepening my understanding of Sun Duk and synthesizing my ideas.

Wonderful, wide-ranging discussions with Katie Gilmartin and Peggy Pascoe helped me place the experiences of the Sun Duk women in a larger context. They—together with Carole Arrett, Peter Ginsberg, Marlon Hom, Miriam Locke, Sonia Ng, Jan Venolia, Ellen Lai-shan Yeung, and Judy Yung —also helped shape the manuscript through their careful, insightful readings of early drafts.

Others who contributed to the development of *The Moon*

Pearl are: Catherine Brady, Chu Moon Ho, Deng Ming-Dao, Marco Fong, Robin Grossman, LeVell Holmes, Steven Kahn, Lee C. Lee, Shelley McKenny, and Marianne Villaneuva.

The extraordinary commitment of my agent, Peter Ginsberg, and the support of my editor, Tisha Hooks, brought the project to fruition.

As always, my husband, Don, was involved from conception to publication, and it is to him I owe my largest debt of gratitude.